IRONWOOD

ALSO BY MICHAEL CONNELLY

FICTION

The Black Echo
The Black Ice
The Concrete Blonde
The Last Coyote
The Poet
Trunk Music
Blood Work
Angels Flight
Void Moon
A Darkness More Than Night
City of Bones
Chasing the Dime
Lost Light
The Narrows
The Closers
The Lincoln Lawyer
Echo Park
The Overlook
The Brass Verdict
The Scarecrow
Nine Dragons
The Reversal
The Fifth Witness
The Drop
The Black Box
The Gods of Guilt
The Burning Room
The Crossing
The Wrong Side of Goodbye
The Late Show
Two Kinds of Truth
Dark Sacred Night
The Night Fire
Fair Warning
The Law of Innocence
The Dark Hours
Desert Star
Resurrection Walk
The Waiting
Nightshade
The Proving Ground

NONFICTION

Crime Beat

E-BOOKS

Suicide Run
Angle of Investigation
Mulholland Dive
The Safe Man
Switchblade

IRONWOOD

A Catalina Novel

MICHAEL CONNELLY

LITTLE, BROWN AND COMPANY
New York Boston London

Little, Brown and Company
Hachette Book Group
1290 Avenue of the Americas, New York, NY 10104
littlebrown.com

First Edition: May 2026

Little, Brown and Company is a division of Hachette Book Group, Inc.
The Little, Brown name and logo are trademarks of Hachette Book Group, Inc.

ISBN 9780316595384 (hc) / 9780316607308 (lp) / 9780316610650 (signed)
LCCN 2026935219

Printing 1, 2026

LSC-H

Printed in the United States of America

To all the lost angels out there …

PART ONE

The Grove

1

STILWELL COULD HEAR the plane but couldn't see it. The moon and stars were behind cloud cover, and the plane was no doubt running without lights as it circled above the island. The radio crackled and Quigley's voice came through.

"Boss, you hear that?"

Stilwell brought his rover up to his mouth and keyed his two-way.

"Affirmative," he said. "Hold your position. Be ready."

He stopped looking up at the sky and used the binoculars to look down from his position toward Airport Road. He picked up an approaching vehicle, also running without lights, as it ascended to the mountaintop airstrip. He keyed the two-way again.

"Ground vehicle on approach," he said. "No lights."

"Copy," Quigley said.

It was an ATV. It entered through the open gate and drove directly out to the airstrip. It sped down to the runway's threshold, turned around, and backed into the brush. Then its lights came on—high beams from the front of the ATV and a powerful set of halogens across the top of its roll bar. The first third of the eighteen-hundred-foot runway was sufficiently lit for the plane circling above. Stilwell went back to the radio.

"Okay, we go as planned," he said. "Move on my call."

"Copy that," Quigley said.

This would be Alton Quigley's first test. He was two months new to the island, and Stilwell didn't know what he had in him yet. But he believed that pairing him with Ilsa Ramirez was the right move. She was Stilwell's most dependable deputy, something he could not have said a year ago. But now, after almost two years under Stilwell's command, Ramirez had turned into a solid member of the Catalina substation's team.

The drone of the plane's single engine grew louder and Stilwell knew the pilot was bringing it down. He felt his pulse quicken with anticipation and the electric sense of possible danger.

Quigley and Ramirez were in an SUV parked in the shadows at the rear of an open hangar, out of sight from the air. Stilwell was in an unmarked hardtop ATV parked next to an equipment shed. There was nobody else. There hadn't been time. The tip came in too late to recruit backup from the mainland. He had to make do with what he had while also keeping one deputy on post in Avalon should the tip be an effort to draw all law enforcement away from the town.

The plane's engine throttled back as it floated down out of the dark sky to the partially lit runway. It landed softly, a testament to the pilot's skill, and coasted toward the southern terminus of the airfield. The ATV pulled out of the brush behind it and followed it down the strip, its lights still blazing.

"Should we go?" Quigley said over the radio.

Stilwell shook his head in annoyance. Quigley was so hyped

on adrenaline that he had either forgotten or was ignoring the plan.

"No," Stilwell radioed back. "Stick to the plan, Deputy. We need to see the drop first."

Stilwell had the binoculars to his eyes, watching what played out in the lights of the ATV on the airstrip. The plane had turned around at the terminus and was now in position to take off again. The pilot did not kill the engine; the plan was obviously to spend as little time on the ground as possible.

The cockpit door opened and an orange duffel bag was dropped to the tarmac. Someone wearing a black safety helmet with a smoked face shield got out of the ATV and approached the plane, staying clear of the still-spinning prop.

The man in the helmet came in under the overhead wing and grabbed the duffel bag. Stilwell keyed the mic.

"Okay, go," he said. "Block that plane!"

Stilwell pinned the pedal down, and the electric ATV leaped from its position by the shed blind, and soon he was racing toward the lights on the airstrip. He could see the deputies' SUV break from the hangar with its lights flashing. It moved down the center of the runway, making it impossible for the plane to take off.

Stilwell saw the man in the helmet drop the duffel bag and sprint back to his ATV. He then did something Stilwell had not expected when he had hastily drawn up plans for the surveillance. He drove the ATV off the airstrip and into the brush that ran down the side of the mountain.

As the ATV plowed through the manzanita bushes that lined the airstrip, its lights went out and it disappeared into the darkness.

"Shit!" Stilwell said.

He followed, keeping his vehicle's lights on. As soon as he

was in the brush, the terrain dropped off and he went bouncing down the mountain at a forty-five-degree angle. He followed the sound of the fleeing ATV and the dust kicked up into his lights. He almost lost control on a sharp left turn when his front right wheel caught a rut. He overcompensated by jerking the wheel right, and the back end swung around in a 180 skid before coming to a hard stop. He started up again, and his lights came upon the runaway ATV now on its side next to the thick trunk of a live oak. Stilwell slammed down the brake pedal, skidded to another stop, and jumped out, pulling his weapon and flashlight from his belt holsters as he moved.

Gun up and wrist braced over the hand holding the flashlight, Stilwell approached the back of the upturned ATV.

"Sheriff's department," he called out. "Put your weapons down and your hands in the air!"

There was no response. He kept moving. Realizing that the flashlight made him an easy target, he flicked it off as he came around the end of the ATV and then turned it back on and focused the beam on the two seats. The driver was gone.

Stilwell swept the light across the thick brush but saw no sign of the man in the safety helmet. He knew it would be impossible for him to adequately search the mountainside for a runner on his own. As he stood there, annoyed with himself for not catching the man, he heard the rising sound of a plane's engine and instinctively knew it was running down the airstrip to take off. He ran back to his ATV and grabbed the two-way out of the charging mount.

"Quigley, what is—"

His voice was drowned out as the plane flew about seventy-five feet overhead.

There was no response on the radio.

"Quigley, Ramirez, copy me on your status."

He waited. Nothing.

Stilwell jumped behind the wheel of the ATV and pointed it up the mountain. But the angle was steep and its wheels spun on the loose soil. It slowly made its way up, then popped out of the brush onto the tarmac. He saw the SUV with its doors open and lights on. In the beams of its headlights he saw two bodies on the tarmac. Neither was moving.

2

STILWELL KNEW THE fastest rescue would be from the US Coast Guard out of the Port of Los Angeles. Their chopper crossed the bay and got to the airstrip twenty-two minutes after Stilwell made the call. Quigley was dead, the back of his head blown off, but Ramirez was hanging on despite massive blood loss from a bullet that had clipped the top of her vest and gone into her neck. Stilwell was holding a dressing from the SUV's first aid kit to the wound when the red-and-white chopper landed and the medical team came rushing across the tarmac.

It took them less than six minutes to stabilize Ramirez and get her on the chopper. Stilwell watched it take off and bank toward the mainland, then looked at Quigley's body. He'd been taken down by a shot that entered through his left eye.

Stilwell felt nauseated. Quigley had a family. They would never see him again.

His thoughts were interrupted by a call on his cell phone. It was Captain Corum. He said that he and a homicide crew were heading to the sheriff's air base and would be arriving by helicopter within the hour.

"Stil, you okay?" he asked.

"I'm okay," Stilwell said.

"What the fuck happened out there?"

"Captain, I don't know."

3

AS SOON AS the homicide team took control of the crime scene, Stilwell was brought down to the substation and sequestered in the interview room until one of the detectives could get away and begin the first of what would be several debriefings. Stilwell spent the time reviewing as many details of the surveillance operation as he could remember and writing them down on a legal pad. Because a deputy had died and another had been seriously wounded, Stilwell knew he would be on the hook for every decision, good and bad, made at the airstrip. Though still reeling from the loss of life that had occurred, he had to consider his own situation. He had the option to request a representative from the union to advise him and sit in on any interviews, but he'd decided not to go that route and told Captain Corum upon his arrival that he would fully cooperate with the investigation.

After he had written down every salient fact of the past six hours on the yellow pages, he got up and started stacking the boxes that cluttered the interview room. Because the space was so infrequently used for interviews, it had become the unofficial lost-and-found area for the island. There were boxes of lost cell phones, backpacks, purses, and cameras, three full suitcases, fishing rods and reels, camping and diving equipment, and other detritus left behind by tourists. Every three months Stilwell ordered a deputy to sort through the accumulation and either find the owners of the left-behinds or donate the items to St. Catherine's, which held a quarterly rummage sale to raise money for the island's struggling families. Organizing things in the room helped Stilwell burn off nervous energy.

He had the room neat and orderly by the time the first investigator came from the crime scene. His name was Ernie Simon. Stilwell knew him from his previous posting in the homicide squad. He knew that Simon was a capable and fair investigator who was methodical in his approach to his work and thus was known as a tortoise—as opposed to a hare—among his colleagues.

"What's the status on Ramirez?" Stilwell asked as soon as Simon entered.

"Still kicking, at last report," Simon said. "What's all this?"

He gestured at the boxes stacked against the wall.

"Lost-and-found stuff," Stilwell said. "I turned the storage room we used to use for that into a bunk room. It's made the rest of the sub kind of cramped, but we needed a place for people to sleep."

Simon took a seat at the table across from Stilwell. He had shaggy white hair and a paunch that came from too much fast food and a fondness for vodka after work. He held a clipboard with a blank sheet of paper on it.

"The captain says you're okay talking to me," he said. "That right?"

"Right," Stilwell said. "Whatever you need."

"What I like to do is have you tell your story and then we'll turn on the recorder and you tell it again, the same thing. Seems to work best that way."

"You can record the whole thing as far as I'm concerned. The story's not going to change."

"Let's do it my way, see how we go."

"Sure."

Simon pulled a mini-recorder out of his pocket and put it on the table but did not turn it on.

"The room's wired too," Stilwell said. "I can turn that on if you want."

Simon ignored the suggestion and dove into the interview.

"Let's start at the start," he said. "How did tonight's operation begin?"

"It began with Quigley getting a tip from one of his mainland CIs," Stilwell said. "The guy knew Quigley was working out here now and he said that there was a plane coming in tonight. Coming up from Mexicali. They make the drop out here where nobody's watching and in the morning it's on the first ferry to overtown."

"Overtown?"

"What they call the mainland over here."

"This confidential informant, did Quigley give you a name?"

"Wouldn't be confidential if he did. He did say the guy was a one-hundred-percenter. All his tips were money."

"And this was a guy he knew when he worked the narco unit?"

"That's what he said. You guys make the notification to his family yet?"

"They're handling that from . . . overtown."

"He had a wife and kids."

"So I hear. When did Deputy Quigley get the transfer out here?"

"A little over two months ago."

"And this CI calls him out of the blue and says a plane's coming in and it happens to be landing on the island where Quigley now works. That sound a little convenient to you?"

"Maybe."

"Do you know why Quigley was transferred out here?"

"I only know what he told me. I'm allowed access to basic personnel records on the people they move out here, but I don't see the disciplinary files."

What Stilwell knew but didn't need to say was that the Catalina substation was a transfer destination for deputies who had somehow run afoul of the department's command staff. This could be due to anything from a political misstep to an improper show of force to accepting a free meal to getting your shirts pressed for free. It was a form of punishment and everyone in the LASD knew it. If you were transferred to Catalina, you had fucked up. That was how Stilwell got here.

"What did he tell you?" Simon asked.

"He said it was because he was working a nightclub in West Hollywood and busted a guy selling coke in the restroom who turned out to be the sheriff's nephew. Whether that was a true story or not, I don't know."

"The story might be true but it wasn't the reason he was transferred out of narcotics."

Stilwell didn't respond. He hoped his silence would lead Simon to reveal more, but it didn't.

"So, you get this tip," Simon said. "It's short notice and not enough time to get anybody from narcotics out to handle it, so that leaves you, Quigley, and Ramirez."

"Correct," Stilwell said. "Quigley said his CI was a hundred-percenter but what's that mean to me? Nothing. So I also left a deputy in the sub to handle calls in case this whole thing was a decoy op."

"You mean to draw you up the mountain to the airstrip while they hit a target down here?"

"Exactly."

"Very smart."

"SOP."

"Maybe, but still a good move. When did this tip come in?"

"Deputies out here work twelves, changing on the sixes. Quigley worked three days on, four off. He stayed in the bunk room because he thought he'd be a short-timer out here and his family was embedded with schools and a house and all of that in Gardena. He had clocked out but was hanging around the sub because I guess he had nowhere else to go. His CI called him and he came to me at seven twenty with it—I wrote it down. His guy didn't have an ETA but said the plane was already in the air."

"From Mexicali, that's, what, about three hours?"

"Depends on the plane and the flight path, I guess. I don't know planes but it was a single prop with an overhead wing and a blue stripe down its side. No tail number. And judging by the sound, it came in from the west, probably flying outside the twelve-mile limit till it got up here."

"Did you call the narco unit after this tip came in?"

"I did. They were running an op in Compton last night. They said they couldn't get anybody out here but they'd follow up on it in the morning. But by then it would be too late, so I told

Quigley to suit up and I took Ramirez off the second shift to make three of us."

"What happened up there?"

Referring to his legal pad, Stilwell began to give a detailed account of the events up at the airstrip.

4

STILWELL SPENT FOUR hours in the interview room repeating his story to Simon and then two other investigators on the team. The windowless room was rank with bad breath and body odor by the time Captain Corum came in. He left the door open.

"Let's air this place out," he said. "What's all this?"

Like Simon, he was looking at the collection of stacked boxes and other belongings lining the wall. The captain was tall and thin. He always dressed in a sharp black suit to match his unnaturally black hair. He completed the ensemble with a white shirt and a colorful tie. He was in his mid-fifties and had a two-tone face—deeply tanned from his eyes down, his forehead a hat-protected pearl white. He spent much of his weekends on a golf course.

"Lost-and-found," Stilwell said.

"You sure there isn't something dead in there someplace?" Corum said.

"Maybe. Am I clear?"

"You're clear. For now. But you're grounded until we see how this shakes out. I want you staying in the sub."

"Twiddling my thumbs?"

"You know how it works. Give us a few days to put the package together and send it up to the boss."

Stilwell knew that the elected sheriff would need to sign off on any after-action discipline.

"Am I getting thrown under the bus, Cap?" Stilwell asked.

"You, no," Corum said. "As far as we can tell, they probably didn't clear the plane properly. There was somebody besides the pilot hiding on board and he got the drop on them."

Stilwell did not nod, though he was thinking the same thing.

"You really didn't hear any gunshots?" Corum asked.

Stilwell paused for a moment. Was Corum suggesting he needed to change his story?

"No, I didn't," he finally answered. "But like I told everybody, I was chasing a gas-powered ATV and was down the side of the mountain. Not sure I would've heard the shots."

"It's just that if a suppressor was used . . ."

"Why would a guy have a suppressor on an airdrop?"

Corum didn't answer. Stilwell changed the subject.

"What about the guy I chased?" he asked. "He's probably still on the island. I should be out there looking for him."

"That's not happening, Stil," Corum said. "You're on the bench."

"So nobody is looking for him?"

"We're looking for him. We're just a little short on manpower at the moment. But in the morning we'll have people at the docks in Long Beach and San Pedro checking everybody who gets off the boats from here."

Stilwell thought about that and decided not to criticize the plan. He changed the subject again.

"Did you talk to Quigley's wife?" he asked.

"I did not," Corum said. "Notification of the family was handled by Ahearn and Sampedro over there."

"Great. They're on this?"

"They're not. I just needed somebody to make the notification. I know enough now to keep your orbits separate."

"Thank you."

There was long-standing enmity between Stilwell and Ahearn, going back to Stilwell's prior posting in the homicide unit. It was their dislike of each other that had led to Stilwell's transfer to Catalina. And things had only gotten worse last year when they both worked a murder case on the island.

"They trace the ATV yet?" Stilwell asked.

"They did," Corum said. "It was reported stolen last night before the shit hit the fan."

"I didn't get any report on that."

"It came in while you were up there on the stakeout. The owner called it in, and the deputy you left down here — who was that?"

"O'Connor."

"O'Connor went up and took the report."

Stilwell just nodded. He knew he could get that report and talk to O'Connor for further details. Corum seemed to be able to read him.

"I know what you're thinking, Stil," he said. "But you're staying away from this. You're a witness, not an investigator. Clear?"

"Yes," Stilwell said. "Clear."

"Good. So, let's talk about media. Same thing. You are not part of this. Direct all inquiries to me or the media unit. I don't want to see your name in any paper, including that little rag they publish out here. *Comprende?*"

"*Comprendo.* What about reporters from the mainland coming out here and poking around?"

"Let them do what they do but don't help them and don't talk to them. Like I said, refer all media requests to the mainland."

"Roger that."

"Last thing—you have space in your bunk room for Simon? We're taking the chopper back but he's going to stay here so he can check out the crime scene when the sun comes up." Corum looked at his watch. "Which won't be for a few hours," he said. "If there's room, I'll tell him he can catch some sleep until then."

"There's room," Stilwell said.

"Good. The rest of us are leaving and you're clear to go home."

"Okay."

Corum raised his chin toward the lost-and-found wall.

"And I would use some of your downtime in the sub to clean all this up," he said. "Make things more professional around here."

"Good idea," Stilwell said.

5

AFTER CORUM AND everybody but Simon left to fly back to the mainland, Stilwell showed Simon the bunk room and the locker where clean sheets, blankets, and pillows were kept. The bunk room was a make-your-own-bed facility. He went to the desk shared by the on-duty deputies and found a copy of O'Connor's report on the theft of the ATV used the night before in the airdrop.

The ATV was reported stolen by a man named Art Sellers who told O'Connor the vehicle had been taken from the driveway of his home on Clarissa. Coming up on two years since his transfer to the island, Stilwell was familiar with many of the residents, particularly those who lived in Avalon. More than a million people visited the island every year, but there were fewer than six thousand residents, and Stilwell, the lone detective on the island, had done his best to get to know as many of the locals as possible. Art Sellers was not a familiar name to him, but he knew that Clarissa was a street where a lot of long-term and multigenerational families lived in century-old row houses built as close together as teeth in a smile. It seemed to Stilwell that someone on that street would have heard a gas-powered ATV being taken from a driveway.

Sellers told O'Connor that he had had the ATV for two years and usually left the key in it because he had never been worried about it getting stolen. This was the practice of many residents on the island as they tried to cling to the idea of Catalina as a crime-free atoll cleanly separated from the ills of society by twenty-two miles of ocean. There would be a rude awakening for Sellers and others when word of the murder of a deputy spread in the days ahead.

The ATV in question was still lying on its side up on the mountain by the airstrip. Though it had been processed by the criminalist who came with the homicide team, extricating it would have to wait until daylight. The vehicle was clean as far as fingerprints and other evidence went. The driver in the full helmet had apparently worn gloves.

Before going home, Stilwell pulled a radio from the wall-mounted charging station and called Deputy O'Connor, who was out on patrol, and told him he was leaving the sub and that there was an overtown detective sleeping in the bunk room.

"Roger that," O'Connor said.

Stilwell left the sub, made sure the door was locked, and drove his ATV up the hill to his home. Tash had left the front door of the house unlocked despite his repeated requests over the year they had lived together to lock up at night. He entered quietly and found her asleep and snoring in the bedroom. Though it was a mid-range snore, he knew it would keep him up. He grabbed his pillow and retreated to the living-room couch. It was just past four and he had to get back to the sub early. He set a timer on his phone for two hours and was asleep within minutes of putting his head down on the pillow. He was too tired to dream.

In the morning he was up before Tash and managed to shower, shave, and get dressed without waking her. Before leaving, he watched her sleep for a little while. Stilwell had hated everything about his transfer to the island until he met her. Now he knew he had stumbled into the right place at the right time and didn't think he'd ever want to leave. But that did not stop a sense of foreboding that had descended on him in recent months, a feeling that something bad was coming to his island idyll. He didn't know what it was, but he had taken to calling it "the dread" in the once-a-month therapy sessions he secretly attended on the mainland. It was why he insisted that Tash lock the door at night.

His first stop was the sub to pick up a fully charged two-way and look in on Simon, but he found the bunk room empty. Stilwell assumed he had already gone up to the airstrip to view the crime scene in daylight. He checked the vehicle log and saw that Simon had signed out the SUV.

Stilwell walked from the sub to the ferry dock, where people were lined up to board the 7:50 boat to Long Beach. It was the first of the day, and the second did not leave until 10:00. Stilwell thought that if the man in the black helmet was trying to get off the island, he might go for the first boat out.

Stilwell was wearing green cargo pants and a black polo shirt with LASD printed on the breast pocket. The gun and badge on his belt further announced him as law enforcement. He walked along the line of travelers, checking for any sign of nervousness caused by his presence.

But no one flinched or took off running as Stilwell walked by. He also didn't see anyone carrying a black motorcycle helmet with a full windscreen. That would have been too easy.

He moved on to the ticket window of the Catalina Express office and saw a familiar face behind the glass. Lindsey Fordham was a source he had started cultivating soon after he arrived on the island. He asked her for the 7:50 boat's manifest and she pushed a clipboard through the window slot.

"We're sold out and I have a waiting list if you want to see that too," Fordham said.

"Got it," Stilwell said. "Let me look at this first."

He stepped away from the window and looked at the clipboard. It held a printout with the names of customers who had purchased advance tickets for the 7:50 ferry. The morning trips to the mainland regularly sold out and it was best to buy tickets ahead of time. He ran his finger down the list of buyers. None of the names were familiar.

Stilwell slid the clipboard back to Fordham and asked to see the waiting list. There were seven names and cell numbers on it. These were likely new visitors to the island who hadn't known the early boats sold out and now were scrambling to get a ride home. After each name there was a plus sign and a number, indicating how many seats were needed. Only one of the names was a solo passenger: Kalas.

Stilwell slid the list back to Fordham.

"Lindsey, the solo guy on there, Kalas?" he said. "Is that a first or last name?"

"I don't really know, Stil," Fordham said. "Sorry."

"Not a problem. Do you remember if he was a white guy, Black guy, any accent?"

"Definitely Latino. He had an accent."

"Do you know where he is?"

Fordham leaned over the counter toward the glass to get a better look at the outdoor waiting area. There were several people sitting on benches or milling about near the last-chance souvenir stands as they opened for the day.

"I don't see him," Fordham said. "You want me to call him?"

Stilwell had to think about that for a moment. He had nothing other than his instincts to confront the man called Kalas with.

"He's fourth on that list," he said. "Do you think he'll get on the boat?"

"Probably," Fordham said. "We usually have ten or fifteen no-shows."

"Is the ten o'clock boat sold out?"

"Not yet."

"What if I told you I don't want Kalas to leave on the first boat?"

"Not a problem, Stil. I'm sure you have your reasons."

"Okay, so call him and ask him to come back to the window. When he gets here, don't mention me, but tell him he's not going to get on the early boat. I'll take it from there."

"But why wouldn't I just tell him by phone instead of making him come back to the window?"

"Say that the ten o'clock is going to sell out and he needs to buy a ticket before it does."

"Good. I'll do that."

"Okay, and when he gets here, tell him you need his full name for the manifest or you can't sell him the seat."

"Will do. That's actually the rule anyway."

"Good."

Stilwell walked away from the window and used a souvenir

kiosk as a blind. He kept his eye on the ticket window, and when a call came in on his cell, he answered without checking the screen. It was Tash.

"Thank God!" she exclaimed when she heard his voice. "You didn't come home last night, and I just saw the news. You're all right?"

"I'm fine. It was Quigley."

He guessed that the name of the fallen deputy had not been put out to the media yet, giving rise to Tash's panic.

"Oh, no," Tash said. "What happened?"

"Well, we don't really know yet," Stilwell said. "I was chasing a runner down the side of the mountain and didn't see what happened on the landing strip. But Quigley and Ramirez both got shot."

"Ilsa? Is she okay?"

"I haven't gotten an update yet today. The Coast Guard flew her to the hospital and she was stable when she got there. But that's the last I heard."

"When I saw you hadn't come home, I thought it was you."

She was trying to control her relief and worry. Stilwell could hear it in her voice. Maybe some anger too.

"I'm all right, Tash. Really. And I'm sorry, I should have called you. But I actually did come home for a couple hours. I slept out on the couch so I wouldn't wake you."

"You mean so you could get away from my snoring."

"Not really. You weren't bad last night."

"You're a terrible liar, Stil."

Stilwell watched a man walk up to the ticket window. He wore sunglasses and a wide-brimmed hat. Stilwell saw that he was Hispanic and thinly built. Stilwell thought about the man who'd jumped out of the ATV to retrieve the duffel bag last night. The body size seemed close. So did the black jeans and the dusty boots he was wearing.

The man carried only a backpack, no suitcase. This told Stilwell that he was a short-timer on the island. The backpack bulged and sagged off the man's shoulder like it contained something heavy and bulky.

Stilwell watched as the man slid cash through the slot. He was buying a ticket.

"Maybe," Stilwell said to Tash. "But listen, I'm in the middle of something and I need to go. Can we talk later when I know more?"

"Of course," Tash said. "I'm about to head in."

Tash Dano was interim Avalon harbormaster, elevated from the assistant position when the longtime harbormaster resigned. Tash was hoping that the city council would give the job to her permanently, but she had competition from applicants in overtown yachting centers.

They said their goodbyes and Stilwell watched as the man at the ticket window turned and started walking back toward town. He had a slight limp, maybe from an injury he had gotten when he dumped the ATV on its side last night.

Stilwell hurried back to the ticket window.

"Was that Kalas?" he asked.

"Yes," Fordham said.

"You get his full name?"

"Yes, Gonzalo Kalas."

She slid the clipboard with the manifest to the window and put her finger on the handwritten name.

"Got it," Stilwell said. "Thanks."

"I'm glad you're okay, Stil," Fordham said. "I heard what happened up at the airstrip. Terrible thing."

"It was. Thanks."

Stilwell stepped away from the window, got a bead on Kalas, and started following. He was aware that he was advertising that he was a cop with his exposed gun and badge. He hung back even though the docking area was now crowded with travelers who had just gotten off the first ferry in. He stayed a hundred feet away and watched as Kalas left the pier and turned onto Crescent Avenue. Many of the shops and restaurants were not open this early. Kalas raised a cell phone to his ear but it was not clear if he had called someone or received a call.

Kalas turned abruptly onto Catalina Avenue. Stilwell got to the corner and glimpsed him slipping through the door of Original Jack's Country Kitchen, which was open for breakfast.

Stilwell crossed the street and stepped into the entry alcove of a closed shop. He pulled the two-way off his belt and called the substation.

"Avalon One to base."

"Go ahead, One." It was Mercy, the office manager. The sub had its own radio channel and she had a stand-up microphone on her desk.

"Is our visitor from overtown there?"

"No, haven't seen him."

"Copy."

Stilwell pulled out his phone. He had Simon's number in his contacts from when they both worked homicide. Simon answered, and Stilwell could tell he was driving.

"You left the airport?" Stilwell asked.

"Just did," Simon said.

"Where to now?"

"I was going to interview the owner of the stolen ATV. You want to come with me?"

Stilwell wondered if Simon knew that he was supposed to be on the bench.

"Yeah, I'll go with you," Stilwell said. "But before we go, I have eyes on a guy who might have been the one driving that ATV last night."

"What makes you think that? You never saw his face."

"True, but this guy has the right size and the right boots. Plus he's trying to get off the island."

"I'll meet you. Where?"

6

WHILE STILWELL WAITED for Simon, he called Mercy back and asked her to run the name Gonzalo Kalas through the computer. She did so and learned that there was an ICE hold on a Gonzalo Kalas, age thirty-four. Stilwell guessed that he was looking at the wanted man and asked if there was an ICE contact listed on the hold.

"Agent Jerry Gordon," Mercy said. "Santa Ana office."

"Got it," Stilwell said. "Is there a contact number?"

Mercy gave it to him but with reluctance in her voice, and Stilwell knew why.

"I'm not crazy about calling ICE," he said. "But I need some intel on who this guy is."

"I get it," she said, though the reluctant tone was still there.

He hung up and called the number she'd given him. The phone was answered right away.

"Agent Gordon. How can I help you?"

Stilwell identified himself and said he had eyes on a man he believed Gordon was looking for.

"I'm looking for a lot of people," Gordon said. "Which one are we talking about?"

"Gonzalo Kalas," Stilwell said.

Gordon responded quickly, apparently without having to check the name in his files. "You have him in custody?" he asked.

"No, I said I have eyes on him," Stilwell said.

"Where?"

"Catalina."

"The island? No shit. Not where I expected to get him. Thing is, I'm not going to be able to get out there for a bit. Can your gang take him down?"

"I'm waiting on backup. Can you tell me anything about this guy?"

"Yeah, he's a dirtbag and we want to send him back where he came from."

"Which is where?"

"Sinaloa, Mexico. He's a courier for the cartel. Maybe even a sicario."

"A hitter? If we have the right guy, he was involved in a drug drop at the airport over here last night. Two deputies got shot."

"Oh, man, I just saw that on the news. And this guy was the shooter?"

"Not the shooter. But he was there. Can you send me a picture so I can make sure we're talking about the same guy?"

"We don't really have a good shot of him but I'll dig up what we have and send it. Text it to this number?"

"Yes, that would be good. Thanks."

"And you'll let me know when you have him in custody? We'll come take him off your hands."

"Uh, we'll stay in contact, but he's going to face charges here. We have a dead deputy."

"Right, yeah, there's that. Just keep me in the loop, then. And if we can be of service, you know where to find me."

"I do."

After disconnecting from Gordon, Stilwell looked at his watch and wondered where Simon was. He checked the restaurant and saw Kalas sitting in a booth by the front window. It looked like there were two glasses of water on the table.

"Where's the guy?"

Stilwell turned and saw Simon coming from Crescent. Stilwell nodded toward Original Jack's. "Front table by the window," he said. "I think he might be waiting for someone."

"What makes you think that?"

"He either made or got a phone call while walking over from the ferry dock. And there are two glasses of water on the table."

Simon checked the restaurant to confirm Stilwell's report, then nodded.

"What boat did he buy a ticket for?" he asked.

"The ten o'clock," Stilwell said.

"Then maybe we watch and wait. Did we get a name on this guy?"

"Gonzalo Kalas. I ran the name and there's an ICE hold on him. He's a courier and suspected hitter."

"Surprise, surprise."

"He's carrying a backpack that might contain a weapon."

"We'll need some backup. Who do you have that won't fuck it up?"

Stilwell took that as a slight aimed at Quigley and Ramirez and maybe even himself. He ignored it—for the moment.

"I've got two deputies on," he said. "I can pull them over here."

"Do it," Simon said. "But if they're in uniform, tell them to hang back till we need 'em."

"They're in island uniform—like me."

"Then tell them not to wander into our surveillance."

Stilwell used his two-way to call Deputies De Giorgio and Mason and direct them to stage at Crescent and Catalina until needed. When he turned back he saw that Kalas was still sitting by himself in the booth at Original Jack's.

"I think it's bullshit," Simon said. "I think he just said it would be two so he could get the booth."

"Maybe," Stilwell said. "He did have a call."

"That could have been anything. Maybe he was arranging his pickup on the other side."

"So what do you want to do?"

"I want to see what he's got in that backpack you mentioned."

"Then as soon as we have backup, we go in."

Ten minutes later Stilwell and Simon crossed the street and approached the door to Original Jack's from an angle to Kalas's back. They entered the restaurant with Simon in the lead. He slid into Kalas's booth opposite him, and Stilwell slid in next to Kalas.

"Keep your hands on the table," Simon said.

"What is this?" Kalas said.

Stilwell shifted his position so he could put his hand on his holstered weapon.

"Are you armed?" he asked.

"No, I'm not armed," Kalas said. "What is going on here?"

He spoke with a heavy accent.

"We just wanted to speak with you," Simon said. "And—oh, I'm sorry, did I just kick your leg?"

Simon leaned back to look under the table.

"Oh, your backpack," he said. "Let me get that out of the way."

"It's not mine," Kalas said quickly. "It was already there."

"Really?" Simon said.

He reached down and pulled the backpack up onto the bench next to him. Stilwell wondered if Kalas understood the mistake he had made by denying ownership of it.

"You sure it's not yours?" Simon asked. "It's a nice backpack."

"It's not mine, and I must go now," Kalas said. "I am on the next boat."

"Then you've got plenty of time," Simon said. "Doesn't he, Stil?"

"At least an hour till boarding," Stilwell said.

"You must really want to get off the island," Simon said.

"I have business," Kalas said.

"Tell you what," Simon said. "If this isn't yours, then we're going to have to open it up to see if we can figure out whose it is."

Simon unzipped the main compartment of the backpack and spread it open. It revealed the shiny black crown of a safety helmet with a full wind visor. He looked at Stilwell, who nodded, confirming it matched the helmet worn by the runner the night before.

At that moment Kalas threw his shoulder into Stilwell and knocked him out of the booth onto the floor. Kalas climbed out of the booth to run, but Stilwell recovered enough to grab his leg. Kalas tripped and fell into a table where a family of four were sitting. Water glasses and mugs of coffee crashed to the floor.

Both Stilwell and Simon were on him then; they pulled him off the table and took him down.

"Help!" Kalas yelled. "I'm a citizen and they're taking me away!"

Stilwell pulled his cuffs from a belt holster and quickly secured Kalas's hands behind his back. Kalas kept yelling.

"This is ICE! They can't do this! I'm a citizen! Help!"

People were standing up from their tables to get a view of the man lying face down on the floor. Stilwell saw a woman recording the scene on her cell phone.

Stilwell held Kalas on the ground and used the two-way to call De Giorgio and Mason in.

Simon got up, out of breath.

"Sorry about that, folks," he announced to the restaurant. "Just a little excitement to start your day with."

"We are not ICE," Stilwell told them. "We're L.A. County sheriffs. Please be seated and enjoy your breakfast."

The deputies arrived and Stilwell issued orders.

"Take him to the sub and put him in the interview room," he said. "Make sure you search him for weapons and lock him down."

"You got it," Mason said.

He and De Giorgio walked Kalas out of the restaurant, holding him by both arms. Stilwell went over to the family sitting at the table Kalas had crashed into. They had either finished their breakfast or were still waiting for it, so the only damage was to water glasses and coffee mugs.

"Everybody okay?" he said. "We're sorry that happened."

He got four looks of wide-eyed shock in response.

"We're okay," the father said. "We weren't expecting that."

"Neither were we," Stilwell said.

7

SIMON BORROWED STILWELL'S office to call Captain Corum and update him on the morning's activities. When he stepped back out, Stilwell was waiting.

"You didn't tell me you're supposed to be riding the pine," Simon said.

"I thought you knew," Stilwell said. "The captain's upset?"

"He'll get over it. I told him it was you who came up with Kalas. What's he going to say to that?"

"Thanks."

Simon pointed to a video screen on the wall that showed Kalas waiting in the interview room, his arms locked behind his back.

"What's our strategy here?" Simon asked.

Stilwell noted that he called it "our" strategy and appreciated Simon's decision to keep him involved despite what Corum might have told him.

"I was thinking that he doesn't know what he doesn't know," Stilwell said.

"Meaning what?" Simon said.

"He took off last night and was down the mountain when whatever happened on the landing strip happened. He probably knows the plane got away, but he's been hiding all night and doesn't really know what went down. Maybe we can use it to bluff him."

"Maybe. We need him to talk his way into a charge, because that helmet isn't going to be enough."

"What I was thinking."

"Okay, then. Are you ready?"

"You want me in there with you?"

"I want you to ask the questions. You were up there last night. You know more than anybody else around here."

Stilwell wondered if Simon was giving him the lead as a way to insulate himself from failure should Kalas take the Fifth and clam up.

"Okay," he said. "Let's do it."

"Are we recording this?" Simon asked.

"We're recording."

"Excellent."

Two minutes later they entered the interview room. Stilwell took the chair across the table from Kalas while Simon leaned against the wall to his left.

"Mr. Kalas, we are recording this session," Stilwell began. "You have been read and understand your rights. I'm Detective Stilwell and this is Detective Simon. You are under arrest and being held on a warrant from the Immigration and Customs Enforcement agency. But we want to speak to you about your activities last night at the airstrip."

"I don't know what you are talking about. What airstrip?"

"You know what I'm talking about, Gonzalo. We tracked you by camera from the moment you stole the ATV on Clarissa Street to the top of the mountain last night. If you cooperate with us, we might be able to work something out with ICE. Witnesses don't get detained and deported."

"I don't know, man. I'm thinking I should talk to a lawyer about all of this."

"Well, if you want a lawyer, we'll get you a lawyer. But that ends things today. You go into a cell and we're done."

Stilwell paused for a moment and waited for a reaction. He got none.

"So what do you want to do, Gonzalo?"

"I want to call a lawyer."

"Then we're done here."

Stilwell stood up and used his leg to push his chair back to the wall. He went around the table and behind Kalas. He used a key to open the handcuff linked to the metal frame of the chair.

"Stand up," he said.

Kalas stood and Stilwell cuffed his wrists together behind his back. He walked Kalas out of the interview room, through the squad room, and to the booking section of the jail. He took mug shots of Kalas and scanned his fingerprints with a digital reader. He then moved him into cell one, which had two sets of bunk beds but was empty.

"You get your choice of beds, Gonzalo," he said.

"What are the charges against me?" Kalas asked.

"Right now, we're going with the no-bail hold from ICE, but that's the least of your problems. We'll talk to the district attorney's office and ask for a conspiracy-to-commit-murder charge. That's the big one, Gonzalo. We get that and you're gone. And I don't mean back to Mexico."

"What about my call?"

"Almost forgot."

Stilwell pulled out his cell phone and handed it through the bars. Kalas didn't take it.

"I want a real phone," he said.

"That is a real phone," Stilwell countered.

"A landline. I don't want to use your phone, man. You could be recording shit on it."

"All calls on our landlines are recorded."

"Then bring me my phone. I'll use that."

Stilwell stared at him for a long moment, hoping to convey hesitancy.

"All right," he finally said. "One call."

Stilwell went out to the squad room and found Kalas's phone in a bag in the evidence locker. He had checked it earlier and knew it was password-protected. There was also a money clip in the bag and a key fob with a Jaguar logo on it.

Simon was at a desk looking at a computer screen.

"What's happening?" he asked.

"I'm giving him his phone to make a lawyer call," Stilwell said. "Hoping I get it back unlocked."

He walked the bag over to Simon and held it up so he could see the key fob.

"Looks like he's probably got a car in the Express lot in Long Beach," he said.

"What about San Pedro?" Simon asked.

"He bought a ticket to Long Beach."

"I'll call the guys over there and let them know. I'll take the key and check it out when I go back."

"You sure?"

It would go against protocol. The key wasn't evidence; it was property. He assumed Simon would not try to get a search warrant unless he knew there was something of evidentiary value in the car.

Stilwell gave him the key.

"How much money's in the clip?" Simon asked.

Stilwell looked at the notations on the plastic bag. It said the property inventory had been handled by Mason.

"Six hundred," he said.

"Nice stash," Simon said. "Did you notify ICE that we have him?"

"Not yet, but I told them I had eyes on him. Thought I'd wait on that till we decide what we want to do."

"Yeah, good idea. The captain texted and I need to call him. I'll see how he wants to handle it."

Stilwell took the phone into the jail and handed it through the bars to Kalas.

"You have one call and five minutes," he said.

"It might take longer to get him," Kalas said.

"Then leave him a message. I'll be back in five for the phone."

Stilwell went into the squad room and saw that Simon was on his phone, most likely talking to Corum. He went into his office and pulled up the sub's camera grid. It showed eight camera angles from inside and outside the sub. He enlarged the jail camera and turned the volume up. He knew it was illegal for him to listen to a suspect's communication with an attorney, but he suspected that Kalas wasn't calling an attorney.

But Kalas had apparently seen or anticipated there was a camera. He was huddled with the phone in a corner of the cell talking in what sounded like Spanish in a low voice. Stilwell could not make out a word of what he was saying in any language.

"Well, fuck you," he said.

When Kalas finished the call, he stood up and held the phone up to the camera located on the opposite wall.

"I'm done," he announced.

"Funny guy," Stilwell said.

He left his office and went back to collect the phone. Kalas had locked it.

When Stilwell returned to the squad room, Simon was off his call. He averted his eyes from Stilwell's, and that was a tell.

"What's up?" Stilwell asked.

"The captain wants me back there," Simon said. "He's sending an air unit. You think somebody can give me a ride over to the heliport?"

"Yeah, I can do that."

"No, he wants you here. He's a little bit pissed off and told me to remind you that you're on the bench."

"Did you remind him I came up with Kalas this morning?"

"I did but he still got upset."

"Whatever. Are you taking Kalas with you?"

"No, he wants to leave him here for now."

"Why?"

"He thinks ICE won't come all the way out here for just one guy, so we keep him here for now. But if we hear ICE is coming for him, the captain will send an airship and we can do the shuffle."

He was talking about the so-called sheriff shuffle, which was a means of hiding a suspect in custody from lawyers and other agencies by constantly moving him from one detention facility to another in the department's massive jail system.

"What about the follow-up with Sellers?" Stilwell asked.

"The captain doesn't think we need him since we got Kalas," Simon said.

"I could do it."

"I don't advise it, Stil. The captain got pretty hot. He's even pissed at me. Said he was going to call you. And, uh . . ."

He gestured at the video camera mounted on the ceiling in the front corner of the room.

"He wants the link to the cameras you got here," he said.

"Are you kidding me?" Stilwell said. "He wants to watch me?"

"Sorry. You know how he gets."

"I guess I do now."

Stilwell walked over to Mercy's desk and asked her to radio one of the deputies on patrol to come pick up Simon and take him to his rendezvous with the sheriff's helicopter.

"You also want me to send the camera link to the captain?" she asked.

"Yes, go ahead," Stilwell said.

"Everything—interior and exterior links?"

Stilwell thought about that for a moment before answering.

"Just the interior cameras," he said.

The sub was covered by six interior cameras: two in the holding area focused on the cells, and single cams in the squad room, kitchen, interview room, and entryway. Stilwell's office, the bunk room, and the restrooms weren't covered. If Corum thought he was going to be able to monitor every move Stilwell made, he was wrong.

8

FIVE MINUTES AFTER Simon was shuttled to the heliport, Stilwell took a call from Captain Corum, who dove headlong into his upset.

"I thought I was clear with you, Stil," he said. "You are on the bench until the investigation of the shooting is complete."

"You were clear, Captain," Stilwell said. "I just thought I had to check the morning boat to see if anybody caught my eye. Someone did, and now we have him in a cell. Would you rather we didn't have him?"

"The question answers itself. But you could have sent Simon or any of your deputies out there to check the boat. Instead, you chose to disregard my order. So I will give it again: You are benched until further notice. If you are on duty, you are in the substation. Do you understand?"

"I understand."

"Am I being clear?"

"You're clear."

"Good."

"Uh, Captain, what about court?"

"What about it?"

"The Allen trial? I'm supposed to go to Long Beach next week to talk with the prosecution team about my testimony. What if I—"

"This will be wrapped up by the end of the week, so don't worry about that. Until then, just stay at the sub. Handle the phones, clear that junk out of the interview room. Oh, and one other thing."

"What?"

"Give me a heads-up if you hear anything from ICE. If they come and grab our guy, he'll be out of the country before we know it."

"Will do. And Captain?"

"What?"

"What's the latest on Ramirez?"

"Last I heard, she was hanging in, but we can't talk to her. They got her on a ventilator. Hoping for tomorrow."

"Okay."

After the call, Stilwell put his phone down on his desk and thought about Ramirez fighting for her life. He had gotten close to her in the past year as he mentored her and had watched her become the most capable and dependable deputy on his team. Now it seemed possible that her days as a deputy were over, and this made Stilwell feel both sad and guilty. It didn't matter whether the review of his actions resulted in him getting a slap on the wrist or an all-clear from the department. His own review left him wondering what he could have or should have done differently.

He used a key to unlock a desk drawer and took out the folder on Quigley. It was Stilwell's practice as the supervisor of the substation to keep a file on all deputies assigned to the island. Each folder was thin, just transfer orders and a basic info sheet that included the deputy's address and phone number and, if applicable, the spouse's name and phone number and children's names and birth dates. Now he made the call he'd always dreaded making when he worked homicides. Quigley's wife already knew he had been killed, but that didn't make this any easier. He almost hoped no one would answer so he could put it off for a while, but it was picked up right away.

"How can I help you?" A man's voice.

"This is Sergeant Stilwell. I was Deputy Quigley's supervisor. I'd like to talk to Adriana Quigley if she's available."

"Can you hold for a moment while I check?"

"Sure."

Two minutes later he heard a woman say weakly, "Hello?" Stilwell spoke fast, following a subconscious urge to get the call over with as quickly as possible.

"Mrs. Quigley, this is Sergeant Stilwell," he said. "I was Alton's supervisor here on Catalina. I'm calling to express to you how sorry I am for the loss of Alton. He was new out here, but I could tell he was a good and dedicated man."

The truth was that Stilwell barely knew Quigley and hadn't yet formed an opinion of him as a man or a law enforcement officer.

"What happened out there?" Adriana Quigley said.

"Ma'am, I'm not part of that investigation," Stilwell said. "But I'm sure you will be kept—"

"Why was he out at the airport? I know your name. The captain said you were there."

"Uh, yes, I was there but I didn't see what happened. I was chasing a suspect down the mountain."

"Then you should have been with him. You could have saved him."

Stilwell wasn't sure if she meant that he could have prevented the shooting or that he could have saved Quigley if he had been with him.

"Anyway, I have to go," she said. "Goodbye, Sergeant Stilwell."

She disconnected before Stilwell could respond.

He thought about the conversation for a few minutes before he was interrupted by a call on the desk line from Mercy.

"The tow guys went up and pulled the ATV up to the top," she said. "They want to know where to take it."

She was talking about the ATV Stilwell had chased down the mountain the night before. It had been processed and towed out of the brush. It could now be returned to Sellers, its owner, but Stilwell didn't want to make that call because Corum might give him a hard time for working the case.

"Tell them to put it in the city equipment yard," he said. "I'll take care of it later."

He stepped out of the office and checked the deputies' report-writing desk, then went over to Mercy.

"What happened to O'Connor's report on the ATV?" he asked.

"Oh, right here," Mercy said.

She handed him a sheet from the top of a stack on her desk. He checked the info boxes on the reporting party and saw that Art Sellers was a quality-control supervisor at the desalination plant located on the south side of the island. There were cell phone and work numbers for Sellers, but Stilwell wasn't interested in interviewing him by phone. He decided he would attempt an in-person interview later, when he was off duty and technically not violating the captain's order to work in the sub.

"Mercy, I'm going to start clearing out the lost-and-found," he said. "Do you mind calling Father Braxton and telling him that we'll be ready tomorrow for him to pick up donations for the church sale?"

"Glad to," Mercy said.

Stilwell looked up at the camera mounted in the corner of the squad room and imagined the captain sitting at his desk watching him.

"Did you send the captain the camera link?" he asked.

"I did," Mercy said. "The six-pack."

"Good."

Stilwell went into the interview room to assess the boxes and other property he had neatly stacked against one wall. When lost or forgotten items were brought to the sub, the official procedure was to write a report on anything with a value of a hundred dollars or more. This report contained a description of the item, the date it was turned in, who received it, and what efforts had been made to locate its owner. Mercy did most of this work, but it was a low priority on the list of her many duties as office manager. More often than not, what actually happened was that they waited to see if someone came into the substation looking for their lost property.

The biggest item in the lost-and-found was an eight-foot paddleboard that had been left on Descanso Beach seven weeks earlier. Mercy had taped the property report to it. Stilwell simply moved it to the other side of the room, where he planned to place everything that would be picked up for the church rummage sale. He then started going through the other items. There were folding beach chairs, a high-end fishing rod and reel and a tackle box to go with it, and assorted items of clothing, none of which had any visible indications of ownership. Stilwell moved all of it over to the donation wall.

There was a plastic box containing phones that had been found and turned in. They were password-protected, leaving

Mercy no way to trace them. A whole plastic carton was filled with various pieces of scuba-diving equipment left behind at the diving steps near the casino. He moved these cartons over to the donation wall too.

There were three backpacks, including what looked like a fairly new Hyperlite Unbound camping pack. Stilwell knew it was top of the line and went for over three hundred dollars because he had priced backpacks the Christmas before as a present for Tash, who camped several times a year on the island. The property report Mercy had written was slipped into a netted pocket on the side of the pack. Stilwell pulled it and saw that it had been brought into the sub two months earlier. A person named Lenore Beaupre had turned it in after finding it on a bench on Crescent Avenue near the pier.

He unzipped the pack and dumped its contents onto the interview table. It contained mostly women's clothing — T-shirts, jeans, and underwear — which did not surprise Stilwell, because the packs came in male and female torso sizes and this one was the shorter size.

Also among the contents were small pieces of camping gear, including a mini-flashlight, a waterproof container filled with matches, a first aid kit, a compass on a wristband, and an insulated water bottle. Stilwell started going through the pack's zippered compartments looking for anything that might lead to the identity of its owner. He found a small makeup compact, four individually wrapped tampons, a ChapStick, and a key ring with five keys attached.

One of the keys had a Ford logo on it. It was an old-style key that turned in the ignition, not the electronic fob that most contemporary vehicles came with. Of the four other keys, only one stood out. It was a Medeco key with a large square head. The name and number of a locksmith was imprinted on it along with the words DO NOT DUPLICATE. Stilwell was familiar with the Medeco brand from prior investigations and used them himself. They were expensive, but you got what you paid for: a secure, tamperproof lock.

The locksmith's area code was 562, which covered most of southwest L.A. County, including Long Beach and the northern beach towns of Orange County. His curiosity was piqued by the fact that nobody had come to claim this expensive pack and its contents. Stilwell took out his phone and called the number on the key. The phone was answered right away by a man whose voice had been cured over time with cigarette smoke.

"Gold Coast Lock and Key, how can I help you?"

"Yes, my name is Stilwell. I'm a detective with the L.A. County Sheriff's Department. Who am I speaking with?"

"This is Barn. This is my business."

"Barney?"

"No, just Barn. I'm sort of a big guy. People call me Barn, short for Barn Door. What can I do for you, Detective?"

"I'm conducting an investigation and I'm looking at a key with the name and number of your shop on it. I'm wondering if it's possible to trace it to its owner."

"Uh, that depends. What kind of—"

"It's a Medeco and there are some numbers printed on the head under the shop name."

"Then you're in *lock*, as I like to say. We keep Medeco records in case somebody needs a replacement key made."

"Even if it says *Do not duplicate* on it?"

"We keep the name of the customer and that's the only one who can order a copy. What reference number do you have there?"

Stilwell gave him the six-digit number and waited as the man typed it into a computer.

"This is weird," Barn said.

"How so?"

"I remember this one because the police came around asking about her."

"About who?"

"The customer's name is Angela Metier. That's in our records. The police came in here and asked about her because she was missing."

"When was this?"

"Oh boy, it must have been . . . three or four years ago? They found a receipt for the keys we made for her and wanted to know if she'd said anything about needing the Medeco locks because of a security issue. They were thinking she might have had a stalker or something."

Stilwell was silent for a few moments as he considered this information. Something about what Barn said didn't make sense.

"You're sure it was three or four years ago?" he asked. "Not more recently?"

"No, I'm looking at it here on my screen. We did the work at her place in March of '22. And it was pretty soon after that that the cops came in here asking about her."

"Long Beach police?"

"No, actually, it was LAPD. She lived up there."

"Do you know if she later showed up or was found somewhere?"

"No, I don't think so. At least not that I heard. It was in the papers for a while, and I remember thinking, *Pretty girl like that, I hope she's okay.* I heard they traced her out to Catalina but then the trail went cold."

Four years ago was before Stilwell had been posted on the island. He had not been told about the Angela Metier case when he arrived. It was not part of the briefing he got from the outgoing sergeant.

"I think, if I remember right, that the conclusion was that she had gone off on her own somewhere," Barn said. "You know, like it was a voluntary thing."

Stilwell asked Barn where the work for Angela Metier had been done. He was given an address on Pacific Avenue in San Pedro. Stilwell was familiar with the area and knew the address was close to the Lighthouse, a jazz club he'd frequented when he was living on the mainland. The address also confirmed that it had been the LAPD that came asking about the key. San Pedro was in the city of Los Angeles.

"You don't happen to remember the name of the LAPD detective, do you?" he asked.

"No, but if you give me a minute, I can probably find his card," Barn said. "Don't get many visits from the cops, so I think I kept the guy's card in my desk."

"Sure, take a look."

"Hold on."

Stilwell heard the phone being put down on a hard surface. While he waited, he thought about the incongruity of Angela Metier being missing for four years and her keys and backpack showing up on a bench in Avalon two months ago. He held the backpack up to study it again and noticed that the cushioned panel that went against the spine of the wearer had a jagged line drawn on it with a Sharpie. It looked like an EKG tracing or a seismogram of a mild earthquake.

"Okay, got it," Barn said. "The card says 'Detective Bryce Kaufman, LAPD Missing Persons Unit.'"

Stilwell put the backpack down.

"Is there a phone number?" he asked.

He wrote down the number Barn gave him.

"You've been a big help," he said.

"What are you thinking, that she's alive out there somewhere?" Barn said.

"That I don't know. But I'm going to try to find out."

9

STILWELL RETURNED THE items to the backpack and then carried it to his office and called Kaufman. The call went to voicemail and Stilwell left his number and said the inquiry was about Angela Metier.

"I found her backpack," he added.

He hoped that dropping the name of the presumably still-missing woman and mentioning her backpack might spur a quick return call. While he waited, he called Tash over at the harbormaster's office at the end of Green Pleasure Pier.

"How far back do you archive the harbor cameras?" he asked.

"I think it's ninety days," Tash said. "Three billing cycles. That way if anybody disputes their days here, we can just go to the video and show them."

Stilwell knew from a prior investigation that there were several cameras offering a view of Avalon Harbor from many angles.

"Do you have any cameras that show the beach and the benches on Crescent?" he asked.

"Uh, yeah, we do," Tash said. "There's a camera over the first kiosk on the pier. It's really focused on the skiff dock but it gets a lot of Crescent."

Stilwell looked down at his notes.

"Good," he said. "I need to see that angle from February ninth. Can you set that up for me?"

"Sure," Tash said. "When are you coming?"

"I can be there in ten minutes if you'll have it ready."

"Come on over. I'll have it ready to watch. It's pretty slow around here even for a Tuesday, and it will give me something to do."

After disconnecting, Stilwell left the office and crossed the squad room to the restroom. He didn't have to use the facilities but wanted to show up on camera should Corum be keeping visual tabs on him. Afterward, he announced loudly for the camera as well as Mercy that he would be making calls from his office and didn't want to be disturbed unless it was necessary. Mercy acknowledged the request and he returned to his office, shutting and locking the door behind him. He then went to his office window, cranked it open, and removed the screen. He climbed through and dropped down behind the hedge that ran the length of the building. Soon he was walking down Catalina Avenue to the pier.

Tash had a screen with the camera angle on Crescent up and ready for him when he arrived. He put the recording on high-speed playback for the first viewing. Mercy's report noted that the Unbound backpack had been turned in at 2:15 p.m.

The camera angle Tash had set up for him was from a distance of fifty yards. With Tash looking over his shoulder, he pointed to the benches on the screen.

"This is the best angle you have on these benches?" he asked.

"Yes, sorry," she said. "But as I said, it's focused on the skiff dock, not really on the benches."

The video review was tedious. Stilwell had to stop the playback every time he saw somebody sit on one of the four benches that lined the seawall in the plaza. The view from the benches was one of the best on the island, so Stilwell was stopping and starting the playback often.

It wasn't until he had run the video back to 11:15 a.m. that he caught sight of the Unbound backpack. He slowed the playback to normal speed and watched as a male figure sat down on the last bench in the line and placed the distinctive black-and-white pack next to him.

Stilwell froze the video.

"Okay, can we blow this image up?" he asked.

"Let me sit there," Tash said.

Stilwell got up and Tash took his place. She expanded the image on the screen. The pixels spread and the image became blurry. Still, he could see that the man on the bench was wearing a baseball cap with an indistinct logo on it, sunglasses, and a face mask. It had been more than five years since the COVID pandemic, and although some people still used masks, they were rare enough for Stilwell to think that the man was trying to hide his identity.

"You want a hard copy of this?" Tash asked.

"Yes, please," Stilwell said. "And then let the video run."

After sending the still image to the printer, Tash started the playback again in real time. The man sitting on the bench seemed to be taking in the beauty of the harbor. But five minutes after he sat down, he calmly got up and walked away, leaving the backpack behind. None of the other people in the plaza or sitting on the other benches seemed to notice that he had left it. Stilwell watched as the man crossed Crescent and started walking up Catalina Avenue. Soon he was out of the camera frame.

"Stop it?" Tash asked.

"No, take it to about one thirty and then let's watch," Stilwell said. "It was turned in to the lost-and-found a little after two."

Tash did as instructed, and at 1:42 on the playback, a woman eating an ice-cream cone sat down on the bench and noticed the backpack. She swiveled her head, looking around for the owner. She even stood up, turned to the plaza, and held the backpack up, appearing to call out to the other tourists. But no one claimed the pack.

"Let's watch the drop-off again," Stilwell said.

Tash reversed the video to the 11:10 mark and they watched as the masked man sat down on the bench and then got up and left the pack behind.

"What do you think he's doing?" Tash asked.

"I don't know," Stilwell said. "But it's almost like he knew he was on camera and wanted the backpack to be found and turned in."

"Like he's getting rid of evidence?"

"Like he wants us to find it."

"That's kind of creepy."

"Yeah."

Stilwell thought it was more than creepy. It seemed to be about engagement. The psychology was disconcerting. Four years after Angela Metier disappears, this man places her backpack in a spot that will surely lead to the reopening of the case. Why? Was he taunting law enforcement?

"Can you shoot me a link to this video?" Stilwell asked.

"Sure," Tash said. "And I'll go get the still we printed."

She got up and went to the printer. When she came back, she asked Stilwell if they were cooking or going out for dinner.

"Uh, I was actually thinking about going overtown and visiting Ilsa," Stilwell said. "You could come if you want."

"No, thanks," Tash said. "How is she?"

"Last I heard she was hanging in there. But she's on a ventilator and sedated."

"That doesn't sound good. How much longer will she be on it?"

"I don't know. I'd like to go over whether she knows I'm there or not. You sure about staying here?"

"Definitely. I'll be fine."

"Thanks for understanding."

"Sure."

Tash religiously avoided going to the mainland. She believed that only bad things happened over there, and there was evidence to support that belief.

"Okay, I'm going to get back to it," Stilwell said. "I'll let you know if I go across."

Tash walked him to the door and gave him a quick kiss, and he headed down the pier to Crescent. Along the way his phone rang. It was Lionel McKey, a reporter from the weekly *Catalina Call*. Stilwell answered his question before he could ask it.

"If this is about the airstrip shooting, I can't talk about it, Lionel."

"But you were there when it all went down."

"Doesn't mean I can talk about it. You need to speak to Captain Corum."

"He never calls me back."

"The life of a reporter."

"Yeah, tell me about it."

Stilwell didn't respond.

"I hear you have somebody in the jail. Is that related to last night?"

Stilwell had to respect McKey—the reporter had the island wired. Stilwell would have liked to know who McKey's sources were, beginning with whoever had given him Stilwell's cell number. But to ask the question was to reveal that it bothered him, and Stilwell didn't want to give the reporter that.

"No comment," he said.

"Come on, Stil," McKey said.

There was a definite whine in his voice, but Stilwell didn't care.

"Call the captain," he said. "I've got to go."

He hung up as he approached the open window to his office. He slipped in, put the screen back in place, cranked the window closed, then stepped into the squad room to put in an appearance on camera. He went over to Mercy's desk.

"Anybody looking for me?" he asked.

"Not lately," Mercy said.

His phone buzzed and he dug it out of his pocket, expecting it to be McKey again. But he recognized the number as belonging to Bryce Kaufman of the Missing Persons Unit.

"I've got to take this," he said.

He headed back to his office, answering along the way. "Sergeant Stilwell. How can I help you?"

"Kaufman, LAPD. You left me a message about Angela Metier."

"Yeah, hold on a sec."

Stilwell closed the door to his office and took a seat behind the desk.

"Yes, I wanted to see what was going on with that case," he said.

"Tell you what, why don't we start with what you've got going on," Kaufman said. "You said you found her backpack? Where?"

"I'm on Catalina. It was in our lost-and-found. I started clearing things out today and came across a camping pack. There was a set of keys in one of the pockets and I traced a Medeco back to Metier. At least, the locksmith told me it was hers."

"And you've had this sitting there in the lost-and-found for four years?"

"No, more like two months. It was turned in on February ninth. A woman found it on a bench overlooking the harbor."

That brought silence from Kaufman.

"I know," Stilwell said. "She's been gone four years, why's the backpack showing up now?"

"Doesn't make sense."

"I have a grainy photo off a camera in the harbor that shows the guy who left it, but he's not identifiable."

"Send it to me anyway."

"I will. But tell me what happened with the case and what I can do from out here."

There was another long silence from Kaufman before he responded.

"Look, I don't know you and you don't know me," he said. "You're at the sheriff's station in Avalon, right?"

"That's right," Stilwell said.

"Okay, let me call you back on the station's landline."

"You want the number?"

"No, I'll find it. Give me a few."

He disconnected. Stilwell thought it was a good move on Kaufman's part. But it also made him wonder if Kaufman had previously been burned in some way on the case.

Five minutes went by before Stilwell saw one of the outside lines on his desk phone light up. He let Mercy answer it, then his direct line buzzed.

"Detective Kaufman from the LAPD calling you back," she said.

"I'll take it," Stilwell said.

He picked up the line.

"Okay, where were we?" Kaufman said.

"I think you were about to tell me why you were taking the precaution of calling me back," Stilwell said.

"Just wanted to make sure I was talking to the real thing."

"Because?"

Another long beat of silence.

"Okay, I'll tell you," Kaufman said. "This isn't the usual missing persons case. There's a guy out there somewhere who calls me from time to time asking about her. Always on a burner, untraceable. And he says things that make me think he's the one who took her."

Stilwell looked at the blurry photo of the man on the bench that Tash had printed out for him.

"What things does he say?" Stilwell asked.

"Oh, I don't know," Kaufman said. "I'd have to get the file back from the Cold-Case Unit."

"You guys have a dedicated missing persons cold-case team?"

"No, but this case had a little heat on it. It was one of those where we kind of thought she wouldn't be coming back. You know what I mean? It didn't fit with her profile that she'd just split of her own volition. And then about a year ago, the Cold-Case Unit asked for the file to see if it matched up with something they were looking at."

"And did it?"

"I never heard back. And you know how it is, I had other cases to work."

"Right. Who had it in that unit?"

"They're mostly volunteers over there. Everything goes through the OIC, Ballard. Renée Ballard. She asked for the file."

"You have a number for her?"

Kaufman gave Stilwell a number. "Don't expect them to have done much with it," Kaufman said. "They've got like six thousand unsolveds over there. And those are with bodies that have been found."

"Right," Stilwell said. "Let me ask you a couple basics before I let you go. I heard there was a search over here for Angela four years ago. Before my time. What pointed you out here?"

"Her car. We found it in the Catalina Express lot. She was a camper and a hiker and had been going out there since she was in Girl Scouts. This backpack you're talking about was missing, as was some other camping equipment, so we thought she'd gone out there. But we never found anything to confirm that. There was no credit card purchase for the Express either. Nothing but the car in the lot."

"And no evidence in the car?"

"None. No blood evidence, no sign of a struggle."

"What kind of car was it?"

"Uh, it was a... Mini. Yeah, a Mini Cooper."

"You sure? It wasn't a Ford?"

"No, it was a Mini. Why'd you think it was a Ford?"

"The keys I found in the backpack. There was a key with the Ford logo on it. An old-style key, not a fob."

"That's strange. I don't remember anything about a Ford. You could ask Ballard."

"I will."

10

STILWELL CALLED THE number Kaufman had given him for Renée Ballard. The phone was answered by a man.

"Cold-Case Unit, Laffont."

"Yes, I'd like to speak to Detective Ballard."

"She's tied up. Can I help you?"

"I want to talk to her about a case she's working."

"Which one would that be?"

"Angela Metier. It's a missing persons case."

"I can help you with that. Who am I speaking to?"

Stilwell hesitated. He knew that squad rooms could be as competitive as any office environment; there were backstabbings and fierce loyalties and employees with trust issues. He didn't know what the LAPD cold-case squad was like.

"Detective Sergeant Stilwell, L.A. County Sheriff's," he finally responded.

"And you have information on Angela?" Laffont said.

"I want to speak to Detective Ballard about it. Can I leave a message?"

"Can I ask what made you call here?"

"I called Kaufman in Missing Persons. He told me to call Detective Ballard in cold cases because she'd taken it over."

"And why did you call Kaufman, Sergeant Stilwell?"

"I work out on Catalina and found her backpack. I heard that years ago Kaufman worked her case in Missing Persons."

"Okay, can you hold on a second?"

Stilwell was put on hold before he could reply. He waited nearly a minute before the connection went live again.

"Sergeant Stilwell?" Laffont said. "You're on speaker with Detective Ballard and myself."

"Hello, Sergeant, this is Renée," Ballard said. "My colleague says you think you have Angela Metier's backpack."

"I know I do," Stilwell said.

"I admire your certainty, but she's been gone a long time," Ballard said. "Where did you find it?"

"It was turned in to the lost-and-found at the Avalon substation two months ago," Stilwell said. "A black-and-white Hyperlite Unbound pack. There was a key ring in the bag with a Medeco key that I was able to trace to Angela through a locksmith stamp. I reviewed video from the harbor cameras and I have grainy video and stills of a man leaving the backpack on a bench so it would be found."

There was no response from Ballard or Laffont. Stilwell guessed that they were looking at each other and silently debating whether to bring him in or shut him out. He decided to push things further.

"You obviously took the case away from Missing Persons because it matched up with or at least had similarities to something you were working," Stilwell said.

Still no response.

"Probably it was a case with bodies on the ground," Stilwell continued. "I might be able to help you with that. I worked homicide in the past."

"You're making a lot of assumptions, Sergeant," Ballard said.

"I call them hunches," Stilwell said. "And my hunch is that one of your victims drove a Ford. An older model."

This time there was no hesitation in the response.

"What makes you say that?" Ballard asked.

"Because the key ring I found in the pack had five keys on it. One was the Medeco," Stilwell said, "and there was also a key with a Ford logo on it, which doesn't make sense, because Angela Metier drove a Mini Cooper."

Back to the silent treatment.

"Anybody there?" Stilwell asked.

"We're here," Ballard said. "You have a first name, Sergeant?"

"I do," Stilwell said. "But people call me Stil."

"Well, Stil, I think we need to see the backpack and the key ring," Ballard said. "When can we come pick them up?"

"I'll bring them to you," Stilwell said. "As long as you bring me into the case."

"I'm not sure how that would work," Ballard said. "We've been working this case for over a year now and I can't—"

"I get it," Stilwell interrupted. "You know the case and I don't. But I know the island and you don't. So talk to whoever you need to talk to about this and give me a call once you decide what you're doing."

He started to give the sub's telephone number.

"Hold on, hold on," Ballard said. "I'm sure we can work something out. Interagency cooperation is always a good thing."

This time it was Stilwell who went quiet.

"Did we lose you?" Ballard asked.

"No, I'm here," Stilwell said. "I nailed it about the Ford key, didn't I?"

"You did," Ballard said. "When can you bring the backpack to us?"

"I'm off tomorrow," Stilwell said. "I'll take a boat over."

"Perfect," Ballard said.

11

THE LAPD COLD-CASE Unit was located at the Ahmanson Center training facility near the airport. Stilwell had never been there. He took the first boat over from Catalina, carrying Angela Metier's camping backpack in a drawstring trash bag from his kitchen. He kept an old Bronco in the long-term lot at the Express dock, but it had been two weeks since he'd been there, and the fifty-year-old engine failed to start. This was becoming routine. He called to the lot attendant, who eventually came over with a battery pack and cables and jump-started the car for twenty bucks. Stilwell didn't arrive at Ahmanson to meet Renée Ballard and Tom Laffont until ten a.m.

The cold-case investigators worked in a pod of desks that were dwarfed by the rows of unsolved-case files surrounding them. So many cold cases kept coming in that the shelves were on tracks that could be pushed together like a giant accordion to make room for more. Stilwell noticed that someone had used a Sharpie to write *Library of Lost Souls* over the entrance. Ballard and Laffont were waiting for him. Ballard was a dark-haired, deeply tanned woman in her early forties. She looked like a surfer and was dressed informally in a black polo and cargo pants. Laffont looked like a stiff. He was in a jacket and tie, his arms folded as he stood next to Ballard, who was seated at the head of the pod. There was no one else present.

After shaking hands all around, Stilwell held up the trash bag.

"Here it is," he said.

"Has it been processed?" Ballard asked.

"Not yet," Stilwell said. "I went through it before I knew what it was, and our office manager looked through it when it was first brought in."

"Okay, we should process it," Ballard said, taking the bag. "What about the key ring?"

Stilwell pulled a zip-lock bag containing the key ring from his pocket and held it out. Ballard took that as well and told him to have a seat. Laffont also sat down.

"So," Stilwell said. "Where are we?"

"I talked to my captain and we are good to read you in on this," Ballard said. "We just need to be clear that LAPD is lead. We're already a year and a half down the road on this guy."

"Not a problem on my end," Stilwell said. "I'll do anything I can on Catalina. If it's anywhere else, my captain is going to get hives. He's kind of allergic to me leaving the island."

"How'd you end up on Catalina?" Laffont asked. "You've got a lot of experience that probably doesn't get tapped out there."

The question told Stilwell they had checked him out before bringing him into the fold. He believed that his history, especially the eight years he'd spent in the homicide unit, would work in his favor.

"It's a long story," Stilwell said. "But if you checked me out, you probably heard a version of it. I got some people upset with an investigation I was on. They sent me out to Catalina to cool my heels for a little while, but something happened—I liked it out there. I told them I wanted to stay."

"Well, we don't know how much of this involves Catalina," Ballard said. "But we're going to run it down for you and maybe something will pop up now or later."

"Sounds good to me," Stilwell said. "And by the way, for what it's worth, I have this."

He unfolded the printout of the fuzzy still from the harbor video of the man who'd left the backpack. He handed it to Ballard.

"Damn, it would have been perfect if we could ID the guy," she said. "You think it's worth turning the video over to our photo techs to see if they can clean it up?"

"The camera was at least a hundred and fifty feet away," Stilwell said.

"Probably not, then," Laffont said.

Using a tag-team approach, Ballard and Laffont proceeded to describe the investigation they had been working on for the past eighteen months.

"This whole thing started in Griffith Park," Ballard said. "A hiker up there, just below the observatory, found some bones that had been disinterred by animals."

"Excavation led to the recovery of the full skeletal remains of a young woman," Laffont said. "Cause of death was likely strangulation—her hyoid was crushed—but the date of death was unknown. Near as we could tell, she had probably been in the ground eight to ten years before the animals found her."

"That made it a cold case," Ballard said. "We got stuck with the bones."

"But the lab was able to extract DNA from the marrow," Laffont said. "It connected to a missing persons report. Increasingly with missing persons cases where foul play is considered a possibility, they put the DNA into the databank. Our victim was named Candace Neary. She was twenty-eight, lived in Los Feliz, and loved hiking in Griffith Park. She went up there often by herself. She was reported missing in 2016. There was a search but nothing was found. Except for her car, which was parked at the observatory. A Ford Mustang. Locked, no key."

"This didn't look like a one-and-done," Ballard said. "So we profiled Neary and started looking for other cases that might be similar. Angela Metier was one of the cases we found."

"We were looking for women who were hikers, in their twenties, dark hair, athletic, confident, known to hike and camp on their own," Laffont said, ticking things off on his fingers. "When these women were reported missing, it was thought that they were lost. No foul play was suspected at first."

"And sometimes not for months or even a year, the thinking being that their bodies would eventually show up in a crevasse or at the bottom of a cliff," Ballard said.

"How many did you come up with that matched the Neary profile?" Stilwell asked.

"Four," Ballard said. "Neary, Metier, a woman who went missing on a hike in Angeles National nine years ago, and a 2011 case where a mother of two young children disappeared in Malibu Canyon."

"But there are five keys on the key ring," Laffont said. "We might be missing one."

That brought a somber moment of silence before Stilwell spoke.

"Those last two you mentioned," he said. "Malibu Canyon and Angeles National. They're in the county. Have you brought in the sheriffs?"

"Actually, they're National Park Service jurisdiction," Ballard said. "We're working with them, but they don't have a homicide team."

"And what about the suspect?" Stilwell asked. "Do you have enough to profile him?"

"We thought we did until the backpack showed up," Ballard said. "We had him as very smart, likely some kind of professional. A planner. A hiker himself. He probably stalked these women for weeks before the kill. The grave where he buried Neary was four feet deep. That took some work and planning. He clearly didn't want her found. Usually four feet is below foraging depth. That tells us a lot—or we thought it did. We figured he was an untraceable—a killer who flies below the radar, whose psychological gratification comes from the hunt and the kill, not from the public horror and fear generated by the discovery of the victims."

"And not from engagement with law enforcement," Laffont said. "They don't care about the cat-and-mouse, I-am-smarter-than-you of it all."

"But that whole profile seems to be wrong now," Ballard said. "He apparently wanted that backpack and key ring found. Something with him has changed. I think he's trying to engage now. He wants our attention. He's got a big ego."

Stilwell nodded.

"So where do we go from here?" he asked.

"Our focus has been on connecting the victims," Ballard said. "Trying to find commonalities beyond the fact that they were all hikers. They didn't know one another, as far as we've been able to determine. But there has to be a nexus where they crossed paths with our bad guy."

"We think we're looking for a guy who knows these trails and encounters his victims as a fellow hiker," Laffont said.

"Have you thought about going public?" Stilwell said. "You know, putting it out there and seeing if any hikers come forward with encounters they've had on the trails?"

"Until now, no," Ballard said. "We haven't wanted him to know we're onto him. But given his backpack move, that might be the way for us to go. The thing is, we don't have evidence tying these cases together. It's all circumstantial and based on similarities between the victims. I'll talk to my captain about it. Maybe we'll put out that grainy photo and see what comes in."

"That will undoubtedly be a circus," Laffont said.

"Yep," Ballard said.

"What do you want me to do?" Stilwell asked.

"I think go back to Catalina," Ballard said. "Do a deep dive on Angela Metier and find something that was missed before."

"Her roommate told us she was going to hike something called the Trans-Catalina Trail," Laffont said. "You know it?"

"That's thirty-eight miles all over the island," Stilwell said.

"She was covering it in pieces," Laffont said. "It was her third time out there when she disappeared."

Stilwell knew through Tash about the TCT. She had hiked it numerous times over the thirty-five years she had lived on the island, also doing it in pieces.

He nodded.

"Okay, I can do that," he said.

"Good," Ballard said.

"Do you have a media file you can share with me?" Stilwell asked. "I'd like to take a look at the news coverage these cases got."

Ballard looked at Laffont and nodded.

"Give Tom your email and he'll get it to you," she said.

"Any sense in me reinterviewing the roommate?" Stilwell asked.

"I won't stop you, but I think we got what's there," Ballard said. "Tom will also send you summaries of the interviews so far."

"Excellent," Stilwell said.

"We appreciate it," Ballard said. "This is an all-volunteer unit—except for me. We'll take all the help we can get."

"Copy that," Stilwell said. "I'll stay in touch."

"We will too," Ballard said.

12

ILSA RAMIREZ WAS in the critical care unit at Torrance Memorial. Stilwell went by on his way from the Ahmanson Center to the Catalina Express docks at Long Beach. He had been told she was in a medically induced coma, but he wanted to go and show his support even if she didn't know he was there.

She was in a single room with an observation window. A uniformed deputy was posted at the door, not that anyone seriously thought that Ramirez was in danger from a threat outside the room. Her biggest threat was the possibility of her own organs shutting down.

Stilwell stood at the window thinking about the twenty minutes it had taken for the rescue chopper to get to them and all the blood he could not stop flowing from her body. Her neck had been torn up by the bullet. He'd tried to slow the bleeding with a dressing from the first aid kit, but it had soaked through.

"Do they need blood, do you know?" he asked the deputy at the door.

"Nah, people have been lining up to give blood," the deputy said. "She probably could use some prayers, though."

"Right. What about her family?"

"Yeah, they've been here. A bunch of them came up from San Diego."

"Good."

Stilwell's phone buzzed and he pulled it from his pocket. It was Captain Corum. He started walking down the hallway as he answered.

"Captain."

"Stil, I haven't seen you on the cameras today. Why is that?"

"Because I'm off Wednesdays and Thursdays, remember?"

"Right, right. Are you at home?"

"No, I took a boat over to the mainland. I'm at the hospital checking on Ramirez."

"How is she?"

"No change. Still in a coma, breathing tube, the whole thing."

"A goddamn shame. Even if she makes it, she's done."

"Maybe."

"So, listen, I'm calling to tell you you're off the bench. Return to full duty starting Friday."

"That was fast. Are they dinging my file?"

"No, not this time. It was clear there was a fuckup at the airport, but your efforts to save Ramirez balanced things out for the review team. No punishment, no penalty. You should be happy."

"I am, Captain. How goes the investigation into the criminal side of it?"

"They're working all angles."

"They looking at Quigley?"

That brought a beat of silence from Corum.

"Why should they be looking at him?" he finally asked.

"It was his tip, his CI," Stilwell said. "I figured they would want to run that down, see if they can figure out who his guy was. Should be in the CI file, right?"

"I'm sure they're looking at all of that."

"Captain, can I ask you something?"

"Go ahead. I may not answer it, but go ahead."

"What did Quigley do that got him transferred to Catalina?"

The captain took his time answering.

"That's above your pay grade, Stil," he said. "But why would you ask that?"

"Just thinking about the possibilities," Stilwell said. "He comes out here a couple months ago, then he gets this tip about a drop out here. I'm sure it's happened before, but it seems kind of coincidental, don't you think?"

"I'm sure all of that is under consideration. But it's not your case, so why are you so interested?"

"Not my case, but it is my island, Captain. I just wish I knew a little more about the people I get sent. Speaking of which, I'm down two deputies. I'm going to need replacements or overtime authorization."

"You'll get replacements with the next deployment. Meanwhile, I'll give you eighty hours of overtime to spread around. Be tight with it."

"Got it."

"Good. Now, remember, you are off the bench but you are not working this case. *Comprende, mi amigo*?"

The captain always dipped into his rudimentary Spanish when he was trying to sweet-talk Stilwell into going along to get along.

"*Comprendo, Capitán*," Stilwell said.

13

STILWELL CAUGHT THE last Express back to the island. Along the way, he sat in the enclosed commodore cabin and caught up on email and texts. He sent Tash a message asking where the third leg of the Trans-Catalina Trail started. Her response came quickly: Hermit Gulch.

Stilwell decided he would go up there the next day to get a feel for the area where Angela Metier had been heading. It was Tash's usual day off and he would invite her to come, as she was the experienced hiker and he wouldn't have to worry about getting lost. Plus he would enjoy her company.

As the boat cruised into the harbor, Stilwell pulled up the substation's cameras on his phone so he could see who was on duty and what was going on. Mercy made the schedule for the island's deputies, and with two officers down, that was not an easy task. He planned to tell her in the morning about the eighty hours of approved overtime from Corum.

He saw no one in the squad room. Mercy's desk was empty, but it was after five, and that was not unusual. But the standard protocol was to keep a deputy in the sub whenever anyone was held in a cell. He switched to the jail cameras and saw that cell one was empty. He checked the second cell and saw that Kalas had not been moved to it.

Kalas was gone.

Stilwell immediately called Mercy's cell. She answered right away and Stilwell didn't bother with a hello.

"What's going on at the sub?" he asked. "Where is Kalas?"

"Uh, nothing's going on, far as I know," Mercy said. "And the ICE agents picked Kalas up."

"What? When?"

"About three. They came in with the transfer order from a federal magistrate."

"Who let them take him?"

"Deputy Mason was in here. He dealt with them and the paperwork."

"Mercy, I'll call you back."

Stilwell disconnected and went into his call history to find the number for the ICE agent he had spoken to about the hold on Gonzalo Kalas. The ferry was now docked and he got up from his seat to join the tourists disembarking. He made the call as he was crossing the gangway.

"Agent Gordon, how can I help you?"

It sounded like Gordon was in a moving vehicle.

"It's Stilwell out on Catalina. I want Kalas back."

"Uh, what are we talking about here?"

"Gonzalo Kalas. You guys came and picked him up."

"That's news to me."

"Bullshit. It might not have been you, but you sent guys to grab him. He's the suspect in the murder of a sheriff's deputy and I don't want him on the next bus to Tijuana."

"Look, as far as I'm concerned, I was waiting on you. You said you had eyes on him and you were supposedly going to call me once you had him in custody. Funny, I never got that call."

"You're saying you didn't have him picked up?"

"Exactly. But he is on our pickup list. If you booked him, his name could've come up on the computer."

Stilwell was silent as he walked toward the substation.

"You there, Stilwell?" Gordon asked.

"I'll call you back," Stilwell said.

He disconnected. He didn't have a two-way with him so he called Mason's cell phone. It went directly to voicemail, but the message box was full. He dictated a text telling Mason to return to the sub ASAP.

Two minutes later Stilwell entered the substation through the unlocked front door to find Mason already there.

"Sorry, I was in the can when you called," he said. "I was about to call you back."

"Tell me about ICE coming for Kalas," Stilwell said.

"Uh, yeah, two ICE guys came in and said they were here to pick him up. They had the pickup order from the judge."

"What judge?"

"A federal magistrate, actually."

"Did they leave it?"

"No, but I made a copy of it."

"Show it to me."

Mason went over to the deputies' report-writing desk and took a document off the top of a stack of papers. He handed it to Stilwell.

"What about badges and IDs?" Stilwell said, looking at the document. "You check them?"

"They had badges," Mason said.

"Did you get their names?"

"Yeah, but I didn't write them down. One was Rivera, like the pitcher. I remember that. Not sure I remember the other one."

At first glance, the custody-transfer order looked legitimate. But then Stilwell noticed that it had a seal from the magistrate of the US District Court for the Southern District of California. Los Angeles County was in the Central District. It didn't mean the order wasn't valid, but it made him suspicious.

"This is from the Southern District," he said.

"So?" Mason said. "Is that a problem?"

"Just seems odd that they'd come all the way up from San Diego to pick the guy up. Did they say anything about where they were taking him?"

"No, they just said that they were here for him and showed me the transfer order."

The order was two pages, and the magistrate's signature and seal were on a third page.

"Take a look at this," Stilwell said. "Does this look like a different font on the signature page?"

He handed the document to Mason, who flipped between the pages and studied the font on each. "Uh... maybe," he said. "Hard to tell."

"I think they're different," Stilwell said, taking the transfer order back.

"Then what's it mean?"

"They could have used the signature page from another order and clipped it to this one."

"Why would they do that?"

"I don't know yet. What time did they come?"

"Around three."

"They come on a chopper?"

"Uh, I don't know."

"And you're sure they were ICE?"

"Well, pretty sure. Like I said, they had badges."

"Did they take his property?"

"Yeah, they took it. Did I do something wrong, Sarge?"

"Not as far as I know."

"Then can I go back out on patrol?"

"Of course. I'll probably stick around here for a while."

Mason grabbed a set of keys. As he headed to the door, a new thought came to Stilwell.

"Hey, you worked shifts with Quigley when he first transferred here, right?" he asked.

"Yeah, a few," Mason said.

"Did he ever talk about what happened to him back on the mainland? You know, like what got him the transfer out here?"

"No, not really. I mean, I asked him about it. You know, Island of Misfit Toys and all that. I asked him who he'd pissed off over there and he claimed he didn't do anything to anybody. He just said he asked to transfer out to the island so he could lie low for a while."

"'Lie low'—you're sure he said that?"

"Hundred percent."

"And you didn't ask why he was lying low?"

"No, I didn't. It was just conversation, you know?"

"Yeah. Sure."

"Can I go now?"

"Yes, you can go."

14

AFTER MASON WAS gone, Stilwell went into the kitchen, took a Diet Coke from the refrigerator, and checked the pantry for something to eat. There was little to choose from and that reminded him to ask Mercy to restock the shelves. He found a bag of pretzels with a clip holding it closed and a Post-it Note saying the bag belonged to Ilsa. It hit Stilwell then that she would probably never be back to the station. Either the injury and recovery time would prevent it or the attractive injured-on-duty pension would make coming back a financial mistake.

He went into his office, sat down at the desk, and pulled up the sub's cameras on his computer screen.

He backed up the recordings to 2:20 p.m. and started the playback. At 2:26 two men entered the sub through the front door. They were wearing the dark, nondescript, and unmarked raid attire Stilwell had seen on television reports showing ICE roundups of immigrants on the mainland. They also wore baseball caps reading ICE.

Stilwell switched to an interior camera. The two men entered and Mercy greeted them, then turned them over to Mason. The conversation was muffled because the two visitors stood with their backs to the camera and kept their voices low. He did hear Mason ask for verification of the removal order from the magistrate. One of the two visitors produced the document, which Mason read quickly.

"Do I keep this?" Mason asked.

The man's answer was unintelligible no matter how many times Stilwell replayed it at various volumes.

"Then okay if I make a copy?" Mason said.

He must've received an affirmative response, because he got up and went to the copy machine. Once he had a copy, he led the two men to the jail. On the jail cameras, the men waited for Mason to unlock the cell. They then entered and cuffed Kalas's hands behind his back. When Kalas was walked out of the cell, Stilwell had his best view of the visitors. But the brims of their baseball caps hid much of their faces from the camera mounted in the upper corner of the room.

With each of the ICE agents holding one of his arms, Kalas was walked through the squad room and out the door. Stilwell called ICE agent Gordon back.

"I'm looking at video and I see two guys with ICE hats walking Kalas out of the station," he said.

"Hey, after you called, I checked on this," Gordon said. "As far as I can tell, it wasn't us. I can't find Kalas on the computer. That means either he's still in transit or it wasn't us."

"Then keep checking the computer and let me know if he turns up."

"Will do."

"This is a murder of a law enforcement officer. They need to bring Kalas back here."

"Got it, got it."

Stilwell disconnected and stared at his computer screen while he thought about his next moves. He didn't know if he could trust anything Gordon said. He could be lying about not having Kalas. But if he was telling the truth, then Kalas had escaped. In that case, Stilwell had just been cleared in one investigation of his actions only to face another. While Mason would be the fall guy for actually allowing the prisoner to be walked out of the jail, the buck would stop with Stilwell as the station supervisor. He would go back to the bench or worse just as the investigation of the missing hikers was picking up speed.

He couldn't let that happen, but he also couldn't ignore the possibility that Kalas was in the wind. He decided to start with a call to Ernie Simon at the homicide bureau.

"Stil, what's up?" he said. "Did our guy confess his sins?"

"I actually have some bad news about him, Ernie," Stilwell said.

"All I need on this case. Lay it on me, brother."

"I was off today and went over to the mainland to visit Ramirez. While I was gone, ICE showed up out here and took Kalas."

"Those motherfuckers—they didn't know he's our suspect?"

"We were only holding him on the ICE warrant, remember? They either didn't know or didn't care about our case."

"That's fucked up. Who gave him to them?"

"We had a deputy on duty. They had a transfer order from a magistrate. I can send it to you if you want to take a look."

"What good would that do? This is some serious bullshit. Did you try to find out where they took him?"

"I called the agent whose name is on the hold and he claimed he didn't know about the pickup. I told him we want Kalas back but I don't know how motivated he'll be to find him."

"Text me his name and number. I'll call him and light a fire."

"Will do."

"And give me the name of the magistrate. We might have to get him involved in producing the body."

"You got it."

"What I ought to do is leak to the *Times* that ICE stole the suspect in the murder of a sheriff's deputy."

"That might cause more trouble for you than them. There was something off about the pickup."

"Like what?"

"Just the way they did it. The pickup order is from a magistrate in the Southern District."

"That's weird. Does it look legit?"

"Yeah, it looks legit, but the deputy only made a copy of it, he didn't keep it, so I'm not looking at the original."

"All right, send me that too. I'll talk to the captain about what he wants to do. Anything else happening out there? I heard you were cleared back to full duty."

"I was, and thanks for whatever your part was in that. So, anything you need from out here, give me a call."

"Right now, what I need is our prisoner back. How do you think they got him off the island?"

"Helo, government boat—take your pick if they were legit. If not, they could have just jumped on the Express. You want me to try to run that down?"

"Um, not yet. Let me see what I can find out first."

"Okay."

"I'll get back to you."

"I'll be here."

Stilwell was satisfied that he would be able to operate until it was determined whether Kalas was in federal custody or had escaped. After the call ended, he got up and stood in front of the map of the island that was mounted on the office wall. It showed the island's established hiking trails and campgrounds as well as their elevations. As he looked at it, he pulled out his cell and called Tash.

"Hey, what's up?" she asked.

"I need to ask you another TCT question," he said.

"Sure."

"Just looking at a trail map here. You said you think the third leg would be at the gulch."

"I do, yes."

"That looks like it would work if you went straight from the second to the third leg. What if you were breaking it up? Hermit Gulch would be kind of hard to get to, wouldn't it?"

"Hmm. You mean like on different days or visits?"

"Exactly."

"Then I guess it would depend on what kind of hiker you were. You know, experience level and skill, equipment, all that stuff."

"Okay, let's say experienced. Pretty highly skilled. Top-of-the-line equipment."

"Then probably you'd start at the campground at Black Jack Mountain on the third leg. If it were me, that's where I would start."

Stilwell ran his finger along the trail on the map until he found Black Jack Mountain.

"Okay," he said. "And how far would you plan to go from there in a day?"

"It depends on how often you stop to rest or eat or just enjoy the views," Tash said. "But if it were me, I'd get to Soapstone Quarry. It's not that far, but it's pretty rugged up there. And high. Soapstone's only a few miles, but they're slow miles. A lot of switchbacks. But if you're ambitious, you could go all the way down to Little Harbor."

Stilwell followed the trail with his finger to Little Harbor on the back of the island.

"And you can get a ride up there to Black Jack?" he asked.

"Sure, easy," Tash said. "You can arrange it. Why are you asking about the TCT?"

"I wasn't out here then, but do you remember Angela Metier, the hiker who went missing about four years ago?"

"Of course. I helped look for her. Is there something new?"

"No, not really, but I'm looking into that case."

"Don't get obsessed like Lionel."

She was referring to McKey, the reporter for the *Call.* They had grown up together, attended twelve grades of school together, and Stilwell wasn't really sure how close they were.

"Why is Lionel obsessed?" Stilwell asked.

"I don't know," Tash said. "He just wrote about it a lot when they were looking for her up there. He seemed to care more about her than your predecessor did."

Stilwell had inherited the post on the island from an investigator named Dan King who'd treated the assignment as a punishment and therefore did little to integrate himself into the community and generally got low marks in the protect-and-serve part of the job.

Stilwell changed the subject.

"Are you still off tomorrow?" he asked.

"I am," Tash said. "You want to go up there and look around?"

"I was thinking about it. Just to get a feel for it. But only if you would be my guide."

"Love to. We should go early, though. When you're up that high, the sun is superhot by midday."

"Fine by me. I'm off tomorrow and I can go up anytime."

"We also need to register with the conservancy and get passes."

"Can you handle that?"

"Yes, and I'll put together a pack tonight. We're going up and back, right? No camping?"

"No camping. I'll need to get back."

"Deal. When am I going to see you tonight?"

"I'm heading home in a little bit."

"Me too. See you then."

15

AFTER THE CALL Stilwell remained standing and studying the wall map. He located Soapstone Quarry on it and saw that it did appear — at least on the map — to be only a short distance from Black Jack Mountain. He and Tash had gone on several hikes over the eighteen months they had been together, but most of those were along the coast. Hiking the interior of the island was less appealing to Stilwell, largely because he feared he wouldn't be able to keep up with Tash, who was eight years younger and not carrying an ounce of extra weight. Not wanting to embarrass himself, he always chose the hikes that didn't involve climbing mountains.

Tomorrow would be different.

While he was looking at the elevations printed on the map, he noticed a road that cut away from the Trans-Catalina Trail, went east toward the mountaintop airport, then connected to Echo Lake Road. There was no name on the map for the cutaway road, but it was a black line as opposed to the yellow line for the TCT. According to the map's legend, a black line was a road accessible by vehicle.

Without taking his eyes off the unnamed road, he called Tash back.

"I'm looking at a map that shows the TCT, and there's a road that cuts away from it on Black Jack Mountain," he said. "Any idea what that road is?"

"It sounds like you're talking about Black Jack Road," Tash said. "It goes east?"

"Yeah, directly east."

"Then, yes, that's Black Jack Road. It goes down to the ironwood grove and Echo Lake."

"What's the ironwood grove?"

"It's just a protected area because the Catalina ironwood tree is slowly disappearing. There are supposedly only about a hundred groves left on the island. The one you're talking about is the oldest."

"Well, doesn't *grove* mean a bunch of trees?"

"Ironwood trees share an underground root system. So basically, a grove is really one tree. Everything is connected."

"Then why are they disappearing? Aren't they called ironwood because they are strong and durable?"

"Climate change—rising temperature, drought. They may be hard on the outside but they're vulnerable on the inside. Like you."

"I don't know about that. But can we get to this grove on the hike tomorrow?"

"Sure, but it's off-trail. You think it has something to do with Angela?"

Stilwell noted her use of the missing woman's first name.

"I don't know," he said. "I'll see you at the house and explain more. I've got to get back to this."

"Okay," Tash said. "See you at the house."

Stilwell disconnected and went to the desk. He took a black marker from a drawer and tore a page from the scratch pad he kept next to his keyboard. He then went back to the map, held the white paper against it, and traced Black Jack Road with the marker.

He pulled out his phone and called the cell number Renée Ballard had given him. She answered right away.

"Stilwell?"

"Yeah, listen, are you still at work?"

"I'm here."

"Do you have the backpack there?"

"Uh, no. Laffont took it downtown to the crime lab on his way home."

"Did you take photos of it?"

"No, but I'm sure they'll do that at the lab. What's going on? You sound hyped up about something."

"I am. Hold on. I'm going to send you photos."

He took the phone away from his ear and put the call on speaker so he could use his hands. He sent Ballard the photos he had taken of the backpack before he'd sealed it in the plastic trash bag for transport to the mainland. Then he took a photo of the paper he had just traced Black Jack Road on.

"Okay, you still there?"

"I am."

"Did the photos of the backpack come through?"

"Yes, they did. What's going on?"

"This is kind of crazy but I noticed that on the panel under the straps of the backpack, there is kind of a squiggle made with a permanent marker. You see it?"

There was a pause.

"Yes, I see it. A squiggle. What does it mean?"

"Okay, hold on. I'm sending you another photo."

He texted the photo of the scratch paper.

"You get it?"

"Got it."

"Okay, you see the mark on the backpack? Compare it to the mark on the paper I just sent."

He waited.

"Okay, they're the same," Ballard said. "What does it mean?"

"The mark on the paper is what I just traced off a map of Catalina. It's a road up in the mountains that connects to the trail that Angela Metier told friends she was going to hike."

Ballard said nothing.

"I think our killer put a map on the backpack that he left for us to find."

"A map to where he put her?"

"What I'm thinking."

"You're right. This is kind of crazy."

"But it works. It fits. I mean, what are the chances the two lines would match up perfectly like that? For whatever reason, he's reaching out to us."

"Like he wants to play a game of I'm-smarter-than-you."

"Exactly."

16

THEY FOUND THE bones buried beneath the canopy of an ironwood tree in the grove at the end of Black Jack Road. The line drawn on Angela Metier's backpack provided the heading for the search. It was led by a cadaver dog named Sniffy whose owners volunteered their animal's services to Ballard and her cold-case team. After the dog alerted them, his nose was replaced by an electronic nose—a gas probe that detected chemical compounds released in the soil during the decomposition of human remains.

With Ballard and two rangers from the conservancy observing, an excavation proceeded. Stilwell did most of the careful digging until he uncovered small bones from what looked like a hand and the deteriorated sleeve of a shirt almost four feet down. At that point, everyone backed out and waited for an excavation team from the medical examiner's office to be flown out to document and recover the remains. While he waited, Stilwell paced along the line set by the crime scene tape strung between trees in the grove and quietly seethed. A primal anger was growing in him over the apparent murder of a woman who had thought she would be safe while hiking on the island.

The medical examiner's team arrived, and although official confirmation that the remains were what was left of Angela Metier was withheld pending comparison to dental records, Stilwell and Ballard had no doubt. They had been led to the spot by her killer and now the game was on.

It was impossible to keep the coordination of the search-and-recovery efforts radio silent, and they knew the media was onto the story when several news helicopters from the mainland crossed Santa Monica Bay and circled overhead. Lionel McKey from the *Call* was the lone reporter on the ground, dutifully standing at the yellow tape that the two rangers, Kent Middleton and Bo Meriam, had used to cordon off the grove and keep reporters and passing hikers back. The medical examiner's team had erected a tent over the dig location to protect the diggers from the sun and the site from the cameras on the helicopters.

Stilwell knew it was time to inform the captain of what was going on. Corum wasn't happy that Stilwell had not told him much earlier in the process of his work on the case and the joint investigation with the LAPD.

"When did you bring the LAPD into this?" Corum asked.

"Just yesterday," Stilwell said. "When I identified the owner of the backpack in the lost-and-found, I connected it to their investigation. Things moved pretty quickly after that. But it was more like they brought me into it, Captain, not the other way around."

"Semantics. You should have told me when you reached out to them."

"Captain, when I called them, I had nothing. Do you really want me checking with you every time I make a call?"

"Of course not. But this is different. Now I'm going to have to run interference to ensure that we don't get pushed out of a case on our own turf."

"I don't think that's going to happen. The detective in charge of the cold-case squad needs all the help she can get. She's working with a bunch of volunteers."

"How many cases is this connected to?"

"Three that we know about. Maybe four."

"You are using the word *we*. There is no *we* here. I know her boss, Larry Gandle. I'll talk to him and make sure we don't get mushroomed—kept in the dark."

"Does that mean I can follow this off the island?"

"I was thinking of putting somebody from the squad here on it."

"Great. I put this together, and somebody else gets to run with it. That makes sense."

"You forget that you are in charge of a substation out there. You have management duties and you can't be leaving the island to chase a murder case. It's as simple as that."

"It still doesn't sound right."

"Well, that's the way it is. I have no problem with you working the Catalina angle on this, but I don't want you crossing the bay to follow leads. Let the LAPD handle that. Agreed?"

"You're the boss. And I have to get back to this."

"Then we're done. Let me know where we are on it at the end of the day."

"Roger that."

Stilwell pocketed his phone and returned to the excavation.

"Trouble?" Ballard asked.

"Why do you say that?"

"Because of the way you were head down and pacing while you spoke to the boss."

"Yeah, well, he's not happy I brought LAPD into this, even though I explained that it was sort of the other way around. He'll probably call your captain. I think he said Candle."

"Gandle. I always love that, when two guys who don't work the cases decide how the cases get worked. But don't worry, Stil, I'll keep you in the loop. As far as I'm concerned, this is the biggest break in the case we've had. And it came through you."

"I appreciate that."

Stilwell looked at the dig site. The two techs from the ME's office were down to using spoons and brushes to reveal the bones. It was a tedious process. He looked back at the yellow crime scene tape stretched between limbs of the ironwood grove. Lionel McKey was waiting there patiently. To his left were two hikers who had stopped to watch.

Middleton, one of the conservancy rangers, beckoned Stilwell over with a wave.

"That one guy there is a reporter for the *Call,*" he said. "You want me to get rid of him?"

"Uh, no," Stilwell said. "He's got every right to be there just as long as he doesn't try to get closer."

Stilwell left Middleton and walked over to Ballard.

"I'm going to go talk to the reporter," Stilwell said.

"How well do you know him?" Ballard asked.

"He's not a problem. They don't go to print till tomorrow anyway."

"Before you go, let's talk about holdbacks."

Stilwell stepped closer to her so they could speak without even the rangers hearing them.

"The mark on the backpack?" Stilwell asked.

"Yes, and also the keys," Ballard said. "Let's keep that stuff to ourselves."

"You got it. I'm actually going to try to get more from him than he gets from me. He was here when Angela Metier disappeared. I wasn't."

"Okay. Good idea."

Stilwell walked to the yellow tape at an angle that would pull McKey farther away from the lookie-loo hikers.

"Lionel," he said. "How'd you hear about this?"

"Hard to keep the arrival of the LAPD and sheriff's choppers quiet," McKey said. "Is that Angela Metier you're digging up?"

"You know I can't confirm that. They are definitely human remains, and it appears to be female clothing—what's left of it. You can put two and two together but I can't confirm until we have an official identification made by the ME's office."

"Cause of death?"

"Same answer."

"I just called her mother to see if she had heard anything. It was news to her. But she's going to fly down from Spokane."

"That's all we need, the media jumping the gun. I hope you're the one who gets to call her if it turns out not to be her daughter in the ground over there."

"Come on, who else could it be?"

"You tell me. You've been out here your whole life. Tash told me you were all over this story originally."

"I was and I still am. What led you to this spot?"

"Sniffy did."

"Is that the cadaver dog?"

"Yes. Maybe you should go interview him."

"Funny. But what made you bring Sniffy out?"

"Can't say."

"What about LAPD? Will they talk to me?"

"I kind of doubt it."

"Why are they here?"

"Because if it's Angela Metier, then it's their case."

"Come on, Stil. You gotta give me something. This is my story, not the big shots' from overtown."

"You don't even publish till tomorrow. Why don't you check with me in the morning. Then you can get the freshest update, if there is one."

"My deadline for tomorrow is today."

"All right, check with me later. If I can give you more, I will."

"What do you mean, *more*? You haven't given me anything."

"All right, so when you call me later, ask me about the backpack."

"The backpack? That's it?"

"For now, that's it."

"It better be good."

"You wrote the story when she went missing four years ago, right?"

"I did, yeah. A lot of stories. But I thought you weren't confirming it's Angela."

"I'm not. I'm just asking you questions. Do you remember if this grove with the ironwood trees was searched back then?"

"I think it was. But I was mostly up at Black Jack and then Hermit Gulch."

"Why Hermit Gulch?"

"They got a tip from another hiker, who said he thought he saw Angela on a trail over there. It was unsubstantiated, and obviously it was wrong." He gestured toward the excavation.

"So, in all your reporting, did you find any confirmed sightings of her?" Stilwell asked.

"No, not really," McKey said. "It was all based on what she had told her parents and friends—that she was going back to Catalina to hike—and the permit she got online."

"She had been out here twice before to hike?"

"Yeah, the conservancy had issued two other hiking permits to her, in May and October of the previous year. She was doing the Trans-Catalina Trail in parts. Like the way people do the Appalachian Trail in the East."

"Any of the park rangers remember checking her for a permit?"

"No, that would have been big. And look at me answering your questions when you should be answering mine."

"How's it feel?"

"Not good."

Stilwell smiled and clapped him on the shoulder.

"Call me later," he said.

"Right," McKey said. "And I'm sure you'll answer."

"What's with the sarcasm? I told you I would."

"Yeah, we'll see."

Stilwell approached the rangers.

"Either of you guys here four years ago?" he asked.

"Not me," Middleton said. "Got the job about two years ago."

"Me neither," Meriam said.

"I'm just wondering what records might be in your office from the search for Angela Metier," Stilwell said.

"I can certainly look and get back to you," Middleton said.

"That would be great," Stilwell said. "Thank you."

Stilwell looked past Middleton. There was a blanket of pink flowers growing in the shade of one of the ironwood trees. The flowers looked beautiful, but they couldn't lighten the tragedy of the moment and the dread Stilwell was feeling now.

17

THE EXCAVATION WENT on until dusk. The bones and clothing were collected and cataloged and secured in a plastic box for transport to the medical examiner's office. Ballard flew back in the LAPD helicopter shortly after the sheriff's airship took off with the ME's team. Stilwell got home to the smell of Tash's gumbo. That plus the music she was playing on the kitchen Bose—Steely Dan's album *Gaucho*—told him that he was forgiven for reneging on their plans to hike Black Jack Mountain that morning in light of Ballard's plan to come with a cadaver dog and a gas probe.

She was at the stove with her back to him, stirring a pot with a wooden spoon, when he entered the kitchen.

"Hey," she said. "How did it go up there?"

"Good and bad," Stilwell said.

"You found her, I heard."

"Yeah."

"Sad."

"Yeah."

She turned around to check him and saw the bouquet of flowers in his hand.

"Flowers," she said. "You thought I'd be mad?"

"I don't know," Stilwell said. "I guess. Mad or sad. She liked to hike on her own. Like you. I hope it doesn't change your love of walking trails."

"I hadn't thought about it that way. But it won't."

"Good."

She put the wooden spoon down on a plate on the counter and came over to him in the doorway. She took the flowers.

"How did you know?" she asked.

"Know what?" Stilwell asked.

"These are wishbones — my favorite. Did you pick them up there in the grove?"

"Yeah. Away from the dig."

"I hope so."

He realized it was the first time he had ever given her flowers.

"Do you mind stirring the roux while I find a vase for these?" Tash asked.

"As long as I can take a taste," Stilwell said.

"Don't you dare."

She went out to the dining room and came back with a wine carafe from the shelves. She filled it with water and arranged the flowers in it. She saw him raising the spoon from the pot.

"No," she said.

"Smells so good," he said.

"My grandma's Catalina gumbo."

"I know. Why can't I try it?"

"Because it's not ready. Why don't you go get cleaned up. It'll be ready when you're back."

"Perfect. I definitely need a shower."

She came to the stove and took the spoon from him.

"I know," she said. "So go."

She pushed him toward the hallway.

"Yes, ma'am," he said.

"You want red or white?" she called after him. "I'll open a bottle."

"Uh . . . red."

"Red it is."

A few minutes later his head was under the hot shower. He raised his face into the spray. He knew that it couldn't wash away everything. But he was home and he felt the dread he had been carrying start to lift.

PART TWO

The Impenetrable Darkness

18

ALTON QUIGLEY WAS buried on the Sunday after his death at Oakwood Memorial Park in Chatsworth. More than a thousand people attended, most of them in uniforms from various law enforcement agencies throughout Southern California. Even Stilwell was in uniform, as dictated by department regs. He also saw officers from Las Vegas and Phoenix. The bagpipes were played, seven rifles were fired three times, and a flag was precisely folded and presented to his widow. And the media was there to record it all.

Stilwell had been to more cop funerals than he could remember and knew the protocol. The only thing different this time was that he knew and had worked with the fallen deputy and carried the lingering regret and guilt over not preventing the death.

Quigley's former boss in the narcotics unit, Lieutenant Gavin Lambert, gave the eulogy. Lambert was a tall man with a jutting Dudley Do-Right jaw, a thick black mustache, and an even thicker mane of dark hair. He gave a somber and heartfelt speech about the loss of a close colleague, whom he referred to by his nickname. "Quigs" was only thirty-six years old and had so much more life ahead of him. It was a familiar theme at cop funerals. The widow, dressed in black and hiding her eyes behind dark sunglasses, stoically lasted through the ceremony without a tear streaking her face.

When it was over, Stilwell watched as Lambert stood with the other members of his unit to commiserate about the loss of Quigs and tell stories about their fallen comrade. Pretty soon there was laughter to go with their memories and tears.

Ernie Simon joined Stilwell and they watched the narco group for a few moments before Simon said what was on his mind.

"I need to give you fair warning," he said. "I'm pretty sure ICE didn't take our suspect."

"Why is that?" Stilwell asked.

"Because I can't find the guy anywhere, and the magistrate's clerk tells me he didn't issue a pickup order for him."

"Shit."

"Yeah, and I'm not going to be able to contain it once I tell the captain that ICE can't cough the guy up because they say they don't have him. It isn't going to look good for you or your deputy who let him escape."

"Thanks for the warning. When do you plan to tell Corum?"

"I can't sit on it for much longer. We've got to put out the BOLO."

Stilwell nodded. "You got anything else working to brief him on?" he asked.

"Not much," Simon said.

"What about Ramirez? I heard she's off the vent and is going to make it."

"I talked to her. Tried to. She doesn't remember a fucking

thing. Plus she's got to write everything. Her vocal cords were damaged by the fucking round that hit her."

"Shit. Permanent?"

"That's what I heard."

"That's bad."

"Tell me about it."

"It could come back to her. Her memory, I mean."

"Yeah, that's what the medical staff say. I'll stop by again in a few days. We'll see."

They stood in silence for a few moments, watching the mourners crossing the lush grass of the cemetery to their cars.

"Have you identified the CI who set the whole thing up at the airstrip?" Stilwell asked.

"Not yet," Simon said. "But I have a second sit-down with Lambert tomorrow morning. He said the other night he'd look into it."

"The way he just talked about Quigley, he was a hero. But why did he get shipped out to Catalina?"

"In our first interview, Lambert said Quigley came to him and asked for the transfer."

"To Catalina?"

"To anywhere. He wanted out of narco."

Stilwell thought about the cold way the widow had reacted when he called with condolences. And now at the funeral, no tears.

"Have you interviewed the wife?" he asked.

"No, the captain said to give her a few days," Simon said. "Maybe tomorrow."

"What about Kalas?" Stilwell asked. "Any connection to Quigley? Or to narco?"

"None that we know about. So far."

"Well, good luck."

"Yeah, I'll let you know how it goes."

"Anything I can do for you out on the island?"

"Did Quigley have a locker at the sub?"

"Yeah. Everybody does."

"I didn't think about it when I was out there. You check it?"

"Yeah, just some clothes and boots. I can get it to you if you want to take a look."

"I'll take your word for it. And I'll be in touch if anything else comes up."

Simon walked off and that was when Stilwell noticed that Renée Ballard was also at the funeral. He saw her talking to an old man he didn't recognize. He wasn't in uniform but had the bearing of a cop. He kicked around in the grass as Stilwell watched, then bent down to retrieve something. The old man touched Ballard's arm, apparently said goodbye, and headed off. The touch on the arm told Stilwell that they were close.

Stilwell walked over to her.

"Was that one of your volunteers?" he asked. "A little long in the tooth."

"I wish," Ballard said. "He worked a case for me but I couldn't get him to stay on. But he's a damn good homicide guy. One of my mentors."

"What was he looking for in the grass?"

"A rifle shell. He takes one from every cop funeral he goes to. He's got a jar that's almost full."

Stilwell looked in the direction her mentor had walked off in. He was gone. He turned back to Ballard.

"So how's it going on the case?" he asked.

"We got confirmation on the ID," Ballard said. "Dental records. DNA will come later but it was Angela. What a day. I told her mother this morning, and then I come to a cop funeral."

"You didn't know Quigley, did you?"

"No. But I lost one of my volunteers a couple years ago. It was tough. So I like to honor the fallen."

"I understand."

"You, of course, did know him. Sorry for your loss."

"I didn't know him that well. He had just transferred out there a couple months ago." Stilwell wanted to change the subject. "Anything else from the ME on the bones?" he asked.

"Cause of death matches Candace Neary's," Ballard said. "Hyoid bone fracture. She was most likely strangled."

Stilwell nodded. It wasn't a surprise.

"The lab find anything in the backpack that helps?" he asked.

"Nothing of value to the investigation," Ballard said.

She said it like she was reading the summary from the lab report. Stilwell nodded again. He had something to tell her but wasn't sure how to get to it.

"Well, I guess I'll head back to the office," Ballard said.

"I'm obsessed," Stilwell said.

It came out fast, almost desperate. Ballard looked at him, a hesitant smile on her face. She had taken it the wrong way. He guessed that a woman who looked like her dealt with many unwanted advances. The same happened to Tash.

"Obsessed with what?" she asked.

"The case," Stilwell said. "This case."

"Well, I wish I had you working it. But I'm not sure what else you can do from Catalina."

"I've been back up to the ironwood grove. And I keep looking at the files you sent me. I keep hoping I'll see something that's been missed."

"Welcome to my world."

"You mean you're obsessed too?"

"I want to find the guy."

"Right."

"You know that man who was just here—my mentor? He always says the answer is right in front of us. It's in the book. The murder book. Talk about being obsessed. With *every* case, he studied the book for hours and hours, and you know what? He was usually right. The missing thing was there."

"What's his name, the old guy?"

"Harry Bosch."

Stilwell didn't recognize the name.

"Homicide wisdom, huh?" he said.

"Yeah, in spades," Ballard said. "He never came at the book the same way twice. He would always change it up. Sometimes reverse chronology; sometimes he'd just open the book randomly and start there. He said a fresh angle meant fresh thinking."

Stilwell thought about how he had been reviewing the records himself.

"That's a good idea."

19

AFTER GETTING BACK to the island, Stilwell sequestered himself in his office at the sub. It was early Sunday afternoon and quiet. He opened a file cabinet and took out the murder book he had put together from the reports shared by Ballard and Laffont on the missing-hikers investigation. He had printed everything out and put it in a three-ring binder. He stood it on its two-inch-wide spine, took his hand away, and let it fall open randomly.

"Okay, Harry Bosch," he said, "let's see what you've got."

The binder opened to a section of crime scene photos from the excavation and recovery of Candace Neary's remains. He had previously studied these, noting that the depth of the grave matched that of Angela Metier. Both victims were buried close to the base of a tree—the ironwood with Angela and a live oak with Candace. He had read extensively about the Catalina ironwood, hoping to find a clue as to why it was chosen but had come up empty.

Convinced that there was nothing new to be gleaned from the photos, he flipped to the next section. It was the autopsy report on Neary. He had nothing to compare it to in the Metier case because the autopsy had only recently been completed and Ballard had stopped sending reports to him. He took out his phone and texted her, asking that she continue to share reports as they came in. He ended the message jokingly, saying he needed the reports because he was now looking at the case Harry Bosch–style. He hoped it would at least get a smile from her and persuade her to keep him in the loop.

He pressed on with the review, going through interview summaries with Neary's roommates, coworkers, and family members. These reports he had already read repeatedly, to the point that he knew what each person said before he actually saw it in the summary.

"Come on, Harry," he said. "Give me something."

He came across a topographic map of Griffith Park. He had previously checked to see if there was a correlation between the altitudes where the bodies were buried, but there was not. Metier had been buried a thousand feet higher than Neary. He didn't know what it would have meant if they had been buried at the same level, but checking even these details underlined his need to find something that would advance the case.

The last section of the murder book contained several pages of photographs taken by police, media, and citizens during the search of Griffith Park in the days and weeks after Neary was reported missing. It had been a monumental task. Griffith Park was four thousand acres of up-and-down terrain at the eastern end of the Santa Monica Mountains. Though much of it was landscaped and included the observatory on Mount Hollywood, the Greek Theatre complex, and other municipal facilities, the vast majority of the park's acreage was urban wilderness with steep rises and deep canyons. Neary's disappearance and the publicity around it drew hundreds of citizens and the media to the search effort.

In criminal investigations of violent acts, it was common for the perpetrators to return to the scene as a means of psychological fulfillment—to witness firsthand the horror and fear they had caused. This led law enforcement to collect media reports, photos, and videos for study later. This procedure was particularly successful in cases of arson; the guilty party often showed up to watch the flames and destruction.

But because foul play had not been considered in Neary's disappearance until after several days of searching, the media coverage was not collected until Ballard's team got the case. Though Ballard told Stilwell that studying the visuals had not brought any leads, he had put his own eyes on the photos and videos. He did it again now, hoping to come up with something new.

After studying all the photos, Stilwell moved to his laptop, where he had downloaded a file containing videos from news reports about the missing woman. Something he saw in the fourth video, a segment that was aired on KCAL 9 News, made him freeze the image on his screen. The field reporter was interviewing a woman named Monica Katz, a friend of Neary's and one of the organizers of the park searches. In the background, other volunteers were moving up a hillside in a line, all spaced six feet apart. Also in the background was another news crew pointing a camera and microphone at a park ranger positioned in front of a tree.

It was the tree that made Stilwell stop the video. It was a live oak that had a distinctive split in its trunk from what he guessed was a lightning strike.

Stilwell quickly went back to the front of the murder book and leafed through the most recent reports until he reached the section where he had started, the photos documenting the excavation of the bones. The tree that stood at the foot of the grave showed the same split, though over the years it had healed, and the tree looked much healthier.

Stilwell considered what he had found and what it might mean. First of all, it showed that the searchers had been right there but apparently had not noticed any suspicious disturbance in the terrain. Perhaps the damage from the lightning strike had made a natural variance in the ground that caused no one alarm. Additionally, the news report was from the first search for Neary, before foul play was considered. Searchers were looking for someone who was lost or injured, not buried four feet down.

Stilwell thought about the ironwood under which Angela Metier had been buried. He recalled nothing unique about it like lightning damage. But still he wondered whether the killer had chosen the tree in Griffith Park because of a distinctiveness that would allow him to find it again when he returned, possibly to relive the crime.

Stilwell was tempted to call Ballard, but he was unsure what all this meant. He stared at the tree in the paused video for a long moment before his eyes moved to the man being interviewed beneath it. He wore a uniform of dark green pants and a lighter green shirt and had on an equipment belt. He was clearly a park ranger. The TV reporter holding the microphone to the ranger's mouth was a readily recognizable blonde who had worked in the L.A. market for years. Stilwell even knew her name, Donna Driscoll, because she had been covering pretrial hearings in the mayor's case for Channel 5 News.

He hit the Play button and watched the rest of the KCAL report, hoping to get a better look at the ranger. A moment before the cameras cut away to the studio anchor, the ranger in the background turned his head slightly and pointed in the direction of the line of searchers moving methodically up the hill.

Stilwell froze the image again, studied it, and then his breath caught.

20

STILWELL PULLED OUT his phone and quickly called Ballard, dispensing with any small talk when she answered.

"I think I owe Harry Bosch a beer," he said. "Maybe a whole case."

"Oh yeah?" Ballard said. "Tell me."

Stilwell told her to pull up the Griffith Park news videos on her computer and then directed her to the KCAL report.

"Okay, freeze it at the twelve-second mark," he instructed.

"Got it," Ballard said. "What am I looking at?"

"In the background. Is that the tree where Candace Neary's bones were found?"

"Uh, hard to... is it?"

"It's got a split from what was probably a recent lightning strike at the time she was buried. When the bones were found years later, you can see the split has grown together, but it's scarred. Look at the excavation photos. It's the same tree."

"Okay. So what does that mean?"

"Well, two things. First, I'm thinking maybe the guy picked that tree so he could easily find it again."

"So he could come back and visit his kill."

"Exactly."

"That's good, Stil. I get that. What's the other thing?"

"The interview going on in the background. That's Donna Driscoll from Channel Five interviewing a park ranger. You see the uniform?"

"Yes."

"Okay, take the video to the sixteen-second mark and freeze it when he turns to point at the searchers going up the hill."

There was a long silence. Stilwell waited for Ballard to make the connection.

"Holy shit," she finally said. "Is that..."

"Kent Middleton—our ranger out on Catalina."

"So what are you saying?"

"That I don't believe in coincidences, not like this."

"You sound like Harry Bosch. So he was a volunteer on the Neary search but worked on Catalina?"

"No, he didn't start working on Catalina until two years ago. He was a city ranger during the Neary search and helped lead it. It's what we were just saying—he buries Neary under the lightning-strike tree so he can always find the spot and visit and relive his fantasy. But then what happens? About two years ago, the grave is supposedly disturbed by animals and the bones are found. They're removed and—"

"And there's no more grave for him to visit."

"Exactly. So he applies to the CIC for a job because he's got another victim up there under the ironwood. He's got one he can visit anytime he wants."

"It's a leap."

"Yeah, but I made it across. So can you."

Ballard didn't reply. Stilwell thought she was probably running it through her filters looking for a flaw in the logic. While he waited her out, he pulled up the still photo of the man leaving the backpack on the bench at Avalon Harbor. He compared it to the image on the screen. It was impossible to make a solid connection.

"What is the CIC?" Ballard finally said.

"Catalina Island Conservancy. It's a nonprofit. Fifty years ago, the Wrigley family gave most of the island to the CIC to preserve and protect it."

"And why did you just say *supposedly* about the bones being disturbed by animals?"

Stilwell was surprised she had noticed that, but he had been impressed by Ballard every time he talked to her.

"Okay, hear me out," he said. "He instigated this whole investigation when he left the backpack on the bench for us. He was inviting us to find Angela, and we did."

"That's a contradiction between the cases," Ballard said. "Neary's remains were found because animals got into the grave, but the killer intentionally led us to Metier."

"That's why I said *supposedly*. How sure are you about animals digging four feet down and pulling up the bones?"

"It's a bit of a stretch, I know. But I sent photos to a wildlife biologist at Cal State L.A. and he said coyotes can dig dens as deep as six feet."

"Is that what this was? A den?"

"It could have been. But the Cal State guy said the animal—most likely a coyote—was probably just foraging, which would be a shallower dig. But when it got down a foot or so, it picked up the scent of the remains and just kept going. But it sounds like you're thinking the bones were intentionally unearthed?"

"It's a possibility. It would fit with Metier and there would be no contradiction."

"That's good. Do we have the video of the Donna Driscoll interview?"

"I didn't see it in what you sent me."

"Okay, I'll get somebody on that first thing tomorrow."

"What do you want me to do out here?"

"I need to think about next moves. We don't want to spook this guy."

"When we were up at the excavation, I asked him if there were any records at his office from the search for Angela. He said he'd check but I haven't heard from him. I could follow up on that."

"That might be good. Kind of take the measure of the guy."

"Okay, I'll go see him tomorrow. Very casual, just following up on that request."

"Perfect."

After the call, Stilwell decided to wrap things up for the day. He texted Tash and said he was heading home and suggested that he pick up dinner at Steve's, the island's venerable steak house. She responded with a thumbs-up but told him she was still in the harbormaster's tower waiting for the last two boats to leave their moorings and head out to the open water. Sunday was an exodus day on the island. The hotels emptied out, the non-resident moorings ended, the ferries leaving Avalon were full, and the boats coming back were almost vacant. Stilwell and Tash often ended the weekend with a steak-and-red-wine dinner on the deck of the house they shared on Descanso Avenue.

Stilwell stepped out of his office into the squad room. It was empty and he went to the wall monitor on which all law enforcement and emergency services vehicles were tracked by GPS on a digital map of the island. The screen had been installed after the fires that devastated areas of the county the year before—emergency responses had been slowed by a lack of communication and poor allocation of equipment. Now all vehicles operated by the fire department, sheriff's office, county utilities, and CIC rangers were tracked on the map.

There were two deputies on duty and Stilwell saw that the location icons for their ATVs were stacked. The deputies were supposed to be patrolling the harbor zone separately but they were apparently together and high up on Avalon Canyon Road. This concerned Stilwell. It meant something had happened and both deputies had responded to it. Either that or they were cooping—slang for parking, sleeping, or generally not on patrol. Given the location of the two ATVs on the map, Stilwell thought something had happened.

He checked the deployment sheet on the bulletin board next to the screen and confirmed that Ross McGowan and Dawn Stabile were on duty. He stepped over to the charging rack, grabbed a two-way, and called McGowan, who was the ranking deputy of the two.

"Avalon One, come back," he said.

He waited for a return. Nothing came.

"Avalon Two? Come back."

"Go for One." It was McGowan's voice.

"What do you have up there, One?" Stilwell asked.

"Another five-ninety-four at ABC," McGowan responded.

Stilwell stepped back over to the wall monitor and stared at the map as he cursed to himself. ABC was the Avalon Beverage Company, the corporation that operated the island's only vineyard, and 594 was the state penal code for felony vandalism. In the past year, the vineyard had been the target of repeated acts of vandalism aimed at disrupting its production of grapes for a pinot noir sold under the label Avalon Crest.

The attackers had disabled vineyard equipment and irrigation lines, set fire to a toolshed, and destroyed vine trellises. The campaign of vandalism appeared to have been spurred by the city council's controversial approval of a major expansion of the vineyard. Currently a small operation that made a few hundred cases of wine for local restaurants, the vineyard would more than quadruple production and start exporting its product to the mainland and beyond.

The controversy revolved around water and political influence. Catalina had a Mediterranean climate but was constantly vulnerable to drought. Water was precious and cost five times what it did on the mainland. Avalon had once made its citizens use salt water in their toilets, but the pipes started rusting out and sewage leaked into the groundwater. After that disaster, a desalination plant was built by the electric company and currently provided more than 40 percent of the drinking water on the island.

But still it was not enough. There were strict regulations on water use and steep fines for scofflaws. Many of the hotels shipped their sheets and towels to overtown laundries at high expense to save water. And the *Catalina Call* regularly exposed the top water users on the island in an attempt to embarrass them into cutting back.

Then came what was known as the water war. Grapes take a significant amount of water to grow, and the "little" vineyard was already a top user. Environmental groups and other businesses contested the approval of its expansion. The *Call* published several opinion pieces, all objecting to the expansion. But ABC was owned by one of the five so-called old families of Catalina. They were well established and financially powerful people who for generations had dominated business and politics on the island. Each of these families had descendants who had spread across the island and into all facets of its society, politics, and business. The proposed expansion of the vineyard ultimately received unanimous approval from the council in an up-or-down vote.

Most of Stilwell's knowledge of this had come through Tash, who had been born and raised on the island, and through the substation manager, Mercy Chapa, who was a third-generation member of one of the old families and therefore a vital link in the chain of local gossip and inside information. Her mother had served as the city clerk since the turn of the twenty-first century, and Mercy freely acknowledged that she had gotten the job managing the sheriff's station because her last name was Chapa.

The vineyard expansion had been approved two years ago, but protests at council meetings continued, as had the acts of vandalism at the vineyard.

Stilwell had investigated the prior reports but did not come close to identifying the individual or individuals responsible. That frustrated him, but not as much as it did ABC's owner-operator, Oliver Marquez.

Stilwell keyed the mic and told McGowan he would call him back on his cell. This was to keep the conversation off the radio, which he knew was monitored by several residents of Avalon as well as by Lionel McKey at the *Call*. He phoned McGowan's cell and asked him what kind of 594 had occurred this time.

"Looks like somebody took a machete to a couple rows of the new vines," McGowan said. "Chopped them up pretty good. Mr. Marquez is super-mad. He screamed at us."

Stilwell knew Marquez well from the previous incidents. He was a volatile man used to getting his own way. That no one had been arrested for vandalizing his property was galling to him.

"Okay, I'm on my way," Stilwell responded. "You should have called me out on this."

"Sorry, boss. I thought you were Oscar India."

That was radio code for *off island*. McGowan had a habit of talking in code even when not on the radio.

"No, I'm here," Stilwell said. "And I'm coming up."

"Oscar Kilo," McGowan said.

21

FIFTEEN MINUTES LATER, Stilwell drove his ATV through the open gate of the ABC vineyard and followed an access road that bordered the original vineyard to the grape-processing and wine-production complex. He parked next to the two deputies' ATVs and could see McGowan and Stabile standing in the shadow of the corrugated roof over the production facility. Dwarfed by two huge stainless-steel fermenting tanks, they were speaking to Oliver Marquez, but when Marquez saw Stilwell, the ranking officer on the island, he left the two deputies like they were day-old fish and charged toward him.

"All right, Stilwell, what are you going to do about this?" he demanded. "I am sick and fucking tired of waiting on results from you people."

Stilwell stepped out of his ATV and held his hands up in a calming gesture. Marquez's face was red with anger. He was nearing seventy years old and was deeply tanned with a full head of unruly white hair. He wore blue jeans and a denim work shirt and had a gold watch on his wrist. His jeans were tucked into black rubber vineyard boots.

"Let's just calm down a little bit, Mr. Marquez," Stilwell said.

"Fuck that," Marquez said. "I'm not going to calm anything down. These people are attacking me and my interests with impunity and I've had my fill of it."

"What exactly happened this time?"

"Somebody came onto my private property and chopped the shit out of my goddamn vines."

"Okay, can you show me?"

"What for? You aren't going to do shit about it."

"Look, Mr. Marquez, I understand you're frustrated, but— "

"No, you fucking don't."

"Sir, I've warned you in the past. Do not take your frustrations out on me or my deputies. We all want the same thing here. We want to stop this, and I promise you, we will."

"You said that last time, and here we are."

Stilwell didn't have a good response to that. He held a hand out in the direction of the vineyard.

"Do you want to show me?" he said.

"Get in," Marquez said.

He headed toward a hardtop ATV with the ABC logo on its door. Before Stilwell followed, he spoke to McGowan and Stabile.

"You two can go back out," he said. "Did either of you take photos?"

"Negative," McGowan said.

"Well, you should have," Stilwell said. "It's getting dark."

Stilwell rode with Marquez to the expanded side of the vineyard. The new vineyard was just two years old, not yet mature enough to produce grapes for wine. Marquez had told him that a new vineyard had to be cultivated for three years before there was a usable harvest and at least two more before anybody would buy the wine from it. It was a long-term investment and a gamble, and the constant vandalism slowed the process and endangered the eventual payoff for his family.

"They took out three lines," Marquez said while he drove. "French clones. Do you have any idea what it will cost me to start over?"

"Not really," Stilwell said. "But I'm sure it puts this at a felony level."

"Damn right it does. I want these people in prison."

"Once again, Mr. Marquez, I have to ask you if you have any idea who would do this. There were lots of protests, and the notable names from those have all been checked. No one stood out based on criminal records and, in some cases, media interviews as somebody who would cross the line to this degree of vandalism."

"Then you're naive. Look at all the protesters who crossed lines with ICE. Burning cars, throwing rocks at the cops."

"I think that was a little different. That was about people being grabbed off the streets and families being separated. Let's talk about today. When did this happen?"

"My viticulturist was out checking the vines today and discovered it. So all I know is that it happened before that. Probably last night. I hadn't been out here since Friday afternoon."

"Who is the viticulturist and is he still here?"

"It's a she. Helena Novak. She's from an old wine family in Napa. She stays at the Atwater when she comes over."

"Okay, I'll probably need to talk to her. I take it she's not full-time?"

"No, she comes about twice a month to check on things."

Marquez drove down a bouncy dirt road that ran perpendicular to the rows of the new vineyard. The young vines were just beginning to canopy over the trellises that spread the branches and created the familiar look of a vineyard. Marquez stopped the ATV at the end of the road, where the vineyard bordered protected land owned by the Catalina Island Conservancy. The border was delineated by a green chain-link fence that stood six feet high.

They got out of the ATV and walked into the vineyard. At first glance, nothing seemed amiss, but once they were walking down a row, Stilwell saw that the trunk of each vine had been slashed clean through, essentially decapitating the canopy of the vine and leaving it to die on the trellis.

"You see what they did to my beautiful vines?" Marquez said.

"I see," Stilwell said.

McGowan was probably right—a machete or similar tool had done the damage.

"How many individual plants?" he asked.

"Three lines, forty a line," Marquez said. "You understand what this costs me in time and money? Two years gone. I have to start over and wait three years to harvest over here. Do you know what that means in terms of cases lost?"

"No idea, Mr. Marquez."

"You can cut my pipes, fuck with my tractors and equipment, and I can fix it in a day. This? This is years. And if you don't find who fucking did this, I will."

Stilwell was crouched and using his phone to take a close-up photo of one of the slashed vines. He stood up and turned to Marquez.

"What does that mean?" he said.

"I know people, Stilwell," Marquez said. "It means do your job or I'll do it for you."

"Mr. Marquez, listen to me carefully. I've told you that I understand your frustration. But you need to stand down and let me do my job. You stay on the sidelines, because if you wander off and do something stupid, we're going to have a very big problem."

"Fine, then do your fucking job. Because if you don't get it done, you can be gone with one call. I did more than just vote for your fucking boss."

Stilwell was angry now but knew he had to keep his composure. He offered a smile and shook his head. Then he lied to Marquez.

"If you know people who can take me off this rock, then by all means, call them," he said. "What you don't seem to understand is none of us want to be here. Me, that pair of deputies who responded to your call—none of us are here because we asked to be here. So if you can get me back overtown, then please and thank you. Do it."

"Yeah?" Marquez said. "How'd you like to go from Catalina to Compton? Those gangs over there would eat you alive."

Stilwell caught and held Marquez's angry stare. Finally, he calmed himself and got back to his professional demeanor.

"Did you or my deputies check the perimeter fence?" he asked.

"I didn't," Marquez said. "Why? That's CIC land over there."

Stilwell pointed at one of the damaged vines.

"Because if I'd done this, that's where I would have come in. I doubt they drove down your access road."

Stilwell walked out of the row and turned right toward the fence. With Marquez trailing behind him, he walked the fence line for about forty feet before he came to a breach. There was a four-foot cut in the links from the ground up. Stilwell used his boot to push the fencing apart, and it created an opening easily big enough for a person to crawl through.

"Son of a bitch," Marquez said.

"How often do you have the fence checked?" Stilwell asked.

"Uh, never. It's a fence."

"Okay, I'm going to go through to see if I can pick up a trail or anything else."

"Don't you need, like, a dog for that?"

"Don't have a dog, Mr. Marquez. We could wait for one from overtown, but it's getting dark."

Marquez didn't respond. Stilwell crouched down, pulled the fence open, and crawled through. He kept his eyes on the ground, looking for any disturbance that might be a footprint or an indication of a path. But there was nothing.

He stood up on the other side and looked through the fence at Marquez.

"You don't have to wait for me," he said.

"We came in the same cart," Marquez said.

"I can walk back. I don't know how long this will take."

"Well, don't get lost."

"That's the plan. While I'm doing this, why don't you call your wine person at the Atwater and tell her I'll be coming by tonight for an interview."

"Okay, I'll call her."

Stilwell turned away from the fence. His instincts told him that the vandal would have come to the vineyard from the right. Avalon Canyon Road and most of the hiking trails in the conservancy were in that direction. He started moving that way. He checked his watch and estimated he had a half hour before it would be too dark for him to see.

The chaparral was tall and dry and its blades broke under his feet. The area was thick with manzanita and mahogany bushes as well as prickly pear and barrel cactus. The vegetation forced him to follow a meandering path that snaked in a northwesterly direction. He saw no indication that he was on the same route the vandal had taken, but after ten minutes of steady slogging, he came to a clearing where there were two picnic tables with benches, a trash can, and an ocean view. No one was there, but a hiking trail split off to the east toward Avalon Canyon Road.

Stilwell had no idea where he was. There was no conservancy placard with information about the location, just a sign on a post that said FIRE DANGER! NO COOKING WITH FIRE. He stepped on one of the benches and then up onto the table. It gave him a better view, and to the east he could see the top of the tower he knew was the centerpiece of the Wrigley Memorial and Botanic Garden. It helped him orient himself.

He pulled out his phone and saw that he still had a signal. He dropped a pin on his location and sent it in a text to Tash, asking if she could determine where he was. He took a photo of the picnic area and sent that to her as well.

She answered promptly.

I think you're at the old San Pedro picnic grounds.

Not on many maps. Can you see the channel from there?

The part of the Santa Monica Bay between Avalon and Long Beach was called the San Pedro Channel but that too was left off most maps.

I see it and the top of the Wrigley phallus.

That was her name for the memorial. It always reminded Stilwell of the old Rolling Stones song about men building memorial towers toward the sky to ensure their fame everlasting.

Okay, then yes, that is the San Pedro picnic place.

Say it three times fast. LOL

Stilwell smiled and texted his thanks. He added that he had caught a call as he was leaving the sub and would be delayed but still planned on picking up a steak at Steve's.

Stilwell climbed down from the table and checked the gravel and sand near the entry to the picnic grounds from the trail. There were so many partial footprints going every which way that he knew his effort was useless. It was getting dark quickly now and he wanted to get back to the vineyard before it was too late to see where he was going. He had left his flashlight in the ATV and the last thing he wanted to do was walk into a barrel cactus and spend the evening picking spines out of his shins.

On his way back he saw something he hadn't seen on his first pass: a green plastic box on a wooden post in a small clearing between two manzanita trees. He stepped closer and determined that it was a protective box holding a camera. There was a number stenciled on the top of the box and a latch with a small key lock. He took a photo of the number, realizing that now he had another reason to talk to Kent Middleton the next day.

From there, it took Stilwell fifteen minutes to get back to the split in the fence and another ten in full darkness to walk the road back to the processing complex. McGowan and Stabile were gone, but Marquez was waiting by what Stilwell now knew was a grape press. It had been one of the things damaged in an earlier act of vandalism.

"Anything?" Marquez asked.

"The cut in the fence is about fifteen minutes from the San Pedro picnic grounds," Stilwell said. "From there, a trail leads to the road. It's probably the route that was used by the vandals, but I didn't find any evidence to support that."

"So a waste of time, then."

"Not really. There's a wildlife camera in the bushes out there. I'll check it tomorrow and maybe we get lucky."

"Where exactly is it?"

"About halfway between your fence and the picnic grounds. The conservancy puts them up to track animals and check for fires, that sort of thing."

"You'll let me know if it's got anybody on it, right?"

"I'll let you know when the time is appropriate to let you know. But speaking of cameras, you should think about putting some up in the vineyard. That and a sign up by the road that says there are cameras might be a solid deterrent."

"One step ahead of you there. I already called a guy."

"Good. There's one other thing I wanted to ask you."

"What?"

"Could this be something else, somebody using the water protests to get back at you for other reasons?"

"You mean, like, do I have any enemies?"

"Exactly."

"No, this is not something else. My only enemies are the people who try to prevent me from using my land the way I see fit."

"You're sure?"

"I'm sure."

"Okay, then. I'm going to go down to the Atwater to get a statement from Helena Novak."

"When will I get the report?"

"What report?"

"The crime report on this. I'll need it for insurance."

"Give me a day to get it written up, then you can pick it up at the substation."

"I will."

"Good night, Mr. Marquez."

"Good night, and listen, I'm sorry if I came on a little too strong."

"Like I said, I understand your frustration. I want to get whoever did this as much as you do."

Stilwell got in his ATV, turned on its lights, and headed back down to Avalon to talk to the viticulturist and then pick up dinner.

22

STILWELL WALKED INTO the lobby of the Hotel Atwater on Sumner Avenue and had to marvel at its lush appointments and stylish modern furniture. After a lengthy renovation and refurbishing by its owners—one of the island's old families—the hotel had transitioned from a down-at-the-heels overnighter known by locals as the Ratwater to a place to see and be seen. It was now considered one of the top hotels in downtown Avalon, rivaling the two venerable hillside hotels, the Zane Grey and the Mt. Ada (the old Wrigley mansion), as the best place to stay on the island.

To the left of the registration desk he saw a counter with a house phone. He picked it up and asked the operator to connect him with Helena Novak. When she answered he identified himself, and she said she had been given a heads-up by Marquez and would be down shortly to meet him in the lobby.

They found an empty corner with a sitting area and took chairs across a coffee table from each other. Stilwell was surprised by Novak's age. He thought she could not be much older than thirty. She was dressed similarly to Marquez, in jeans and a work shirt. She had sun-streaked hair and was deeply tanned, presumably from days spent in vineyards.

"I don't know if I can help you," she said. "I mean, I found the damage to the vines today, but I have no idea who did it."

"I understand that," Stilwell said. "I'm actually more interested in what you might have seen on previous visits to the vineyard and whether you've received any odd or offbeat questions from anybody."

"Like what?"

"Like maybe someone asking what would be the worst thing to happen to a vineyard."

She scoffed. "Well, nobody's ever asked me that," she said. "I would remember."

"If someone did, what would your answer be?" Stilwell asked.

"Um, fire. Obviously."

"A fire is not controllable. What is something that would cripple the vineyard without threatening people or adjoining properties?"

"Probably what happened today. Where those vines were cut is devastating."

"Well, aren't the root systems still intact? I mean, I know it will take time, but won't the vines just grow again?"

"Unlikely. Like I told Mr. Marquez, the canopy collects sunlight and sends it down the shaft to the roots. The roots take in water and moisture and send it up. If that connection is severed, both sides will probably die."

Stilwell nodded.

"How did you get the job at ABC? If you don't mind my asking."

"Well, I grew up in Napa and my father was a winemaker," Novak said. "I've been running around vineyards for as long as I can remember. I went to UC Davis to study viticulture and then spent a year at a vineyard in the Rhône Valley. I started making wine with my dad when I came home. When Mr. Marquez called my father to try to hire him, he wasn't available. He was about to retire, in fact. He told him that I was the next best thing and I got the job."

"That's great. And that was two years ago?"

"Yes. I planted the new vineyard."

"And how is it working with Marquez?"

"He's been fine. He's got a lot of other businesses and isn't there a lot. I think he even owns part of this hotel. At least, he gets me a discount."

"How often are you here?"

"Every two weeks I come down for a day or two."

"From Napa? Is that where you live?"

"Yes."

"Are you aware of the other vandalism that occurred up at ABC?"

"Yes, Oliver called me every time."

"And were you involved with the repairs?"

"No, not really. It's not what I do. I'm about growing grapes and making wine."

Stilwell nodded. He had one more thing he wanted to ask but needed to approach it carefully.

"How is the vineyard doing in general?" he asked. "Seems like a huge gamble to plant a vineyard. You have to wait so long before you have wine you can sell, you know?"

"It takes a lot of time and a lot of money," Novak said. "We've had some setbacks because of the vandalism and other things, but I don't think we'll miss our target by much."

"What other things are you talking about?"

"Well, we had some black rot we had to deal with. But our biggest problem is labor. We are one relatively small vineyard on an island. It was already hard to find seasonal pickers. Then all the ICE stuff last year made finding field-workers even more difficult. They're all gone—deported or hiding. We might not have fruit that's mature enough to make wine, but we still need to harvest it every year. That didn't happen at ABC last October, and that set us back, time- and budget-wise. Mr. Marquez had to pay some high-school kids, including his grandson, to come pick grapes. It was a mess because they'd never done it before, so it was very slow."

"And what about the black rot? What's that?"

"It's a disease caused by a fungus."

"How do you treat it?"

"Different ways. We used a fungicide, but you also have to go in and cut out infected leaves and branches. That was another thing we couldn't find the labor for, and that contributed to its spread. We have it under control now."

"Is it going to delay production?"

"Not really. But it means less fruit, which eventually means less wine."

"And less profit."

"Exactly."

Stilwell nodded. He had gotten a good sense of what was happening at the vineyard.

"Can I ask you one last thing?" he said. "Just for my own education."

"Sure," Novak said.

"Marquez mentioned that the damaged vines were French clones. What does that mean?"

"It just means the vineyard was propagated with cuttings

from French vines. You get a genetically identical copy of the mother vine, and the theory is that you will then get the same characteristics in the wine you eventually make."

"Is that expensive? Marquez mentioned filing an insurance claim."

"Oh, yeah. It's much more expensive than germinating seeds and starting from scratch."

"You learn all this at UC Davis?"

"Some of it I did, but most I learned from my dad."

"Well, listen, thank you for taking the time to talk with me. I'll let you get back to your evening now."

"Like I said, I don't know if I was a help, but I hope you catch the people who did this."

"Do you think it was more than one person?"

"Who knows? But whoever it was, they should be locked up. I've never seen Mr. Marquez so upset."

"I think I understand why."

Stilwell stood up. He shook hands with Novak and headed to the lobby's exit. Out on the sidewalk he called Steve's and ordered one rib eye and two rice pilafs. He was told it would be ready in fifteen minutes. He had parked the ATV out front. He got in and headed toward Crescent. Steve's was on the second floor of a building and had one of the better views of the harbor. Along the way, he called Tash to assure her that dinner would be there soon.

"Good," she said. "I'm starved."

"Sorry about the wait," he said. "It was another vandalism up at ABC."

"Really? Then why were you at the Ratwater?"

Old habits died hard. Tash had grown up knowing the hotel by its nickname. It was also apparent that she had been checking his phone location.

"I had to interview a witness there," he said.

"Who was that?" she said.

"The viticulturist who found the vandalism today."

He had intentionally kept Novak's gender out of his answer. It seemed to quell Tash's curiosity and she changed the subject.

"Did you get rice?" she asked.

"I did times two," he said.

"Hurry home."

"I will."

23

THE CATALINA ISLAND Conservancy protected more than forty-two thousand acres of land, dense vegetation, and fragile ecosystems that amounted to nearly 90 percent of the island. The phalanx of rangers who patrolled it worked primarily out of four-wheel-drive vehicles and small stations spread out over the jurisdiction. Stilwell knew many of the rangers by name and had weekly check-ins with Mick Dunaway, who was the captain of the troop and stationed at a headquarters up in Falls Canyon.

Mindful of Renée Ballard's concern about spooking Kent Middleton, Stilwell thought the best way to get to him would be through Dunaway with what seemed like a routine follow-up. He also had fresh business to discuss with Dunaway and called him on his cell.

"Stil, how was your weekend?"

"Not bad, except we had another problem up at the vineyard."

"No shit. That old guy over there must be hot."

"Marquez, yeah, that's putting it mildly. Somebody took a machete to three rows of vines."

"Oh, shit. That ramps things up."

"Yeah, and that's why I'm calling. We think the vandal or vandals came in through the conservancy side. There was a cut in the fence. I went through and looked for a trail, but I'm no Boy Scout. I didn't find anything, but the cut in the fence was pretty close to the San Pedro picnic grounds."

"Okay. I know that spot."

"I'm thinking that was a starting point and then they went through the brush to the vineyard. Like I said, I couldn't find a trail. But on the way back to the fence, I did see one of your wildlife cameras."

"Yeah, yeah, I was just about to say that we have cameras up there. Did you get a number off it?"

"I did. G-fourteen. How can I look at the footage?"

"Well, you're in luck, because all the camera feeds go here. You could come up and take a look."

"All right, then, I'm on my way."

"I'll be here."

"Oh, and one other thing. How old is the camera project? I was wondering if there was one four years ago near the ironwood grove where we found the remains last week."

"Nah, I would've told you if we had cameras at that time. They all went in a couple years ago. Part of a grant UCLA got to study the Channel Islands' animal migration."

"Important stuff. Is Middleton around today?"

"Yeah, he's working. You need him for something?"

"I have to finish the paperwork on that thing up there and I want to follow up with him. He told me he was going to look for some records for me."

"Not a problem. I'll call him in. It might take him a bit. He's up at Eagle's Nest."

Eagle's Nest was at the top of the mountain off Middle Ranch Road. It offered the best 360-degree views on the island.

"What's going on?" Stilwell asked.

"The high-school kids are up there today," Dunaway said. "Senior-class retreat."

"You okay pulling him off that?"

"I've got three rangers there. It's not a problem. I'll tell him to meet you here."

"Thanks, Mick."

After the call, Stilwell left his office and went to the charging rack to get a fresh two-way. Mercy watched him.

"Are you leaving?" she asked.

"I'm going up to the ranger base," Stilwell said. "Not sure how long I'll be."

"Oliver Marquez called and said he was going to pick up a crime report. Do you have that?"

"I haven't written it yet. Call him back and tell him we'll let him know as soon as it's ready."

"He's a man who doesn't like to wait."

"I know that. Call me if anything else comes up."

"Will do."

The drive up to Falls Canyon took fifteen minutes. Inside the ranger base there was a reception counter where hikers could pick up permits and maps of the trails as well as brochures for other island attractions and activities. A ranger named Loretta Petty was posted at the counter to field questions from hikers. She told Stilwell that Dunaway was expecting him and he headed back to the office. He had been there before and knew the way. Dunaway had already looked at video from camera G-14.

"The camera picked up something, but I'm not sure it's going to be helpful," he said.

"Better than nothing," Stilwell said. "Can you show me?"

"I've got it cued up."

Dunaway had Stilwell sit down in his seat behind the desk. He then leaned down over the keyboard and typed in a command with one hand. On a large desk monitor, a grid of camera views appeared. Dunaway highlighted one and expanded it. There was a digital date-and-time stamp in the lower right corner of the screen as well as the camera code, G-14.

"Okay, so this is the angle," Dunaway said. "It's a motion-activated camera, so we just check the images and we find this."

He worked the keyboard and Stilwell watched as he reversed the recording and then quickly stopped it.

"So, there's you," Dunaway said.

Stilwell was looking at a freeze-frame of himself peering at the camera the evening before.

"And then we take it back almost exactly one day and we get this," Dunaway said.

Now the video showed a figure moving from left to right across the screen but obscured by a bushy manzanita and other thick brush. Stilwell knew it was a human because he could make out clothing. Whoever was moving through the brush was wearing a bright yellow-and-blue shirt or jacket. Though the figure was unidentifiable, the colors were significant.

The figure appeared to stumble and then paused for a moment before continuing out of the frame.

"Going back seven days before this, there's nothing but mule deer and the occasional island fox," Dunaway said. "But you can check for yourself if you want."

"No, I believe you," Stilwell said. "But there's no sound?"

"Well, there is—sort of. As I'm sure you saw, the camera's

in a plastic camo box, and that knocks down the sound considerably. I had the volume turned all the way down, but you want to listen?"

"Might as well see if it picked up anything."

Dunaway reversed the video and replayed the segment showing the yellow-and-blue-clad figure. Dunaway was right; there was almost no sound. But when the figure stumbled, there was a yelp followed by a shout: "Fuck!"

"I'm guessing he stepped in a hole, maybe twisted an ankle," Dunaway said.

"Or walked into a cactus," Stilwell said. "I saw a lot of them out there."

"Could be that too."

The voice had sounded young to Stilwell. Not a deep timbre to it.

"So he doesn't come back?" Stilwell asked.

"How do you mean?" Dunaway responded.

"From the way I saw the camera angle, he would be moving toward the vineyard there. But the camera didn't pick him up coming back."

"You mean after he chopped up the vineyard? Well, he could have taken a different path that went behind the camera. You know what I mean? Especially if he was trying to avoid a cactus patch."

"Right."

There was a knock at the door before it was opened by Loretta from the front counter. She told Dunaway that Middleton had arrived and was in the barracks.

"Tell him Sergeant Stilwell will be along to see him," Dunaway said.

24

STILWELL WENT DOWN a hall to the barracks. It was a spacious room that slept six in three sets of double bunks. As with the sheriff's deputies assigned to Catalina, many of the CIC rangers lived off island and used the bunks between their twelve-hour shifts.

The room was empty, but Stilwell heard a toilet flush, and Middleton came through the door of the lavatory, buckling his belt. He was six feet tall with the ruddy complexion that seemed standard with most of the rangers Stilwell knew. He was in his late thirties with reddish-brown hair and green eyes. To Stilwell, he looked normal. That is, he looked like a guy who was ready to tell you about the feeding habits of the mule deer, not like a man hiding an impenetrable darkness.

"Stil, I'm sorry," he said.

"For what?" Stilwell responded.

"I was supposed to get back to you about the records on the search four years ago for Angela Metier."

"Or I was supposed to check back with you about it and here I am. Did you find anything?"

"I found some stuff, not a lot. Nothing that I think will break the case."

"That's okay. You never know what will break open a case. Let's see what you've got."

"It's in my locker."

He walked over to a wall of lockers and started working a combination with his back turned to Stilwell.

Stilwell shifted to his right so he could catch a glimpse of the inside of Middleton's locker when he opened it.

"So, how's the case going?" Middleton said.

"Uh, well, it's not really my case," Stilwell said. "Homicide overtown has it. They've got me running errands—like picking up reports from you."

Stilwell saw a ranger jacket on a hook in the locker. Not much else. No photos or keepsakes like cops often have in their cubbies. There was a shelf, and Middleton took a thin file off it and turned.

"I couldn't find much," he said, handing the file to Stilwell. "Mostly just search sectors and lists of volunteers. I think the actual investigation was handled by you sheriffs."

Something about the way he said *you sheriffs* carried a touch of hostility that Stilwell had heard before when he sat across the table from criminals.

"Yeah, I checked our files already," he said. "Not much there."

He gestured toward the open locker.

"Doesn't look like you bunk here," he said. "You got a place in town?"

"No, I got it better," Middleton said. "I got a girlfriend who has a place in town. I heard you got the same setup."

"Not exactly," Stilwell said.

"Well, that's what I heard," Middleton said.

Stilwell looked down and opened the file. The first page was a call sheet. Names and numbers of the citizens who searched for Angela Metier. Seven entries down, he saw the name Tash Dano and the cell number she still used.

He closed the file.

"You heading up to Eagle's Nest now?" he asked.

"Yeah, Mick wants me to go back," Middleton said.

"It's the seniors there, right?"

"Uh-huh, some kind of retreat where they all sit around and talk about getting off the island. They don't know how good they got it here."

"I need to go up there and talk to a kid. Can I ride with you?"

"Uh, yeah, but I don't know when I'll be able to take you back down."

"I've got a two-way. I'll have one of my guys come get me."

"Okay, then, you ready?"

"I'm ready."

On the ride up in Middleton's 4Runner, Stilwell tried to keep the conversation casual, but he had a purpose to his questions. He knew he had fifteen minutes until they reached their destination and he wanted to make the most of it.

"Your girlfriend, she's a local?" he asked.

"Not originally," Middleton said. "But she's been out here twelve years. I guess the only way to ever be considered local is to be born here. Otherwise, you're an overlander."

"True. She also a ranger?"

"Nah, I don't fish off the company dock. She's a bartender."

"Which place?"

"The Buffalo Nickel."

"My favorite bar. If she works there, she's either Gwen or Melissa."

"Gwen. Funny, I don't remember seeing you in there. And I end up there two, three times a week. Have to kind of keep my eye on her, you know what I mean?"

"Yeah, she's an attractive woman. You think you'll stay?"

"You mean stay together?"

Stilwell laughed.

"No, I'm not trying to get that personal. I meant stay out here on the island. Working for the conservancy."

"Oh, well, I like it out here, but there's no advancement. There's the captain, two shift supervisors, then all of us rangers. I have an application in with the state and hope to get off this rock as soon as something comes through."

"Where will you go?"

"Wherever they send me. I won't really have a say. But I'd love Malibu. That way I'd be able to keep the girlfriend, because it's close to here and she's never leaving the island."

"I got one of those too."

"You're with the harbormaster, right?"

Stilwell realized he had opened a door to his personal life and that was a mistake. He tried to talk his way out of it without letting on that he thought he might be speaking to a serial killer.

"Uh, interim for the moment," he said. "Her job, I mean. She's waiting on the city council to decide between her and an overlander."

"Oh, she'll get it," Middleton said. "Locals always have the inside track."

"Hope so."

Middleton parked the 4Runner next to two vans and two other 4Runners at the Eagle's Nest clearing.

"Why do you need to talk to a kid up here?" Middleton said.

"It's part of a vandalism investigation."

"You must miss working homicide."

"How so?"

"You know, you were working murders and that was important. Now you work vandalism."

"Vandalism is important to the victim."

"Yeah, but I mean important to you. You were after big game before. Now, what—high-school students? What did this kid do, break a window or something?"

"It's a little more involved than that. But, hey, thanks for the ride."

"You sure you have a ride back?"

"I'll work on that now. By the way, when I get up there, I might need to take a few photos—if I'm right about something."

"Roger that. Do what you gotta do."

They got out and Middleton went back to work with the two other rangers. Stilwell keyed the mic on his two-way.

"Base One, come back."

Soon he heard Mercy say, "Go ahead, boss."

"Check the deployment screen. Who is closest to Eagle's Nest?"

There was a pause while she checked.

"That would be Deputy McGowan."

"Is he on a callout?"

"Not as far as I know."

"Copy. Out."

Stilwell radioed McGowan and asked him to come pick him up at Eagle's Nest. He then clipped the radio to his belt and walked up to the clearing. He saw about twenty-five kids sitting on the ground in a circle. Many were wearing shirts or ball caps with the school's colors: yellow and blue.

Marquez's grandson was easy to spot. He was the one wearing shorts and a large white bandage wrapped around his right calf.

25

OLIVER MARQUEZ STEPPED out of the barn as Stilwell pulled to a stop in front. Marquez wiped his hands on a blue rag as he walked to the ATV, expecting a quick transfer of the crime report. He likely didn't want to get the document dirty with grease or grape juice or whatever he had been working with. He nodded a perfunctory hello.

"Thanks for bringing it up," he said.

"Actually, I didn't bring anything, Mr. Marquez," Stilwell said.

"What do you mean? I told you I needed the report for insurance. There's gotta be a million dollars in damages in the vineyard."

He pointed in the direction of the damaged vines. It was late in the day, and the sun was at a low angle over the neat rows.

Stilwell nodded.

"No crime, no crime report, sir," he said. "At least, no crime yet."

"What the fuck are you talking about?" Marquez said. "You saw my vines. You know what happened here."

"I know what happened to the vines, yes. But the only crime will be if you file an insurance claim. That's when I'll have to write up a crime report."

"You better tell me what the fuck you're talking about, Stilwell, or you're going to be explaining it to the sheriff himself, who happens to be a personal friend."

"Yeah, I checked that out. You not only gave him money, you were the Catalina coordinator for his last election campaign."

"Then you know I'm not someone you want to fuck with."

Stilwell climbed out of the ATV so he was eye level with Marquez.

"That's why I'm giving you a major break here," he said.

"You're talking in riddles, son," Marquez said. "And I don't have the patience for it. Where's my fucking crime report?"

"I told you, there is no crime report. But what I do have, though I haven't filed it yet, is a statement from your grandson Oliver the Third. He didn't even try to bluff. He folded like a bad poker hand, even told me where he hid the machete."

Marquez automatically took a step back.

"Look, I don't know exactly what kind of financial stress you're under," Stilwell continued. "I heard from your grape grower that you've had labor issues and other setbacks while you wait for the new vineyard to produce, but since you own the land and the vines, you can do whatever you want with them. Chop 'em down, burn them, that's your business. And if you paid your grandson two hundred dollars to do it, that's fine, even if he did get a leg full of cactus spines for his trouble."

Marquez's deeply tanned face was turning pale.

"So what I'm telling you is, there's no crime here yet," Stilwell said. "But if you make an insurance claim, that's another matter.

That would be insurance fraud. You do that and I'll be back. I don't think you'll want that."

Marquez shook his head as he realized his million-dollar scheme was not going to pay off and he would be left with three rows of dead vines.

"The kid fed you a load of shit," he said. "I had nothing to do with it."

Stilwell paused for a moment, surprised but not too much by the response. In his experience, men of wealth and power had few limits on what they were willing to do and say, few lines they wouldn't cross.

"You sure you want to throw him under the bus like that?" Stilwell finally said. "I just came from watching a video of you with him in the waiting room at an urgent care. I've got a copy of it on my phone if you want to see it."

Stilwell had indeed dropped by the urgent care center to confirm Oliver the Third's confession and had even seen the video.

"Okay, what do you want?" Marquez said.

The wealthy man's response to everything.

"Nothing," Stilwell said. "Except maybe that you leave your grandson alone so he doesn't grow up to be like you. When he graduates and says he wants to get off the island, let him go. Maybe he'll have a decent chance away from you."

"I want you off my property," Marquez said. "Leave. Now."

"Sure," Stilwell said.

He turned to his ATV but then looked back at Marquez.

"Must be tough," he said. "To grow up with money and power and then see it all die on the vine."

"Fuck you," Marquez barked. "Big man with the badge. You think you're Gary fucking Cooper or some shit, but the reality is you're nothing. Just get the hell out of here."

He turned and headed toward the open door of the barn.

Stilwell got in his ATV and drove off. On his way down the canyon to the sub, he thought about Marquez's last words to him. He pulled out his phone, checked for service, and called Tash. He needed to hear a pure and honest voice.

"Hey, babe," she said.

"Hey," he said. "How are things?"

"All good. Slow. Are you working late tonight?"

"No, I'm going to drop by the sub, make a call, then go home."

"Great."

"By the way, you know Gwen over at the Nickel?"

"Sure."

"You know her last name, by any chance?"

"Yeah, Bassett, like the dog but with two *t*'s. Why?"

"She came up in a conversation today. One of the rangers up on the conservancy lives with her."

"Yeah, I heard that."

"Of course—you hear everything. Anyway, I was thinking of watching an old movie tonight. If I can find it."

"Sure. What movie?"

"*High Noon*."

"Is that the doc about cannabis growers?"

Stilwell laughed.

"No, it's an old one. Gary Cooper. From the fifties. A classic."

"Never heard of it."

"Yeah, that's why we should watch it. I think it's on the Criterion Channel."

"Black-and-white, I bet."

"What's wrong with black-and-white?"

"All I'm saying is that I get to pick the next one. Something made in this century."

"That's a deal. I mean, as long as it's about cops and robbers."

"Okay, I'm hanging up now."

"See you soon."

He disconnected. Thanks to Tash, he no longer cared about Marquez and what he had said about Stilwell being nothing.

"Fuck him," he said.

26

AT THE SUB, Stilwell ran down an address for Gwen Bassett. She apparently had no California driver's license and was not in the DMV database, but her name came up in several crime reports because she was routinely listed as the complaining party at the Buffalo Nickel when deputies were summoned to deal with bar fights and other unruly behavior by patrons. The Nickel, located out by the desalination plant, was mostly a locals' bar. It served working-class drinkers who on occasion acted out to the extent that deputies were called in to restore order, if not make arrests.

Though the address of the bar was always listed as the location of the call, Bassett's home address was on most of the reports because she was a witness to the alleged offenses and might need to be contacted for follow-up investigations.

According to the reports, Bassett lived in Bird Park, an apartment complex in lower Avalon Canyon. It was an affordable location for Catalina service workers, and Stilwell assumed that Bassett had qualified for the housing discount if she had, as

Middleton told him, been living and working on the island for twelve years.

Stilwell had been up to Bird Park on various minor calls and was familiar with the layout. It was a complex of two-story town houses and single-level apartments with a community pool and a playground. It was well maintained and possibly the most desirable of the subsidized housing complexes on the island. Its management team had always been cooperative with Stilwell and his deputies. Stilwell knew that its isolated location in the canyon made it a difficult place to surveil without being noticed.

Bassett's unit—where Kent Middleton also lived—was 208, which meant building two, apartment eight. Stilwell believed it was an end unit, which added to the difficulties of surveillance because there were three sides of the structure to cover. He was tempted to make a casual drive through the complex on his way home, but if Middleton saw him on the same day they had talked, he was unlikely to take it as a coincidence.

Once he had established where Middleton was living, Stilwell called Ballard and filled her in on his activities.

"This is amazing," she said.

"What is?" Stilwell asked.

"That you're having conversations with a suspected serial killer. I mean, I know it happens in the movies, but in real life, who does that? The FBI never has. They interview all kinds of killers after the arrests, but who talks to a serial killer while he's still active and thinks he's got the whole world fooled? This is an amazing opportunity. Not that we're going to let the guy run loose, but you know what I mean."

"We still need to prove he's a serial killer. And I should tell you, he's planning to leave the island. He told me he's applied to the state. Wants to be a ranger at the state park in Malibu if he gets his choice."

"That's the location of one of our cases. Alicia Reynoso disappeared in 2011 while hiking in the Malibu state recreation area. He wants to be close to her now."

"Yeah, I was thinking that when he told me. You know, I also think he was playing me."

"You mean he knows you're onto him?"

"No, I don't think so. It was as if he liked dropping these hints. That he gets off on it."

"It's the I'm-smarter-than-you complex. Most serials have it. It's the fulfillment of hiding in plain sight. See, this is what I mean. Most of this stuff comes out after a serial is caught. All these pieces of the puzzle come together. But here, we're getting some of the pieces in real time."

"It still doesn't explain why he changed from being a guy who literally buried everything four feet deep to a guy who wants to lead us to his kills."

"He's clearly changed, but I don't think it will ever be fully explained. He's evolving. Before, it was about not getting caught. Now he seems to want to brag about not being caught and being smarter than us."

"So how do we take him down?"

"That's the question."

"Watching him out here is going to be tough. It's a small town where everybody seems to know everybody. I don't know if this was a strategic move on his part, but he's living with a woman in an apartment complex that's isolated and hard to surveil. He works in a remote location as well. He either lucked into this or he is an off-the-charts planner."

"I'm thinking the latter. But we need to figure this out fast. I'm going to come over there tomorrow and bring some people. We have to start watching this guy. It's too dangerous not to. When can we get together?"

"Name a time. I'm just not sure we should meet here or involve any of my deputies. It could leak."

"Agreed. You figure out a location and we'll be there. If we stay over, where should we stay?"

"The Ratwater."

"What?"

"Sorry, old nickname. The Atwater is right in the middle of town. It's very nice. You can walk to everything and it's less than a block from here. There are nice places up the mountain too, but you need a cart to get to and from them."

"The Ratwater sounds good."

"Don't call it that if you call to make a reservation."

"I won't. I'll also check Airbnb."

"Okay, let me know when you're coming."

He disconnected. Ballard's mention of Airbnb gave Stilwell an idea. He opened a desk drawer and took out the rubber-banded stack of business cards he had been collecting since his posting to the island two years earlier. He shuffled through the cards until he came to Lukas Hernandez. He was the manager of the Bird Park apartment complex. He was also related to one of the island's old families, the one that had built and owned the complex. Stilwell flipped the card over and saw the personal cell number he had written down when he was looking for a place to live on the island. He knew the call would be a long shot, as Bird Park was in high demand because of its location and price, but he was hoping there would be a short-term opening between tenants.

Hernandez answered his call and Stilwell identified himself.

"Lukas, I wanted to see if you happen to have any short-term vacancies at Bird Park."

"Oh, I'm sorry. Things didn't work out with Tash?"

Once again, everybody seemed to know everybody's business.

If Stilwell didn't set Hernandez straight, word would spread like wildfire that he and Tash had split up. Tash had had many suitors on the island, including Hernandez, before Stilwell came along.

"No, it's not for me," he said quickly. "Tash and I are fine. I'm looking for a temporary place to put some friends."

"How temporary are we talking?" Hernandez asked.

"A couple weeks, max, I think."

"Sounds like you need it furnished."

"That would be good."

"How many bedrooms?"

"Two, but they'd take anything."

"Let me call you right back. I want to check something."

"Sure, you've got my number. And Lukas, I want to keep this confidential. Don't tell anyone that it's coming from me."

"Wait a minute—are these people witnesses or something? Are they in danger or dangerous?"

"No, no, they're cops and they don't want people to know their business."

"Okay, got it. I'll call you back in ten."

While Stilwell waited for Lukas to call back, he went into the squad room to look at the deployment screen. While riding with Middleton, he had noted the unit number painted on the 4Runner he was driving. He assumed the vehicle was assigned to him and that Middleton would now be trackable when on duty across the island. He also knew there were qualifiers to that assumption. Locating the vehicle did not necessarily mean Middleton was in it or even near it, and it could be used by a different ranger following a shift change.

His 4Runner was unit five. Stilwell quickly located it at Hermit Gulch, where he knew there was a small ranger outpost. What he didn't know was whether Middleton was still on duty.

Stilwell's phone buzzed—Hernandez calling back.

"You're in luck," he said. "We had a move-out and the new tenant doesn't come in until the first of the month. That gives you a couple weeks. Is that good?"

"Yes, really good," Stilwell said. "How big is it?"

"It's a two. And it's furnished. Moderately. Beds, couches, but no kitchenware. They'll have to bring pots and pans, knives and forks, all that stuff."

"Got it. What's the cost?"

"You said they're cops, right?"

"Yeah."

"Then I'll eat it. We want to cooperate with whatever this is."

"You're the man, Lukas. How soon can they get in there?"

"It's empty right now."

"Which unit is it?"

"Building one, unit three. Two-bedroom town house."

Building one was across a parking area from building two. The apartment would have a direct view of Gwen Bassett's front door.

"Okay, perfect," Stilwell said. "Can I firm everything up and call you first thing tomorrow?"

"Of course," Hernandez said.

"And remember, you have to keep who they are and what they do between us."

"Got it. Not a problem."

"Thank you, Lukas, and sorry about Tash."

"What do you mean?"

"That she's still off the market."

Hernandez laughed as he disconnected.

Stilwell immediately called Ballard back and told her he had found a place where her team could stay and keep eyes on Middleton at the same time.

"Perfect," Ballard said. "We'll be coming out on the first boat tomorrow."

"Who is *we*?"

"Me, Laffont, and Paul Masser."

"I'll meet you at the dock."

27

STILWELL, DRESSED IN plain clothes, waited to greet Ballard and her team at the ferry dock. But he was surprised to see Ernie Simon and his partner, Bob Trestle, come down the gangway first. And they were surprised to see him.

"How'd you know we were coming?" Simon asked.

"I didn't," Stilwell said. "I'm waiting for some people from the LAPD. What's going on?"

"We need to go up to the airstrip, take some measurements, and shoot some photos," Simon said. "Now that you know we're here, you think we can get a ride up there?"

"Not a problem," Stilwell said. "We can go to the sub and get you a ride."

He used his radio to call Dawn Stabile and tell her to come to the sub to take Simon and Trestle up to the airport. By the time he signed off with her, they had been joined by Ballard, Laffont, and Masser, who had been stuck in the crowd getting off the boat because the two men had to wait for their roller bags.

Stilwell made introductions and everybody shook hands. Stilwell explained that they were there on separate murder investigations.

"Little island, big crime, huh?" Simon said.

"Seems that way," Stilwell said.

The group walked to Crescent, then over to the substation. Stilwell wanted to ask Simon what was going on with the airstrip case that required them to return to the crime scene but held back because of the mixed company. He guessed, though, that Ilsa Ramirez might have recovered her memory of the shooting and given them new information. He also guessed that the reason Simon had not informed him of the return trip was that Ramirez's recollections contradicted previous thinking on the case. He was eager to know more but needed to stick with the LAPD investigators as planned.

When they got to the sub, Stabile was waiting in an ATV. But Stilwell told her that she should use the sub's four-seat SUV for the airport run.

"The key's in my office," he said.

"I think Mercy keeps it," Stabile said.

"No, I took it from her," Stilwell said. "Come in, and I'll get it for you."

He turned to the five homicide investigators, pointed to the SUV, and addressed Simon and Trestle.

"Why don't you guys go to the car and she'll be right out," he said. "And you three come with me."

The group split up and Stilwell led Ballard and her men in. Stabile followed. When they got to the squad room, Stilwell pointed to the break room.

"Coffee's in there," he said. "There's a table where we can go over stuff. I'll be right with you."

He led Stabile into his office and closed the door.

"You're right, Mercy has the key," he said, "but I wanted an excuse to come in and talk to you alone. I want you to drive those guys up there and stick as close to them as you can. I want to know what they're doing and what they're saying. Understand?"

"Got it," Stabile said.

"Good. Don't be obvious about it."

"Okay, but why?"

"They didn't mention they were coming out. That tells me something's going on. I want you to find out what."

"Sure, boss. I'll do my best."

"Great. Go ahead."

Stabile left and Stilwell grabbed a file off his desk and headed to the break room. Ballard, Laffont, and Masser were already seated at the lunch table. Ballard and Masser had coffee cups in front of them; Laffont had a Diet Coke from the fridge. Stilwell put the file down on the table and went to the coffee maker to get a cup for himself.

"That's what I have on Middleton," he said as he poured. "You have his photo from a display at the ranger station, and the candids were taken yesterday at a retreat for high-school kids. He didn't see me take them."

There were only three chairs at the table. Ballard was spreading out the printouts of the photos. Stilwell turned and leaned back against the counter.

"So, anything new since we talked?" Stilwell asked.

"Well, these guys have volunteered to take the apartment and watch Middleton," Ballard said. "I'll go back and forth as needed. Were you able to get his schedule?"

"Yeah," Stilwell said. "The ranger captain and I share schedules so we know who's working and when. Middleton is off three days starting tomorrow."

"Then he might go over to the mainland," Laffont said. "Either way, we'll be with him."

"I'm working on putting more bodies together to tag-team him if he goes across," Ballard said. "But here on the island, I think we need to stay small."

"Agreed," Stilwell said. "So you guys are volunteers?"

"We are," Laffont said.

"What were you in your past lives?"

"FBI," Laffont said.

"I worked major crimes as a prosecutor with the DA's office," Masser said.

Stilwell nodded. They were good credentials.

"Have you worked up a cover for them yet?" Ballard asked.

"Yeah. We have a vineyard not too far from the apartment that was just the target of a major act of vandalism, and I heard the owner is facing financial difficulties. I was thinking you guys are in town from the insurance company or maybe as potential buyers assessing the property. Take your pick."

"That could work," Laffont said.

"I like you being buyers," Ballard said. "That way you don't have to say a lot. You're keeping your business on the down-low."

"And you got the apartment short term on Airbnb," Stilwell added.

Laffont and Masser nodded.

"The business is called Avalon Beverage Company," Stilwell said. "People around here refer to it as ABC. They make a pinot noir called Avalon Crest. The owner is Oliver Marquez. That's probably all you need to know."

Laffont took a small notebook out of a back pocket and started to write it all down.

"How's the wine?" Ballard asked.

"I don't know," Stilwell said. "Marquez is a bit of an entitled ass and I don't drink his wine."

"Okay, then," Ballard said, amused.

Stilwell stopped himself before he further denigrated Marquez.

"Okay," he said. "Let's check the screen and see if it's clear to get you into the apartment."

"What screen?" Ballard asked.

"Follow me," Stilwell said.

They walked into the squad room and Stilwell asked Mercy to go to the break room to make more coffee. He trusted her, but the case was too sensitive to talk about openly. He moved to the deployment screen and in a low voice told them it was used to GPS-track law enforcement and first-response vehicles. He explained the colors assigned to sheriff, county fire, and conservancy ranger vehicles. He pointed to a ranger unit.

"Our man is on duty today and in ranger five, a Toyota Four Runner," he said. "At the moment his vehicle is up in an area called Hermit Gulch."

"Perfect," Ballard said. "We should be able to get into the OP without him knowing."

Ballard was already referring to the apartment at Bird Park as the observation post.

"Yeah, but there's a catch," Stilwell said. "His girlfriend works at night in a locals' bar. Her name's Gwen Bassett and she's a bartender. She gets off work late, so right now, she's most likely sleeping. But she knows me and I know her, so if she's awake—"

"You can't take us up there and risk being seen by her," Masser guessed.

"Exactly," Stilwell said. "She tells Middleton, and he'll suspect something's up."

"Are you thinking she knows what he's been doing?" Laffont asked.

"No, there's no reason to believe that," Stilwell said. "But she might see me moving you guys in, and we can't risk her mentioning it to Middleton in conversation."

"Okay, so we go up without you," Ballard said. "How do we get there?"

"Half a block from here is a place that rents golf carts long term," Stilwell said. "You rent a cart and drive up. Then you have a cart if you need it. When you're up there, go into the office and ask for Lukas. He'll show you to the unit like you're new tenants."

"He knows what we're doing?" Ballard asked.

"Just that you're cops. It was the only way to get the apartment," Stilwell said. "We can trust him, but he doesn't know what this is about. Use the ABC cover story if anybody else presses you."

"We're good to go," Laffont said.

"I think you need to hang back with me, Renée," Stilwell said.

He walked over to a desk and grabbed the latest edition of the *Call*. He brought it to her, holding it so she could see the photo on the front page. It was from the recovery of the remains in the ironwood grove. Lionel McKey had shot it from the crime scene tape, and Ballard and Stilwell were clearly identifiable.

"Fuck me," Ballard said. "I guess I'm hanging with you."

Stilwell walked to the charging rack and grabbed a two-way. He handed it to Laffont.

"In case you need it," Stilwell said. "We have two deputies on patrol twenty-four seven. Avalon One and Two. Call them if you need them."

"Hopefully we won't," Laffont said.

"Okay, let's do this," Ballard said.

28

STILWELL WALKED BALLARD back to the Express dock after they got word that Laffont and Masser were settled in at the apartment at Bird Park and had a view through split curtains of Middleton's front door. She was taking the boat to San Pedro at noon so she could get back to work with the rest of her team. They still needed to connect the suspect geographically to the other missing hikers and possibly link the fifth key to a disappearance. She said the analysis of the backpack was due from the lab. She was hoping for DNA or fingerprints but they both knew that such a case breaker was unlikely. The killer was meticulous and undoubtedly had made sure that there was nothing about the backpack that could be traced back to him.

Ballard reported on their efforts to see if the Ford key found in the backpack fit the ignition of the Mustang that belonged to Candace Neary and was found abandoned at the observatory atop Griffith Park. The car had been sold by Neary's family a few years after she went missing.

"We tracked down the buyer, but the car was wrecked in an accident four years ago," she said. "It was sold for parts to a junkyard in the Valley and they had no record of where the ignition switch ended up. Another dead end."

The boat was loading and there was a line of people at the gangway with their luggage and bags of souvenirs. Stilwell had called Kim Krabill, the ferry's captain, and she was holding a seat in the commodore lounge for Ballard, so she didn't need to queue up.

"I hope we're not wrong about this guy," Ballard said. "We have zero evidence against him."

"My gut tells me we're right," Stilwell responded.

"Your gut to God's ear. If we don't find something soon, we might have to bring him in and try to break him."

"He doesn't seem to be the breaking type. Especially if he knows we have nothing solid."

"At least it would let him know we're watching him. Maybe make him stop."

Stilwell was surprised by her thinking.

"What's the hurry?" he asked.

"The hurry is that this guy is active," Ballard said. "We can't let him take another girl on our watch."

"I get that, but why would you pull him in when we might be able to catch him in the act? Then we'd have a bulletproof case."

"Because a thousand things could go wrong with that, and we'd look like shit and feel like shit for letting him terrorize another victim."

Stilwell nodded.

"I hear you," he said. "I'm talking about stopping him before any of that happens, but after we see him cross a line, that lets us put a charge on him."

"It's still risky," Ballard insisted. "And we have no idea how long we'd have to watch him. There are years between these victims going missing. Right now, the cadence is wrong."

"True, but psychopaths change. And the cadence is based only on those we know about. There could be others between those four."

"The reality is that my department won't fund an indefinite surveillance, and those two guys at the apartment are volunteers. I can't ask them to stay with him past a week at most."

"Then let's at least give it till then."

"We'll see."

She was looking past him as she said the last part. Stilwell saw her focus on something, and he turned around to see what it was. Simon and Trestle were hurrying along the dock to make the same boat. They spotted Stilwell and came up to him.

"Is this the one to Pedro?" Simon asked.

"Sure is," Stilwell said. "You leaving already?"

"We did what we had to do," Trestle said.

Simon pointed at the boat.

"But we're on standby," Simon said. "We might have to catch the next one."

"Let me see if I can get you on," Stilwell said.

Stilwell pulled out his phone and called Krabill. He had the names and contacts of all the Express captains. They often called him with suspicions about passengers coming to the island. He called them when he wanted to get a ride either way or on the rare occasion that he had to move a felony custody to the mainland for booking into the county jail.

He saw Krabill come out of the pilothouse and lean on a rail as she answered the call. They spoke into their phones while looking at each other across the dock. She was the only female captain of an Express ferry and had been there for many years. The wind was blowing her curly white hair as they spoke.

"Hey, Captain Kim," he said. "You have room for two more coppers? They're on standby but need to get back across."

Stilwell gestured toward Simon and Trestle.

"Those two?" Krabill said. "You sure they're not prisoners, Stil? They look sort of unsavory."

Stilwell laughed.

"They *are* unsavory but I'll vouch for them," he said.

"I'll make room," Krabill said. "Send them up to the lounge with your lady cop. Peter is on the gangway. I'll let him know."

She waved from the boat as she disconnected and then returned to the pilothouse.

"Okay, you're good," Stilwell said. "The guy checking tickets is named Peter. She'll tell him to let you all into the commodore lounge on the upper level. How'd it go at the strip?"

"All good," Simon said. "We got what we needed."

"Which was what?" Stilwell asked.

Simon frowned at the question and Stilwell realized he had pushed it too far. He was no longer part of the investigation or in the loop. This bothered him, but he knew it wasn't Simon's decision. It went back to Corum.

"Just measurements and photos," Trestle said.

"Sure," Stilwell said. "I get it."

He saw that the line to board the ferry was near its end.

"You guys should probably go before they start calling the standby list," he said. "The commodore lounge is up top. Any issue, ask for Captain Krabill."

"We'll be in touch," Simon said.

He turned to go but threw a wink at Stilwell that his partner didn't see. Stilwell took it as a sign that Simon might keep him informed on a sub-rosa basis. He would call Simon once he was back on the mainland.

"Got ya," Stilwell said.

Ballard started to follow, but Stilwell tapped her on the arm and she hung back.

"So you'll let me know what happens with your guys?" he said.

"Of course," she said. "If Middleton makes a move, you'll know it."

Stilwell nodded in the direction of the boat.

"And listen," he said, "if you end up talking to those guys in the lounge, ask them what they were doing out here. I would love to know."

"I thought it was measurements and photos," Ballard said.

"And I think that was bullshit. They have something they aren't sharing with me."

"Okay, I'll see what I can do."

"*Gracias.*"

"What, you think I'm Mexican?"

"I don't know. Maybe."

"Hawaiian."

"Oh, yeah? Which island?"

"Maui."

"Nice. I spent a lot of time over there when I was in the navy. I'd hop over from the Pearl. A shame what happened to Lahaina. I loved that town. Thought about it when I could see the smoke from the Palisades last year."

"You could see the fire from over here?"

"Just the smoke."

Ballard nodded.

"I'm going to go," she said.

"Aloha, e ku'u hoaloha," Stilwell said.

Ballard smiled as she turned toward the boat.

"You learned something over there," she said.

"A few things," Stilwell said.

He watched her go down the gangway and didn't head back to the sub until he saw the ticket-taker signal her aboard when she opened her jacket to show the badge on her belt.

Ten minutes later he entered the sub to find Dawn Stabile in the squad room.

"What happened up there?" he asked.

"They wouldn't talk to me and told me to wait in the car," she said. "So I did. But I watched them. They were looking at a piece of paper and going to different spots. One would stand there while the other took a picture of him. They also measured different distances and wrote stuff on the paper."

Stilwell knew they were mapping out the double shooting, making sure it was documented should there ever be a prosecution of a suspect. They couldn't have done that if they hadn't found a witness. It meant Ramirez was remembering all or part of that night.

"Okay," Stilwell said. "Anything else?"

"Yes," Stabile said. "First they walked down to the middle of the landing strip and searched in the brush there. Then they walked back up and searched the runway near the end."

"Let's do this one at a time. Tell me about them searching the middle of the runway."

"No, not the runway exactly. They went into the brush on the side and went down where I couldn't see them."

"How far down the runway?"

"About halfway, at least."

This was curious to Stilwell. On the night of the shooting he had chased the ATV into the brush near the end of the runway. This meant Simon and Trestle were searching in a different spot on their return visit to the airstrip.

"How long were they down there out of sight?" he asked.

"Like twenty minutes at the most," Stabile said.

"Okay, and then what?"

"They came back up, spread apart, and headed toward the west end of the runway. They were looking for something."

"On the tarmac?"

"Yes."

"Did they find anything?"

"No. At least, they never picked anything up. I watched them the whole time."

Stabile's report gave Stilwell pause as he thought about what Simon and Trestle had been looking for. It seemed clear that they believed that the shooter had not been hiding on the plane but in the brush off the side of the runway. The search of the tarmac had probably been an effort to find ricochet marks.

"Did you take any photos of them with your phone?" he asked.

"Uh, no," Stabile said. "You didn't ask me to."

"It would have been good if you'd thought of it on your own."

"Sorry."

"Me too."

"Should I go back out on patrol now?"

"Yeah, go ahead. But give me the keys to the SUV."

"I gave them back to Mercy."

At least she did that right, Stilwell thought.

29

AT THE AIRSTRIP Stilwell parked the SUV and climbed the steps to the tower. It was an old two-story wooden structure with an outdoor staircase that creaked under his weight and should have announced his arrival. It had been built when William Wrigley owned Catalina, and back then there was more air traffic, especially when the Chicago Cubs, also owned by the chewing-gum magnate, held spring training on the island. Stilwell knocked once and opened the tower door, rousing Rich Burkhardt from a desk nap.

"Hey, Stil, what's up?" he quickly said, trying to cover that he had dozed off. "Just shut my eyes for a few seconds there."

Burkhardt was manager, maintenance man, and sole full-time employee of the airport. He'd been so for nearly forty years. He had thinning gray hair and a paunch that stretched his red polo shirt, which had AIRPORT IN THE SKY stitched over the breast pocket and RICH on the other side.

"I was wondering if you had your eyes open when my two colleagues were up here this morning," Stilwell said.

Stilwell pointed out the window and down toward the airstrip.

"Sure did," Burkhardt said. "Those guys didn't even check in with me. I'm sitting here and I look down and see them walking across the tarmac like they own the place. A plane could've come in and cut 'em to ribbons."

That seemed an unlikely possibility, but Stilwell didn't challenge Burkhardt on it.

"I got caught up on a call in Avalon and didn't make it up with them," Stilwell said. "I was wondering if you could point me to the spot on the side of the strip where they did the search. If you remember."

"I can do you one better than that," Burkhardt said. "I took pictures. I wanted to document those guys just waltzing across my airstrip without permission."

"Can I see them?"

Burkhardt dug his cell out of his pocket, opened the photo app, and handed the phone to Stilwell.

"There's a few," he said.

Stilwell swiped quickly back through the photos so he could view them in sequence. He came to a photo of a plane in the hangar next to the tower. Burkhardt was looking over his shoulder at the screen.

"Oh, that's Hacker Caldwell's Cessna," he said. "I took that a couple days ago for him. He needed it for insurance."

Stilwell knew Caldwell. He was the patriarch of one of the island's old families. He started swiping forward through the photos.

The first showed Simon and Trestle standing at the edge of the landing strip looking into the brush. There was an ironwood tree about ten yards down the slope. Stilwell swiped to the next photo. In this one they had stepped farther down the slope. This was where Stabile had lost sight of them, but the tower had a steeper angle of view. In the photo, the two investigators were looking down at the ground as if searching for something. He swiped to the next photo, and they were now looking up at the branches of the ironwood, which appeared to be standing alone, not part of a grove.

"Did you watch what they were doing?" he asked. "With the tree, I mean."

"Not really," Burkhardt said. "They were just checking it out, I guess."

"Did they climb it?"

"Not that I saw. But you could ask your girl who drove 'em up here."

"I did."

"Yeah, what'd she say?"

"She was down in the SUV and didn't have the angle on them."

"Well, couldn't you just ask your two buddies what they were doing?"

"I could, yeah. But they're already on the boat back to Pedro."

He returned the phone and looked out the window at the ironwood tree.

"Okay, I'm heading down there, Rich," he said. "Any planes coming in that I should watch out for so I don't get cut to ribbons?"

"Not till four o'clock," Burkhardt said.

"Perfect. Thanks for shooting the photos."

"When you talk to those guys, tell them, next time, check in up here so we know who's on the property and we can keep everybody safe."

"I'll do that."

Stilwell went down the steps, careful to hold the wooden handrail and hoping he didn't pick up a splinter. He crossed the landing strip to the edge in front of the ironwood tree. He slowly stepped into the brush, eyes down on the chapparal, looking for any evidence that Simon and Trestle had missed.

There was nothing. He got down to the ironwood and quickly determined that it was two trees sharing the same root system, one trunk eclipsed by the other when viewed from the tower. Each had branches splitting off from the trunks at intervals that would make climbing difficult. He guessed that this was the reason Simon and Trestle, both men in their fifties and overweight, had not climbed them.

Stilwell reached up to a thick limb and tested it with his weight. It seemed solid. He grasped it with both hands and swung his legs up until he got one foot on a lower, thinner branch. He started climbing, finding that by bracing his back against one of the trunks, he could scale the other.

When he was twelve feet up, he stopped and got his bearings. He looked in the direction of where the plane had stopped on the night of the shooting. There was an opening in the branches that allowed him to see that end of the runway, a hundred yards off. He realized that other branches hid him from the tower and the shed next to where he had parked while waiting for the airdrop.

Holding a higher branch, Stilwell slowly stepped out on a limb below and found the reason there was an opening in the tree's canopy. Several small branches had been snapped off or cut to clear the space. He studied these breaks and saw that the interior pulp of the tree was reddish. The breaks had been recently made.

Carefully taking one of his hands off the limb he was clinging to, he reached into his pocket for his phone and took several photos of the branch breaks and the opening they created in the canopy. He put the phone back in his pocket and began the climb down.

Once on the ground, Stilwell looked in the brush for the broken branches and found them in a heap in the chapparal fifteen feet from the ironwood. The pile was too far from the tree's base to have naturally fallen there. The branches had been discarded there. He pulled out his phone and took more photos.

Stilwell climbed up out of the brush and onto the tarmac. He checked both ways for incoming planes before rushing across the runway to his ATV. As he did so, Rich Burkhardt stepped onto the tower's catwalk and called down to him.

"You find something?"

Stilwell waved up to him but kept going, adrenaline pulsing in his blood.

"I did," he called back.

30

STILWELL WAITED UNTIL he got back to his office to call Simon. He figured that he would be off the boat by then and able to talk without Trestle nearby. Simon picked up immediately.

"Hey, baby, how you feeling?" he said.

Stilwell paused for a moment.

"You can't talk?" he said.

"That's good to hear," Simon said. "You take your meds?"

"Okay, when can you talk? I went up to the airstrip. I found something you missed."

"Set the timer for fifteen minutes and take it then."

"Okay, you have the number."

"Love you too."

Simon disconnected.

With fifteen minutes to kill, Stilwell walked out into the squad room and checked the basket on Mercy's desk where call reports were dropped. When he had entered the sub, she told him there was one that needed his attention.

There were only three call sheets in the basket. The first two were shoplifting reports from souvenir stores on Crescent that had come in within an hour of each other. The stores were less than a block apart, and the suspect descriptions matched: white female, twenties, dark hair with a dyed-pink streak in it. The third was a report of vandalism involving graffiti painted on the chimes tower that overlooked the harbor. Someone had painted FSID at the base of the hundred-year-old tower built by William Wrigley and visible from most spots in Avalon.

This was the report Mercy knew he needed to address sooner rather than later. She had rightfully assumed that such an offense against one of the island's most treasured structures would result in a public uproar, especially if Lionel McKey got wind of it and wrote a story for the *Call*.

"Do you know if they painted over it yet?" he asked Mercy.

"I told them not to until they heard from you," Mercy said.

"Good. I'm waiting on a callback, but then I'll go up and check it out."

"Do you want me to tell Billy Barnes to meet you there?"

Barnes, a local fisherman, was the citizen volunteer who maintained the chimes.

"Not yet," Stilwell said. "I don't know how long this call will take. Any idea what F-S-I-D means?"

"No," Mercy said. "I googled it but nothing came up."

"I can guess what the *F* is."

"I was thinking the same thing."

He took the report with him to his office and shut the door.

When Simon called back, it was from a number Stilwell didn't recognize.

"What, you're calling me on a burner, Ernie?"

"Taking all precautions."

"Why? What's going on?"

" 'Why?' Because I'm smart. So, first of all, why did you go up there after we left?"

"Because I'm invested. If this case goes sideways, I'll go down for it."

"Oh, come on. You really think that?"

"Hey, who's the guy who's already been banished to the Island of Misfit Toys?"

Simon didn't respond, which meant he saw the truth in Stilwell's concern.

"So what did you find up there that we missed?" he asked.

"I confirmed that the shooter wasn't hiding on the plane," Stilwell said. "He was up in that ironwood tree you looked at this morning. This was an assassination, Ernie, and I think that's why you're using the burner."

"I'm not going to get into that. I'm not even supposed to talk to you."

"By whose order?"

"You know who. You're not part of this case anymore."

Corum.

"Come on, Ernie, talk to me," Stilwell said. "Why'd you come back out here?"

"I'm sure your deputy told you what we were doing," Simon said.

"Yeah, and that's why I climbed that tree and found the sniper's nest. It changes things, Ernie. This was an ambush—a planned hit. Quigley was set up because of something he did when he was back on the mainland. And I don't think I'm telling you anything you don't already know."

Simon was silent as he composed a response.

"Listen," he finally said. "Be smart and take a step back. For your own good, Stil, step the fuck back."

"I can't. Quigley was a new guy, but Ramirez was on my team. She didn't deserve to be left on the tarmac like collateral damage. And if I hadn't chased Kalas down the hill, I probably would've been laid out with her. I can't step back from that."

Simon went silent again and Stilwell imagined him shaking his head at his warning going unheeded.

"Is Ramirez the one who told you the shots came from behind them?" Stilwell asked.

Simon answered in a tone of resignation.

"She's telling us stuff," he said. "She's writing it down."

It was a confirmation and a significant give from Simon. Stilwell responded in kind.

"Branches were broken off in the tree you didn't climb," he said. "It opened a window in the tree's canopy. The shooter had a clear view of the end of the runway. I found the branches fifteen feet away from the tree, thrown in the brush. I took photos. I'll send them to you and you can say they're yours."

"I appreciate that," Simon said.

"Did you have your sit-down with Lambert?"

"We did, yeah."

Stilwell waited. Nothing else came.

"Come on, Ernie. What did he say? Who was Quigley's CI? Whoever he was, he set him up."

"Lambert said he didn't know. He said he checked every name Quigley had put in the box. It had to have been someone he hadn't cleared."

Simon was referring to department procedures for using confidential informants. Every CI was supposed to be validated and cleared by the commanding officer of the unit. Way back, those names were secured in a lockbox held by the CO. For decades now, the identities had been kept in an encrypted computer file, but it was still referred to as "the box." In Quigley's case, the identities of the informants he procured and used while in the narco unit would have been kept by Lambert. This procedure was a safety backup but also a way to track informants and determine the level of trust that should be placed in their tips. Stilwell knew it was common practice to test new CIs repeatedly before putting them up for approval and into the encrypted files. The person who had tipped Quigley to the airport drop could have been one of these new, uncleared informants even though Quigley had said he was a hundred-percenter.

Stilwell found himself trying to recall exactly what Quigley had told him about the tip that led to the airport surveillance. He realized that it was another point of vulnerability for him. He had approved the quickly planned operation based on intel Quigley told him his CI had provided.

He decided not to dwell on it and moved on.

"Did you ask Lambert what he knew about Quigley's transfer out here?" he asked. "What did he do?"

"I asked and got the same bullshit answer," Simon said. "He claimed that Quigley asked for the transfer and specifically said he wanted to go to Catalina. Don't take this personally, Stil, but that is bullshit, because nobody asks to go to the Catalina station."

"So Lambert was covering something up. Did you ask Corum to apply some pressure on him?"

"I did, yeah."

He offered nothing else and Stilwell had to read between the lines. If Corum did not pressure or even order Lambert to reveal more, then he was protecting either the department or himself. Stilwell had no reason to believe Corum even knew who Quigley was, at least based on the questions he had asked on the night of the shooting.

Stilwell's conclusion—and he guessed it was Simon's as

well—was that Corum was trying to head off what could be an embarrassing situation for the department.

For Corum, this would be job one. The sheriff's department was obsessively sensitive to image and politics. It was headed by an elected sheriff, and any issue or controversy that might possibly threaten reelection was to be immediately and deeply buried. Status quo kept the sheriff and his command staff comfortably in their positions. It would be career suicide to go any other way.

Part two of Stilwell's conclusion was that Corum's efforts could leave Stilwell hanging in the wind. Should the cover-up need a fall guy, without a doubt it would be him.

PART THREE

The *Game-Over* Look

31

AS STILWELL DROVE up Chimes Tower Road in the ATV, he could see the graffiti on the tower's front wall, positioned to be visible from the harbor below. Graffiti was generally not a problem on the island. There was not a large population of young people and it just wasn't the kind of place that overtowners, including gang members, came to leave their mark. Stilwell thought before he even got there that he would be looking for a local and that the suspect would likely be found at the high school.

During his time in the homicide unit, Stilwell had learned to read graffiti. That is, he had studied the various styles and code words contained in gang tags. Often it led to clues, sometimes the identity of the gang responsible for the murder or even the killer himself. He could tell that the mark on the tower was in what was known as the bubble style, big cartoonish letters meant to be seen from a distance. The letters were blue, outlined in black.

When he got there, Bill Barnes was waiting with painting equipment at the ready. He wanted the message—whatever

FSID meant—to be gone as soon as possible. Stilwell guessed that Barnes had taken the vandalism as a personal affront. He was one of Avalon's floaters—meaning he lived on a boat with a permanent mooring in the harbor. Stilwell had heard two different stories about Barnes. One was that he had been an attorney in Florida and moved to the island when he burned out on the law and wanted to get as far from the Sunshine State as he could. The other story was that he had made so much money in a personal injury case that he retired early, bought a boat, and planned to travel the world's oceans, fishing and exploring, but when he got to Catalina, he fell in love with the place and decided he need not go any further. Either way, he had volunteered to take care of the tower as a means of fitting into Avalon's established social structure and giving something back to his adopted home.

The chimes sang out across the harbor and town every fifteen minutes from eight a.m. to eight p.m. every day. They were custom-made tubular bells that William Wrigley had imported from Chicago. They were sacred to some, including Barnes. He was good and angry when Stilwell hopped out of the ATV.

"I hope you catch the little asshole who did this," he said. "Gotta be some miscreant overtown gangbanger who can't stand the thought of what we have out here."

"Miscreant overtown gangbanger, huh?" Stilwell said. "That's a profile. How do you know it's a he? And that he's from overtown and is a gangbanger?"

"The percentages. You think I'm wrong?"

"I think the first place I'm going to look is up at the school."

"It would pain me to know it was one of our own."

"Well, we'll see. Any idea what it means?" Stilwell pointed to the tag.

"I know what the *F* stands for," Barnes said. "After that, no."

Stilwell pulled out his phone and took several photos from different angles.

"Okay," he said when he was finished. "You can go ahead and paint."

"I shouldn't be the one doing this," Barnes said. "It should be the prick who did it, but I can't stand it being seen all over the harbor."

Stilwell looked down. He saw the harbormaster's tower at the end of the pier and imagined Tash in there watching over the water and all the boats.

"You saw it from the *Bee*?" he asked.

He had heard that Barnes bought the boat with the name *Bimini Bee* already registered. Bimini was an island off the coast of Florida. The boat was an old Carver that looked like it had plowed through too many waves. Based on that, Stilwell believed the first story about Barnes's origins.

"I sure did," Barnes said. "Made my coffee, took it up to the bridge to enjoy, and what do I see?"

He gestured to the tower's lower wall. The tag was centered right below the arched window that revealed the hanging lines of tubular bells.

"Could read it plain as day," he added. "Just like everybody getting off the Express boats. Not cool. Not cool at all."

Barnes already had a one-gallon can of wall paint open. The color matched the tower wall's off-white shade and had been used as part of his previous upkeep of the structure. He started pouring it into a roller pan, muttering about how many coats it would take to cover the blue letters.

Stilwell walked around the tower, looking in the brush that surrounded it for a can of spray paint, hoping that the graffiti culprit was dumb enough to toss his tagging weapon with his fingerprints on it.

There was no such luck. By the time Stilwell had circled the tower, Barnes had one coat of paint over the graffiti. The blue letters were still visible. Maybe not to the boats in the harbor or the tourists on Crescent, but Barnes was right that the offending letters were going to take multiple coats of paint to obscure.

Before he could tell Barnes he was taking off to pursue the case, his phone buzzed and he saw that it was Mercy.

"There's another one," she said.

"Another what?" Stilwell asked.

"Graffiti. The same thing, F-S-I-D — whatever that means — on the casino on the sea-facing side."

"Okay, I'm leaving here and I'll go check it out. Who called it in?"

"My cousin."

Her cousin was Jeff Danzy, the security and maintenance supervisor at the historic casino, the signature structure that graced every poster and postcard sold in the shops on Crescent. It, too, had been built by Wrigley. Mercy and Jeff were part of a widespread family tree that included a former town mayor named Ruth Woods. Though she was long gone, locals still spoke of her with reverence. Affectionately known as "Mom Woods," she was Mercy and Jeff's grandmother and was said to have been a stern taskmaster who'd kept a tight grip on town patronage and politics for more than a decade, from the sixties into the seventies. Among her many accomplishments, Mom Woods was said to have been the force behind the Wrigley family's decision to turn over most of their land to the conservancy.

After disconnecting, Stilwell told Barnes that there was another tag with the same message on the casino. Barnes shook his head wearily in a *What is this world coming to?* way. Stilwell said he would be in touch and headed the ATV down the hill.

The tag on the exterior wall of the casino was located on

the round building's seaward side, so it could be seen by vessels approaching the harbor, including the cruise ships that anchored off Catalina four days a week and transferred their passengers to the island by water taxi. The graffiti was in the same style and colors as the one on the chimes tower, and Stilwell figured it was probably painted by the same hand. Danzy was waiting for him, just like Barnes had been, ready to paint over the blemish as soon as Stilwell gave the word. But this act of vandalism was different. Here, there were cameras.

Stilwell took photos of the tag, then stepped back and looked up at the curving wall of the building. The casino was built like a muffin. Three levels, with the top floor—the grand ballroom—cantilevered over the exterior walls. He saw a camera anchored beneath the third level and asked Danzy to take him to the security office to look at the video.

"I need to paint first," Danzy said. "Can't leave this here."

"Why?" Stilwell asked. "It shouldn't take long. I need to investigate this thing."

"Because the *Princess* is coming, man. We don't want them to see this."

The *Princess* was that day's cruise ship. It would stay overnight, its passengers hopefully filling the town's restaurants and shops.

Stilwell looked out across the water to the south. He could see the midsize cruise ship coming. He knew not to mess with the ebb and flow of the island's fragile tourism industry.

"Okay, one coat," Stilwell said. "It will dry while we look at video."

Danzy went to work with a roller, carefully making small up-and-down strokes to get the paint into the plaster surface of the wall. Stilwell saw a second roller and joined in, following Danzy and making faster and longer strokes.

"You feel like Tom Sawyer, Jeff?" he asked.

"Who?" Danzy asked.

"You know, Mark Twain? Tom Sawyer tricks his buddies into painting a fence?"

Danzy looked puzzled.

"Never mind," Stilwell said.

They finished the first coat quickly thanks to Stilwell's help. But again, the ocean blue of the graffiti bled through the lighter paint. As with the chimes tower, it would take several coats to fully obliterate the tag.

"All right," Stilwell said. "Let it dry while we look at video."

The casino was not a gambling establishment and never had been. It was built in 1929 to be the entertainment center of the island. The first level contained a movie theater that Stilwell and Tash attended often, and the second floor was a theater for live performances. The ballroom at the top included a large stage for a big band. The security office was on the first floor near the movie theater's projection booth. Though in 1929 no thought had been given to camera surveillance, the office had room for a video console, and Danzy sat down there while Stilwell looked over his shoulder.

Danzy brought up the camera that had an angle on the graffiti and expanded it to full screen. He reversed the playback at high speed and they watched until the graffiti tag disappeared from the wall. He stopped the rewind and played the video forward in real time, beginning at 11:22 the night before. They watched as a figure in dark pants and a hoodie pulled tight around his face came into the frame with aerosol cans in both hands. He immediately went to work creating the *FSID* tag. It took him four minutes to make the blue tag with his left hand and then switch to the other can to outline his work in black.

"Left-handed," Stilwell said.

He leaned forward and took several photos of the screen with his phone, even though the painter had his head tilted down and away from the camera through the entire tagging process.

"He knows there's a camera," Stilwell said.

When the tag was finished, the painter backed up to appreciate his work for a moment, then turned and ran out of the frame in the opposite direction he'd come from, heading toward Descanso Beach, which was around the bend. Descanso Beach was where some of the highest-value homes on the island were located. It made Stilwell wonder whether the *D* in *FSID* stood for *Descanso.*

Stilwell and Danzy spent the next half hour looking at video from the other cameras surrounding the casino but didn't catch a glimpse of the tagger in any of them. Stilwell came away from the session with nothing approaching an identification of the vandal, but he did know that he moved like a young person and that he was left-handed, and Stilwell felt sure he was a local.

32

AVALON HARDWARE AND Chandlery was on Marilla. Stilwell drove over from the casino and walked through the store to the back, where the owner, Ned Browning, kept his office.

"I thought you'd be by," Browning said when he saw Stilwell standing in the doorway of his cluttered office.

"Why'd you think that?" Stilwell asked.

"Oh, because everyone's talking about the graffiti on the chimes tower and casino. It's hot news, and I figured you'd come by to see if I was selling spray paint to kids. The answer is no. There's a sign right in the paint department that says you must be twenty-one or accompanied by an adult to buy spray paint."

"Good rule."

Browning was a wiry guy with glasses and a deeply receding hairline. He wore a carpenter's apron over his collared shirt and blue jeans, probably trying to look like the handyman advisers in the Home Depots on the mainland.

"Yeah, but guess what," he said. "I did an inventory of what's on the shelf, what's still in the back, and what's been sold."

"And how'd that turn out?" Stilwell asked.

"Not good. I'm missing three cans total. Two ocean blues and one black."

"Shoplifted?"

"Most likely."

"You have cameras on the paint aisle?"

"Nope. But I'm going to get them."

"Do you remember any kids hanging out in the store and not buying anything?"

"Classic shoplifter profile. No, I don't. But I'm usually back here."

"Take a look at this."

Stilwell pulled out his phone and opened the photo app. He showed Browning the photos he had taken of the graffiti artist. Browning squinted and looked closely but shook his head.

"Nope," he said. "But that's DuPont paint. I see the logo. That's the brand of the three cans I'm missing."

"Thanks for your time, Ned."

School was done for the day, but Stilwell knew that Olester Bryant, the security officer, worked till five thirty. Avalon School, home of the Lancers, was located on Falls Canyon Road, a ten-minute drive from the hardware store. It was referred to as Avalon High, but it actually went from kindergarten through twelfth grade. Falling enrollments in recent years had forced the consolidation of all public schools on the island into one, but even now, the school had fewer than five hundred kids.

Stilwell found Bryant in his office filling out a form requesting supplies from Long Beach Unified, which was the school district that included Avalon. Like most people at the school, and on the island, for that matter, Bryant handled a variety of jobs. Every morning he worked in food prep for the school lunch.

"Olester, I've got a question," Stilwell said.

"I'm here for you," Bryant said.

He said that every time Stilwell had an inquiry about a case with possible ties to the school.

"Take a look at this," Stilwell said. "Tell me if you've seen it before at the school."

Stilwell opened his phone's photo app and pulled up a shot of the *FSID* tag on the wall of the casino. He handed the phone to Bryant.

"Free speech is dead," Bryant said.

"What?" Stilwell said.

"*FSID* stands for 'Free speech is dead.' It's the name of an informal club with the seniors and maybe a couple juniors. They started it last year with all that Charlie Kirk–Jimmy Kimmel stuff. Is this the casino? I heard there was graffiti on the chimes tower."

"Yeah. Whoever did it hit both. How many kids are in the FSID club?"

"It's not sanctioned by the school, so hard to tell. Maybe ten, twelve. They don't meet here—it's not allowed. But I've seen signs on bulletin boards about meetups and stuff. They all said *FSID* and no one knew what it meant, but a teacher got the low-down from one of the kids."

"Have there been any issues with them at the school?"

"None that came across my radar."

"Then why isn't it an official school club?"

"Politics, I guess, but now you're talking about things I'm not read in on."

"Okay, look at one more."

Stilwell pulled up the photo of the tagger he'd taken off the screen at the casino and showed it to Bryant.

"Any chance you recognize him?" he asked.

Bryant looked for a long moment, opened his mouth to say something, then closed it.

"What?" Stilwell pressed.

"You're not going to like it," Bryant said. "But that looks like Matthew Allen to me. The mayor's kid."

Stilwell took the phone back and looked again at the photo. He remembered seeing the mayor's family at a bail hearing and other court appearances, but he didn't recognize the tagger. Still, he believed Bryant's likely identification.

"How sure are you?" he asked.

"It's not a great picture, but I'm pretty sure," Bryant said. "Plus, I know he's got a hoodie like that."

Stilwell knew that the Allens lived in a condo in the Descanso Beach Club. He had served a search warrant there after he arrested Mayor Douglas Allen on corruption and bribery charges.

"That trial's coming up, right?" Bryant asked.

"Jury selection starts next week," Stilwell said. "Unless it gets delayed again. Has the kid been acting out in any way because of what's going on with his father?"

"Nothing that's come to me. Nothing serious like this, as far as I know." He pointed to Stilwell's phone.

Stilwell nodded. This information put him in a bind.

"His father is out on bail," Stilwell said. "If I show up at their place to talk to the son, there is going to be an issue. I'm not supposed to have any interaction with Douglas Allen before the trial."

"You have to get to Matthew outside the home," Bryant said.

"Right. So can you arrange to have him here in your office tomorrow morning?"

"I don't know about that. Arresting a kid on campus . . . I have relationships with these kids. They see me as a friend. If I call a kid in and he gets arrested—"

"I'm not going to arrest him. I'm going to talk to him. It would look bad for me to arrest the mayor's son after arresting the father. It would look like a vendetta. So I'm just going to talk to him, and depending on how that goes, I'll refer it. It will be someone else's call on the arrest."

By saying he would refer the case, Stilwell meant he would submit it to the district attorney's office for the possible filing of a charge.

"How is nine tomorrow?" Bryant asked. "I'll get him between first and second period."

Stilwell was supposed to be off on Wednesdays, but he wanted to put an end to the graffiti spree.

"That'll work," he said.

"If it's at the school, I'm supposed to sit in."

"I want you to. I'll see you then."

On his way back down the hill, Stilwell called Tash and told her he was done for the day and would head home after checking in at the sub.

"You sound down," she said. "Everything okay?"

"Everything's good," he said. "It's just the tin-star effect."

It was a reference to *High Noon* and the thankless job of the man with the badge. If you do the work right, nobody notices, nobody cares. And at the end of the day, what do you have to show for it? A tin star.

He had tried to explain it to Tash, how most days were good, but the badge carried a burden, and sometimes the weight of it made things seem dark in the middle of the day.

33

STILWELL WAS SEATED in a conference room when Olester Bryant arrived with a sullen Matthew Allen in tow. He had sandy-brown hair, an acne-scarred face, and a strong resemblance to his father. In a decision that seemed to confirm Stilwell's belief that most people who break the law are not smart about it, Allen had come to school wearing a black hoodie with a smear of what looked like blue paint on the left sleeve. Stilwell saw recognition flare in the kid's eyes: Stilwell was the cop who was trying to put his father in prison.

"You," he said. "What do you want?"

"To talk," Stilwell said. "Have a seat."

He pointed across the table to an empty chair.

"I don't want to sit," Allen said.

"Just sit down and drop the tough-guy act, Matthew," Stilwell said. "I guarantee this will go better for you if you do."

Allen shook his head like he was being unfairly put-upon and slid into a chair. Bryant took one of the other chairs at the table and sat with his arms crossed over his chest. Stilwell pulled out his phone, opened the recording app, and put it down on the table.

"What the fuck?" Allen said. "You're recording this?"

"Sheriff's department regulations require me to record any conversation with a juvenile," Stilwell said. "It protects you as well as me."

"Whatever."

"So, tell me about free speech. You think it's dead?"

"Don't you?"

"I'm asking the questions. Tell me about your group of free-speechers."

"What about it? We get together and talk about how fucked up the world is. That's it."

"Do you think that marking historic structures and buildings with graffiti is covered by the First Amendment right to free speech?"

"I think that sometimes people need to stand up for their rights. And that's what FSID is about."

"You know, Matt, that hoodie you're wearing? That's evidence that could get you charged with felony vandalism."

"Oh, so putting my father away isn't good enough for you? You want me in jail too?"

"This is not about your father. It's about you making bad choices. I know it's been a rough year for you with your father and every—"

"Fuck my father. You think I care about him? He's a crook. I've known that my entire life, but you people just weren't smart enough to get him till now. As soon as I'm eighteen I am gone. I'm off this rock and never coming back."

Stilwell waited to respond in case there was more adolescent angst coming. He glanced at Bryant, who looked uncomfortable but familiar with the rantings of youth.

"Good luck on the mainland, Matt. I want to see you make it out there. So what I need from you right now is a promise to me and Mr. Bryant that we're not going to see any more damage to your hometown's buildings. You and your friends have to lay off that. Have your meetings, fight the good fight for free speech, but leave the paint cans on the shelf at the hardware store."

Stilwell paused to let all of that sink in. He hoped that Allen would see the good deal he was being offered.

"Can I get that from you, Matt?" he asked.

"You think this makes up for what you're doing to my dad?" Allen said. "Well, it doesn't. He's going to prison, and me and my mom have to live with it."

Stilwell noticed the change. Earlier it sounded like the son despised the father. Now the son was rallying behind him. Stilwell assumed the first response was a front.

"We all make choices, Matt. Your father is separate from you. You need to make a choice now. An important one. I want you to promise me that this graffiti stuff is over. It doesn't mean your fight is over. It's a noble cause, if you ask me. But you gotta be smart and do it the right way."

"Whatever. Fine. I won't do it anymore. You happy now?"

"I want you to promise me and Mr. Bryant. Do that, and this doesn't have to go anywhere outside this room."

"I promise, okay? Can I just go back to class now? I already missed some of it."

"Yes, Matt, you can go. Just know this: If you break that promise, you're going to end up in juvie jail. And that's not a good place to be."

Allen stood up.

"I get it," he said. "I get it."

"Good," Stilwell said. "Good luck."

"Yeah, sure."

Allen left, banging the door closed behind him. Stilwell was not a father, but he had been a son. In this case, he hoped the son would escape the legacy of the father. He looked at Bryant as he turned off the recording app and put his phone away.

"What do you think?" he asked.

"I think he doesn't realize right now what a break he just got," Bryant said. "But don't worry, someday he will."

"Maybe. You never know with people."

"You got kids?"

"No. You?"

"Two. They're all grown up and out on their own. You handled that like a father would."

Stilwell stood up.

"Well, Matt's going to be missing his father soon," he said.

Stilwell thanked Bryant for his help and headed outside. He drove the ATV down to the town. Along the way, he checked his watch and saw he could make the ten o'clock boat to Long Beach. He called Kim Krabill and asked if she had room for him.

"Plenty," she said. "We leave in fifteen."

"I'll be there," Stilwell said.

He stopped at the sub first and checked in with Mercy. It had been a quiet morning, she reported. But he had gotten two calls from Lionel McKey about the graffiti on the casino and chimes tower.

"Can you call him back and tell him it's an ongoing investigation?" Stilwell asked. "No comment at this time. The usual."

"I will," she said. "He won't like it."

"He never does. I'm going over to the mainland. I might not be back till late."

"Are you going to see Ilsa?"

"First stop."

Mercy opened a drawer and pulled out an envelope.

"Please give her this card," she said. "We're all thinking about her."

"Sure," Stilwell said. "That's really nice."

He took the card.

"Call me if anything comes up," he said.

He headed out the door for the walk over to the ferry dock. He was indeed planning to visit Ilsa Ramirez on the mainland, but it wasn't the only stop he would make.

Stilwell was one of the last down the gangway to the boat to Long Beach. It appeared to be half-full. Once aboard, he went up the steps to the commodore lounge. He went directly to the pilothouse and knocked. Captain Krabill opened the door and he gave her his thanks. Afterward, he turned and scanned the lounge, looking for an empty aisle seat. Most were taken but he saw some empties in the two-seat rows that ran along the windows. When he spotted a row where both seats were empty, he headed toward it.

"Stil."

He turned and saw that he had walked right past Kent Middleton, who was sitting by a window with an open seat next to him.

Stilwell forced a smile and went back to Middleton's row.

"Hey, you're going over too," he said.

He didn't have to fake his surprise.

"Yeah, I've got an interview," Middleton said.

Stilwell pointed to the empty seat. "Is Gwen sitting here?" he asked.

"No—sit," Middleton said. "I'm on my own."

As Stilwell took the seat he glanced back across the lounge and saw Laffont and Masser sitting together. They briefly met Stilwell's eyes but gave no sign of recognition. Stilwell, knowing he had stumbled into the Middleton surveillance, ignored them as well.

"Who's it with?" he said. "The interview."

"State parks," Middleton said.

"You going to tell them you want Malibu?"

"I'm going to tell them I'll take whatever they've got."

"Good plan."

"What are you doing?"

"Oh, I'm going to visit Ilsa Ramirez, the deputy who got shot last week. See how she's doing. Then I have to go downtown for a meeting at HQ."

"How is she doing? I haven't seen anything in the news. It's kind of dropped off the radar."

"She's good. I mean, she's fucked up for life, but she's going to live, and that's pretty lucky."

"I guess."

Stilwell heard the thrum of the boat's big motors throttling up and felt the slight initial tug of movement as it started pulling away from the dock.

Over the next forty minutes the two men talked casually about girlfriends and island life. Middleton didn't ask one question about the investigation of the Angela Metier murder. That stood out to Stilwell as much as if he had asked repeated questions.

Forty-five minutes into the crossing, Stilwell said he had to hit the head and got up. As he walked through the lounge, he locked eyes with Laffont and made a slight nod toward the restroom.

Once inside the restroom, he checked under the stall doors. It was empty. He waited, and Laffont stepped in.

"What the fuck are you doing?" Laffont said.

"What the fuck am *I* doing?" Stilwell said. "What the fuck

are *you* doing? Why wasn't I told that he was on the move? I walked into this because I had no idea—"

"Okay, okay, our bad. We should have told you. But you sit down with the guy? What is that?"

"That is maintaining cover. If I didn't sit with the guy, he'd think something was up, that I was following him."

"Jesus, this makes me nervous."

"What's done is done. You got anything you want me to ask him?"

Before Laffont could answer, they heard the outer door of the restroom open. Stilwell immediately turned on the sink faucet and put his hands in the water. Laffont turned and grabbed a paper towel out of the rack. He was wiping his hands when the inner door opened and Middleton entered.

"Yo," he said. "Gotta take a leak."

Laffont grabbed the door before it closed and left. Stilwell finished washing his hands while Middleton went to a urinal.

"You know that guy?" he said as he unzipped.

"What guy?" Stilwell said.

"The one who was just in here. He just moved into Bird Park with another guy. I think they're gay."

"Okay."

"The word is they're looking to buy the ABC vineyard."

"Really?"

"Maybe you should go tell them about all the vandalism happening up there."

"Nah, not my place. I'm sure they'll find out on their own. If they do their due diligence on it."

Stilwell dried his hands on a paper towel, balled it up, and tossed it into an overflowing trash can.

"See you out there," he said.

"Sure," Middleton said.

Stilwell went through the door and headed back to the seats. On the way, he glanced over at Laffont and Masser. Laffont raised his eyebrows. He was asking if they were burned. Stilwell gave a short head shake. He didn't think so.

Middleton had left his backpack to hold his seat. Stilwell was tempted to unzip it and take a quick look inside. He looked back toward the restroom. Middleton was still in there.

But he decided against it. It was too risky and he'd just had one narrow escape. He didn't need another.

34

STILWELL HAD JUST gotten to his Bronco in the long-term lot when Ballard called.

"I heard you almost blew our surveillance today," she said.

"I heard that I was going to be kept informed of his movements," he said.

"Yeah, that's on me. Are we burned?"

"I don't think so. He didn't seem cagey after our encounter with Laffont in the restroom. I think we're good. Just make sure he doesn't run into those guys again. Once is a coincidence. Two and we're burned."

"Lesson learned. We'll do better. Did you get anything good from him?" Ballard asked.

"Not much. He knew about Laffont and Masser moving into Bird Park. He thinks they're gay and want to buy ABC."

"Perfect."

"Where are they now?"

"The state office building downtown. They think he might be applying for a job."

"He already did that. He told me he was going for an interview."

Stilwell turned the key, hoping he wouldn't need another jump. The Bronco's engine rumbled to life. He saw blue smoke in the rearview mirror.

"What was that?" Ballard asked.

"My car," Stilwell said. "It could use a new muffler."

"Well, we'll let you know where Middleton goes next."

"That would be good."

Stilwell disconnected and dropped the transmission into drive.

His first stop was the hospital in Torrance and Ilsa Ramirez's still-guarded room in the third-floor critical-care unit. She was awake and sitting up in bed at a forty-five-degree angle. Her eyes filled with tears when she saw Stilwell enter. He immediately grabbed her hand. She looked very small in the big hospital bed surrounded by various monitors and machines.

"Don't do that, Ilsa," he said. "I know this is tough. But stay strong. You're going to be all right."

She nodded. Stilwell saw that her neck was heavily wrapped in bandages. There were dark circles under her eyes and an oxygen tube under her nose. She reached for a digital tablet that was on the bed next to her hip, activated the screen, then unsnapped a stylus from its side and wrote something. She held the tablet up for him to read.

I'm sorry.

Stilwell shook his head.

"Nothing to be sorry for," he said. "It was a planned ambush. You didn't have a chance."

She nodded.

"They told you that, right?" Stilwell said. "Simon and Trestle?"

Stilwell looked at the room's door. He had told the deputy that he could take a break if he needed to, but he wasn't sure he had left. He turned back to Ramirez.

"What exactly did you tell them, Ilsa?" he said in a low voice. "They came back out to the island to search for a sniper's nest."

She wrote on the screen.

The shooter was behind us in woods.

He yell, Quigley, and open fire.

The message froze Stilwell for a few seconds.

"You're sure he yelled Quigley's name?" he asked.

She used the stylus to underline *Quigley* on the screen.

Stilwell suddenly realized why Ernie Simon had used a burner to call him and tell him to stand down. Ramirez erased the screen, wrote something new, and held the tablet up.

Suspects

Stilwell took it as a question and shook his head.

"I'm not part of the investigation—officially," he said. "But as far as I know, no suspect has been identified."

Ramirez nodded.

"But I'll tell you what, Ilsa," Stilwell said. "Either they find who did this or I will. I promise you that."

Ramirez patted her chest with a hand and the tears welled

up again as she scribbled on the tablet. She held it up forcefully to Stilwell with two hands.

I'm IOD EOW

Stilwell knew what she meant. She would be rolled out of the department on an injury-on-duty pension. Her days as a cop were likely over. End of watch.

"Don't be thinking that," he said. "Not yet. Concentrate on your recovery and let the job stuff come later. You turned into a good cop, Ilsa. High marks all around from me. And remember, it wasn't like that at first. But you worked hard. I saw it. I know it. And I know you'll work hard on getting better."

Ramirez nodded but turned her head away from him, which sent a spasm of pain through her face. He reached down and squeezed her hand again. It was time to go.

"I'll be back to visit, Ilsa," he said. "You hold fast."

Stilwell wondered why he had used a phrase from his days in the navy.

He remembered the card and took it out of his pocket.

"Almost forgot," he said, handing it to her. "Mercy said to give you this."

He was about to leave, when he saw Ramirez start to write on the screen again. She held it up to him.

Wait

He nodded.

"I can stay."

She considered the screen for a while before writing. She held the tablet up.

Trust you?

"Of course," Stilwell said.

She wrote again.

Me and Alton

Stilwell stared for a long moment at the screen.

"You mean..." he asked.

She nodded and held her hand to her chest. Over her heart.

Stilwell was surprised by the revelation. Quigley and Ramirez generally worked the same days, sometimes the same shift, but they were always in separate ATV units and patrolling different zones. They backed each other up on calls, though, and that's where a relationship likely started. It was the way a million cop romances had begun before and would again. Ramirez lived in town in subsidized housing, and Quigley supposedly stayed most nights in the substation dorm, so they could easily have gotten together off-site and off duty, but Stilwell was surprised that they had been able to hide their relationship from him, their supervisor, and apparently everybody else. They'd had to hide it, because it was against department regulations, not to mention that Quigley was married.

A cascade of thoughts and images went through Stilwell's mind, beginning with how empty Quigley's locker was and ending with how his widow had shed no tears at his funeral.

"How long?" he asked.

Ramirez wrote on the screen without hesitation.

New, 5 weeks

That meant their romance had started pretty quickly after Quigley transferred out to Catalina.

"Did his wife know?" Stilwell asked.

Nobody knew

He was already in a divorce

It would have been bad for him

"You're sure no one knew?"

Nobody

"Did you tell this to Simon and Trestle?"

No, only trust you

Stilwell nodded. In a messed-up way it was a compliment. It also put him in a bind. This information was important, and Simon and Trestle should have it. But passing it along could come back on Stilwell because this relationship had gone on under his nose. And if it turned out that it had played a part in the ambush, the consequences for him could multiply exponentially.

Stilwell thought about all this as he tried to come up with the next question. Ramirez's shorthand had carried a lot of new information that came out of left field.

"You said he was already getting a divorce?" he finally asked.

Ramirez wrote.

Since when he transferred

Another secret kept from Stilwell. He was beginning to feel like one of the idiot supervisors he'd had over the course of his history in the department, people oblivious to what was going on around them. It was depressing to think he was like them, but he tried to stay in the moment with Ramirez.

"Did Quigley ever mention who his divorce lawyer was?" he asked.

Ramirez nodded and wrote.

Benny Martinez

Stilwell knew Benito Martinez. He was a former Long Beach cop who'd quit to go to law school and was now a divorce attorney. Remembering his brethren in blue, Martinez offered his services to law enforcement officers at a discount. His business cards were pinned to bulletin boards in every police station and substation in the county. It kept him so busy he didn't need to pay for billboards on the 405 freeway like so many of the other law lizards in town did. Stilwell also knew him because Martinez had been his own attorney when he'd gone through a divorce a year before he came to the island.

"Did Quigley ever tell you why they were getting divorced?" he asked.

Ramirez wrote.

He said she cheated

Stilwell nodded but didn't take that as the truth. The percentages said that in most divorces based on adultery, the husband was the unfaithful one. And what else would Quigley say to a new girlfriend when asked about the reason for his pending divorce? *I'm a cheater*? No; he would throw the shade on his soon-to-be ex-wife.

"Did he say anything else about it?" he asked.

Ramirez shook her head, and once again Stilwell saw that the simple movement of her neck caused her pain.

"Okay, Ilsa, I'm going to go now and let you get some rest," he said. "But I'll be back, I promise. Meantime, you take care. Stay strong."

Ramirez held her hand to her chest again. It was less painful than nodding.

Back in the Bronco, Stilwell closed his eyes when he turned the key in the ignition. He heard the engine start to grind, then finally spark to life. He opened his eyes, pinned the accelerator to the floor, and red-lined the tach. He looked up and saw the cloud of exhaust smoke in his rearview mirror. The old horse was ready to go. He had intended to make the home of the Widow Quigley his next stop, but the new information from Ramirez changed things.

He headed for downtown Long Beach instead.

35

IN CALIFORNIA, DIVORCES are filed under seal, but the initial pleading of the legal action is public. Stilwell went to the office of the clerk of the Long Beach Superior Court, where he knew from experience Benito Martinez handled most cases, and asked for the filing on *Quigley v. Quigley.* He knew he wouldn't get the details of what brought about the divorce, but he would get at least two important pieces of information he needed before he made his next move.

The clerk gave him the cover page of the *Quigley v. Quigley* case, and he confirmed that it was Alton who started the divorce action. The date of the filing showed that Quigley had taken the step to dissolve his marriage a month before he transferred to the Catalina sub and met Ilsa Ramirez. In Stilwell's mind, that absolved Ramirez of any wrongdoing in her relationship with Quigley. And it seemed to confirm what Lieutenant Lambert had told Simon about Quigley asking for the transfer. It appeared that Quigley wanted a fresh start while still remaining in the department and being close—a boat ride away—to his kids.

Stilwell didn't need the Bronco to get to Benito Martinez's office. He worked out of a building across the street from the courthouse. Its address was 100 Magnolia Avenue, and since most of its offices were occupied by lawyers plying their trade in Long Beach Superior Court, it was known as the 100 Lawyers building.

Martinez was on the fourth floor. Stilwell knew this without having to look at the electronic directory in the lobby. When he walked through the door to the one-lawyer suite, he even knew the receptionist's name.

"Hello, Marta, you remember me?"

"Of course, Sergeant Stil. How are you?"

She spoke with a thick Spanish accent, as did her boss, and when she said his name, it sounded like "Sergeant Steel." It could also be "Sergeant Steal," but Stilwell preferred the former.

"I'm doing well," he said. "I was wondering if I could talk to Benny for a few minutes."

"You have an appointment, no?"

"Uh, no appointment. I just need five minutes."

"Hokey, let me check for you."

She got up and disappeared behind a wall that was painted with pithy slogans about divorce.

> Marriage is the chief cause of divorce.
>
> — Groucho Marx

> Half of all marriages end in divorce. Then there's the really unhappy ones.
>
> — Joan Rivers

They had been up there when Stilwell was a client. At the time, he hadn't found them humorous.

Marta came back and told Stilwell that Mr. Martinez was finishing up a call and that he'd be available right after that. Stilwell walked over to a little waiting area where there was a couch and two chairs. The moment he took a seat, Marta said that Mr. Martinez was ready for him.

Stilwell walked around the wall of wit and down a short hall to the door that led to Martinez's office. The attorney stood up from behind his desk when he entered.

"Esteban!" he said. "How are you, my friend?"

"I'm good, Benny," Stilwell said. "It's good to see you."

Martinez always used the Spanish version of his name. He reached across the desk and they shook hands.

"Come," he said. "Sit down. Tell me your problem."

Stilwell took a seat in front of the desk. Martinez sat down across from him, revealing the wall behind him, which continued the motif of the reception area.

> When I got divorced, it was group sex. My wife screwed me in front of the jury.
>
> — Rodney Dangerfield

> The only grounds for divorce in California is marriage.
>
> — Cher

Same quotes as before. Stilwell wondered if Martinez would ever update the walls of the suite. He slid the folded document he had just gotten from the court clerk across the desk.

"I'm not here about me," he said. "I want to ask about that case."

Martinez spread the document out flat on his desk, leaned his arms on the edge of the polished wood, and read. He nodded.

"This is my case, yes," he said. "But, Esteban, you know divorce is filed under seal in California. The judge's order and attorney-client privilege is invoked."

"You know that Alton Quigley was murdered," Stilwell said. "He's dead and all—"

"Yes, of course. I had to withdraw the case from the court. But privilege follows even in death. Very sad about him. Terrible."

As Stilwell was formulating a response, Martinez continued.

"This is what I already told the other detectives," he said.

"Who?" Stilwell asked. "Simon and Trestle? They were here?"

"Here, yes. They asked me the same thing. I told them what I am telling you. This is why I stopped being a cop. Police work is in the gray area. Always, there is blue smoke. That's what we called it. I like the law because it is set in stone."

"Don't tell me that," Stilwell said. "Every lawyer in this building is looking for loopholes in the law on some case somewhere. The blue smoke, as you call it, is everywhere."

"Maybe in your world, Esteban. Not in mine."

"The guy was murdered, okay? And whoever his wife was having an affair with needs to be identified and checked out. If you don't tell me who it was, you might be helping a murderer go free."

Martinez laughed. "Please," he said. "You are trying to make me feel bad in order to get me to break the rules. I cannot do that. I have to have a good conscience. I must feel justified at the end of every day."

Stilwell thought of a line from a western he loved, *Ride the High Country:* "All I want is to enter my house justified." He looked at the stupid quotes on the wall behind Martinez's head. His eyes dropped from the vacuous words to Martinez's face.

"Quigley worked for me," he said. "I was there when he was

killed. The woman he had just started dating was shot too. Did he tell you about her or is that privileged too?"

"He did, yes," Martinez said. "Casually. It had nothing to do with the case, as it was filed before they became involved."

"She worked for me too. I trained her. They got ambushed. He's dead and she'll probably never be able to talk without an electronic device. She definitely won't be a cop anymore."

"I am sorry for her. I am sorry for you."

"But you won't help me find who did it. Don't you owe something to him? To your client?"

"I owe him the confidentiality that is the binding of client and attorney."

Stilwell nodded. He pushed his chair back to get up.

"Were you at Alton's funeral?" Martinez asked.

Stilwell stayed in his seat.

"I was there," he said.

"I was there as well," Martinez said. "But I left before it was over. There was too much hypocrisy."

Stilwell tried to read what Martinez was saying. He was offering something.

"You mean how his wife didn't cry?" he asked.

"I would not begin to have an opinion on why a widow would cry or not cry at her estranged husband's funeral," Martinez said. "That is a psychological determination. It's not hypocrisy."

Stilwell hit on it. The man who'd called him Quigs and choked up as he lamented the lost member of his team.

"Lambert," he said. "Lambert was the speaker. He's the hypocrite."

"It is very unpleasant to hear lies at such a solemn event," Martinez said. "I had to leave. And I did."

"He's the one she had the affair with," Stilwell said. "It was going to come out in the divorce."

It wasn't a question.

"I must leave now for court," Martinez said. "I have a client waiting."

"I need to go now too," Stilwell said. "Thank you for your time, Benny."

"As I said to you last time I saw you, I hope you never need my services again."

"Me too."

Stilwell got back to the Bronco and sat in it without turning the key for several moments as he thought about where he should go with what he knew. Martinez had obliquely given him something that even Ernie Simon didn't have, unless he had gotten it from another source. But it further obscured things in blue smoke and made them even more dangerous. He felt the need to warn Simon on the off chance he hadn't realized Lambert was a person of significant interest.

Before he could make the call, his phone buzzed with a call from Ballard. Stilwell picked up, forcing himself to mentally jump back into the Middleton case.

"Renée, what's up?" he said.

"He's stalking someone," she said.

36

THEY HELD UP the briefing at the LAPD Open-Unsolved Unit until Stilwell could get there from Long Beach. The room was crowded and there weren't enough chairs for everybody. Seven people were left standing, including Stilwell. Ballard handled introductions at the top of the meeting. She first introduced her team—her volunteers. There were Laffont and Masser, a woman named Lilia Aghzafi, a Swedish tech guy named Anders Persson, and a young cop named Maddie Bosch, who Stilwell assumed was the wise old Harry Bosch's daughter. After that, Ballard introduced the captain of the Special Investigation Section, who in turn introduced the eight men he had brought with him. The SIS was LAPD's vaunted surveillance unit, known for its multiple takedowns of violent criminals caught in the act. Many of these takedowns ended in fatal shootings of the alleged bad guys and subsequent wrongful-death lawsuits. The ACLU and other civil rights groups as well as some local bloggers and podcasters had long labeled the SIS a kill squad. And yet it was also the most sought-after assignment in the entire department.

The lead came back to Ballard, and Stilwell was introduced last and in embarrassingly glowing terms. She said that it was his good work that had led to recovering the body of a long-missing woman and identifying the suspect who was the focus of the meeting.

"Some of you know everything I know and some of you don't," Ballard said. "So, to make sure we're all on the same page, we're going to run it down from the top. It's important that we act in concert. There is a life at stake."

Stilwell raised his hand.

"Stil, you don't have to raise your hand," Ballard said. "If anybody has a question, just call it out. There are no dumb questions."

"I was just wondering—if we're all here, who's watching the suspect?" Stilwell asked.

"Good question," Ballard said. "What you see here is only half the SIS unit. The other eight guys are on overwatch on our suspect or prepping tomorrow's op, which we'll get to in a second. At the moment, our suspect, Kent Middleton, is in a room at a hotel in Burbank. If he makes a move, even to get a bucket of ice from the machine down the hall, he'll have eight pairs of eyes on him. He is covered and we don't have to worry about that."

Stilwell waved in a *That answers my question* gesture.

"All right, Tom, why don't you start us off?" Ballard said.

Laffont stood in front of a whiteboard with a map of northern L.A. County, including Burbank, displayed on it. He briefly summarized the activities on Catalina that had made Middleton a person of interest in the missing-hikers case.

"We developed intel that Middleton was looking to leave his job on Catalina and find work as a park ranger somewhere else," Laffont said. "Today was the first of three days off from his job on the island. And this morning he took the Catalina Express to the mainland and rented a car. He was followed to the Reagan State Building downtown, where he presumably had an interview with the state parks service."

Laffont said SIS then took over the surveillance and followed Middleton from the state building to a Hilton hotel near Burbank Airport.

"For those of you not up on your local geography," Laffont said, pointing to the whiteboard, "I draw your attention to the map. You will see that the airport and the hotel are here, situated at the foothills of the San Gabriel Mountains, which of course contain the vast Angeles National Forest. You're talking about one thousand square miles of rugged wilderness. This is of great concern to us because four and maybe five young women have disappeared while hiking in smaller but similar parks over the past fifteen years."

"So I made a call," Ballard said. "Based on the exigent circumstances of Middleton's proximity to the national park and the fact that a previous victim disappeared from this park, we began to infiltrate his electronic media."

Exigent circumstances. Stilwell knew this meant they had justified a warrantless search of Middleton's internet activities when he got near a public park and could be a threat to public safety.

"I'll let Anders tell you how we accomplished that," Ballard said.

In a Swedish accent, Persson explained that after Middleton left his appointment with the state parks service, Ballard went into the office and learned whom he had met with and what job he was seeking.

"With that information, I composed a Trojan horse email, which was sent to the suspect's email address," Persson said. "The message appeared to be from the man Middleton had interviewed with earlier. It was a simple note thanking him for coming in and saying that he—Middleton—would hear from them soon regarding the job."

Persson explained that when Middleton opened the email, it triggered a malware virus that installed keystroke-logging software on his computer. This allowed the cold-case team to set up a computer that mirrored every move the suspect made on his own device.

From there, Ballard took back the narrative.

"We basically watched while Middleton spent the afternoon cyberstalking a woman named Molly Young across multiple social media platforms using a variety of usernames and identities. We're talking about Instagram, X, Facebook, and LinkedIn, as well as groups specifically for outdoor enthusiasts on Meetup, Strava, and Social Hikers. Through these we learned that Molly Young is a hiking guide specializing in day trips into the Angeles National Forest."

Ballard paused there in case there were questions. There was only rapt silence.

"Now, here's the clincher," she continued. "Since we've been watching him, he's responded to two emails from two different accounts reminding him of a prepaid hike reserved for tomorrow morning in Angeles National. In other words, he paid twice under two different aliases for the same trip—a four-hour hike that leaves from the Tujunga entrance to the forest and goes to a remote waterfall and spring."

"Why did he reserve it twice?" one of the SIS men called out.

"Because Molly Young, according to her website, has a safety protocol," Ballard said. "She does not do one-on-one hikes into the forest. Her private tours require a minimum of two hikers. Our thinking was that Middleton reserved the two spots on the private tour under different identities—and by the way, one of the aliases he used is female—and then he's the only one who shows up in the morning. Molly Young then has to decide to cancel or break protocol and take him alone up to the waterfall. If he presents as harmless, maybe even offers to do it another day, then he has a shot at going into the woods alone with her."

Ballard did not have to say what was expected to happen if Young proceeded with the hike.

The next half hour was spent discussing how tomorrow morning's hike would be handled. Ballard told them that the department's command staff had informed the Park Service managers at Angeles National of the investigation and the need for secrecy. Using a map that showed the trail to Switzer Falls, SIS officers were scouting locations and prepping to go into the forest shortly after dawn to set up surveillance blinds along the path that Molly Young would take. Additional SIS men would be posing as hikers along the trail, attempting to restrict the alone time Middleton would have with Young to a short stretch of the trail called the control zone. At no point would Young be out of sight or reach of the SIS.

The first debate that followed the reveal of the operational plan was about when the SIS team should move in on Middleton to make an arrest. There was talk of needing to see an overt act by him before engaging. Ballard countered by saying that an overt act could be a fatal act.

"The previous victims were strangled," she said. "Hyoid bones crushed like potato chips. We can't let it get close to that."

"We won't let that happen," Captain Vance Dawkins, head of the SIS unit, stated confidently. "This is what we do. In sixty years, SIS has not lost a single potential victim under surveillance. Not one. We are going to have men in the trees and on the ground in the control zone. We'll have cameras on the gate and in the zone. Believe me, we are putting all our resources into this. This young woman is going to be safe as a baby. She'll be scared when we move in but abso-fucking-lutely safe. You have my guarantee."

The force with which Dawkins spoke seemed to end the debate right there, but Stilwell could still see a trace of doubt in Ballard's face.

"What's the plan if Molly calls it when the second hiker doesn't show up?" he asked.

"We have to be ready if he makes his move then," Ballard said. "But if he doesn't, we wait and take him once he gets back in his vehicle. Then we get him, whatever he's carrying, and whatever's in the car."

She was talking about evidence. She moved on to what became another debate, this one about whether to tell Young about the operation and give her the option of not going forward with the hike. It was decided pretty quickly that if she was informed and agreed to carry on with the hike, her nervousness might tip off Middleton that law enforcement was onto him.

There was also a brief discussion about replacing Young with a police officer with similar looks and build. But Ballard said that plan was too risky because there were many photos of Young on her website and Instagram feed that showed her hiking in the forest. Many of these were close-up selfies. Middleton had accessed these in his hotel room and might easily spot a stand-in for the real Molly Young. On top of that, finding an officer or even a park ranger who could lead a hike as professionally and as well as the real Molly Young was a long shot, especially on such short notice. It was decided: Molly Young would be a pigeon—SIS parlance for a potential victim who did not know she was under surveillance and was the intended target of a violent criminal.

Ballard finished the briefing by saying the meeting point Molly Young had set for the hike was the gated entrance to the forest on Angeles Crest Highway in Tujunga. She said the command post vehicle for the operation would be in the parking lot of the LAPD's Foothill Division station, which included Tujunga in its patrol zone but was located far enough from the forest gate for Middleton not to stumble upon it. The report-to-duty time for the op was set at 0500 and Ballard finished the meeting with one last point.

"I want Paul Masser from my team to talk about the law and what we will need to make this a solid case," she said. "Paul spent twenty-five years as a deputy DA, so listen up."

Masser had been sitting. He stood up to address the group.

"Essentially, we are going to stop this crime before it happens, right?" he said. "So we have to make sure we have the elements we need to charge this asshole with as many crimes as we can. An overt act was mentioned earlier. That can mean different things. It does not—let me repeat, does *not*—need to be a physical assault. We want to make the arrest before it comes to that. So then, what are we looking for? An overt act can obviously be him brandishing some kind of weapon, which could be anything, even a walking stick. If he stops to look around to see if there are any witnesses near him, that constitutes an overt act."

"Tell them about evidence," Ballard said.

"Right," Masser said. "This guy buries his victims. We expect that he will have the backpack we saw on the surveillance with him and that it will likely contain a shovel or some other kind of digging tool. There will probably be bindings of some kind. Duct tape. Rope. The backpack will be key. If we get that and it has what we think it does, then we've got him and he will go away for a long, long time. Any questions?"

There were none. It looked to Stilwell as if the SIS guys weren't paying attention. It was the first hint that maybe they weren't planning on Middleton coming out of the forest alive. No need to worry about a prosecution case if there was nobody to prosecute.

"Okay, that's it, people," Ballard announced. "Remember, RTD zero five hundred hours. Go home, get some sleep. Be sharp in the morning."

The meeting broke up. The SIS men headed to the exit, and Stilwell moved to the whiteboard to look at the map. Ballard came over to him.

"So, what do you think?" she asked.

"I was thinking about what Paul just said," Stilwell responded. "If the backpack has all the evidence we need, why don't we just take Middleton down at the forest gate?"

"I think we need the backpack plus the overt act to be sure. Paul talked to a filing deputy at the office earlier today."

"All right. I guess so."

"What's wrong?"

"I don't know. A lot of stuff can go wrong during a walk in the woods."

"Then we just have to make sure it doesn't."

"Easier said. Have you worked with SIS before?"

"A couple times. They're good at what they do."

"Killing bad guys?"

"Sometimes. If it goes that way tomorrow, you're not going to see me shedding a tear for Middleton. Only for the victim we haven't identified."

"Yeah, me too."

"You got a place to stay tonight? You're not going back across, are you?"

"Uh, no. But I'll find a place."

"Then I'll see you at Foothill at zero dark early."

"I'll be there."

Ballard went off to confer with Laffont. Stilwell looked back at the map. The Switzer Falls trail was a red squiggle with a lot of switchbacks, indicating an uphill climb. He had a bad feeling about the next day.

He tried to shake it off as he left the building. He pulled out his phone to call Tash and tell her that he wouldn't be coming home.

37

THE TENSION GREW with each minute that passed. Stilwell and Ballard sat in the mobile command post watching the screens on the wall in front of them. Laffont paced on the carpeted floor behind them. On the screen a concealed camera focused on Molly Young leaning against the front fender of her new-model Bronco with her arms folded. It was ten after ten and both her clients, who had paid ninety-nine dollars each to be led through the rugged forest behind her to Switzer Falls, were late. Thanks to minute-by-minute reports from the SIS team surveilling Kent Middleton, they knew the suspect was on his way. The tension was about the timing. Young's website stated there would be only a ten-minute grace period for latecomers. Be on time or your guide would proceed without you on the non-refundable tour. In this case, if two out of two were no-shows, Young would drive off, and all the work that went into the carefully choreographed and expensive operation would be for nothing.

"Come on, come on, come on," Ballard said.

"She's getting her keys out," Laffont said. "We're going to lose her."

On the screen, Young had her hand in the front pocket of a backpack propped on the hood of the Bronco. She indeed pulled out what looked like a set of keys.

"Fuck me," Ballard said. There was a stem mic on the table in front of her. She put her finger on the transmit button at its base.

"Mookie, where are we?" she said.

They were using the names of Dodgers players. The SIS officer in charge of the Middleton surveillance was Mookie. The head of the forest team was Freeman, and Ballard was Ohtani.

"Two minutes out."

Ballard banged her fist on the table.

Stilwell watched Young reach again into the backpack and pull out a phone.

"She's calling them," he said. "We'll be all right."

Young unfolded a printout from the backpack and punched in a number she'd read off it. The team had already checked the numbers Middleton had provided by email for Frida Fanning and Marlon Yates, the aliases Middleton had used to set up the hike. They were both burner phones.

Young was waiting in a gravel parking lot in front of the Tujunga gate. One camera had been mounted inside an animal-proof trash-bin enclosure and was focused on the gate. A second was atop a light pole at the end of the lot and offered a wide shot of the entire area. When the cameras were installed, it was unknown where the two subjects of the operation would park and stand. Camera one showed only the passenger side of the Bronco, so in the command post, they watched the wide shot while listening to the audio from the close shot.

The call clearly went to voicemail, because Young said, "Frida, it's Molly. I'm at the trailhead and it's almost ten fifteen.

I'll wait a few more minutes for you, but call me back and tell me if you're coming."

After referring to the printout again, Young punched in a second number. This one was answered.

"Marlon, it's Molly," Young said. "Where are you?"

They could not hear the other side of the call in the command post.

"Okay," Young said. "I was about to leave but I'll wait. Do you know Frida Fanning, the other hiker?"

There was silence while Middleton presumably said he didn't know Frida.

"Okay, well, hopefully she's coming," Young said. "See you soon."

Young disconnected and put her phone and the printout back into her pack. Something about the action made Stilwell think about Angela Metier and her backpack. The anger he felt about her murder started to well up in him again.

"There he is," Laffont said.

On the screen, a car was pulling into the lot. The SIS had parked three cars in the lot, staged so that Middleton would know there were other hikers on the trail. This was part of the plan to get Middleton into the control zone before he committed an overt act.

Middleton was driving the rental car he had picked up after getting off the Express ferry the day before. He parked next to the Bronco and got out. He slung a backpack over his shoulder as he approached Young. It was the same one Stilwell had seen with Middleton on the Express and had chosen not to inspect.

"Molly?" Middleton said.

He gestured toward her as if unsure it was her. But the

watchers knew, thanks to the keystroke logger, that he had viewed several photos of her on his computer the night before.

"Yes," Young said. "Marlon?"

"That's me," Middleton said.

They shook hands. They still weren't in the close-in camera's frame but the audio from it was clear.

"Um, we might have a problem," Young said. "The other hiker is not here and I can't get her on the phone."

"Really?" Middleton said. "And she paid and everything?"

"Yeah. So let's give it a few more minutes. But if she doesn't show, we'll have to reschedule."

"Oh, no. I came all the way from Catalina."

"Wow. I'm so sorry. But it's sort of a safety thing."

"Yeah, right, I understand. Can you try calling her again?"

"Good idea."

On the screen Young turned from Middleton to open her backpack. With her back to him, Middleton himself turned and did a sweep of the parking area.

"Shit," Stilwell said.

He believed that Middleton might make his move right there. Ballard quickly pressed the radio transmit button.

"Muncy, be ready. This could be it!"

Muncy was the team of four SIS men in two cars parked on a side road less than a minute away; they had timed it during the run-through prep at six that morning.

Ballard and Stilwell watched intently. Laffont leaned in between them to get closer to the screens.

Young turned back to Middleton, holding her phone to her ear.

"She's not answering," she said.

Middleton gestured with a raised arm in frustration.

"Frida, you are now a half hour late," Young said into the phone. "I'm going to have to cancel the hike."

She disconnected and this time slid the phone into the back pocket of her jeans.

"I'm so sorry," she said to Middleton, "but we need to cancel. We can reschedule, or I'll give you your money back. Or I have a sunset hike with a group at four today if you want to join that. It's only twenty-five dollars, so I'd send you the rest back on Venmo."

"Ah, no," Middleton said. "I have something this afternoon. Are you sure we can't just do it? I mean, I get the safety issue. But I'd stay ten feet away or whatever you wanted."

Ballard put her finger on the transmit button, ready to give the go order if Middleton made a move.

"I really can't," Young said. "It's a rule I promised my father I would never break. There've been girls who've disappeared on hikes. In fact, one was found out on Catalina recently. Found dead."

"I know," Middleton said. "I was there."

"What?"

Fear had instantly charged into her voice. On the screen, she took a step back from Middleton. Ballard leaned toward the mic.

Middleton quickly raised his hands in a *Stay calm* gesture.

"No, I mean I was there when they found her," he said quickly. "I'm a conservancy ranger. I got called in. Here, I can show you my badge."

He pulled the backpack off his shoulder as he walked toward the hood of the Bronco.

"I don't like this," Ballard said.

Middleton put the backpack on the Bronco's hood next to Young's. He unzipped a compartment and reached his hand in.

Ballard pushed the button.

"Muncy, go!" she yelled. "Now! Code three!"

Almost immediately, a piercing chirp from a police siren could be heard on the audio. Middleton stepped back from the Bronco and pivoted toward the parking-lot entrance. A full-throated siren wailed as two black SUVs charged into the lot and across the gravel toward Middleton and Young.

Middleton raised his hands and yelled something, but it was unintelligible with the siren jamming the audio feed.

The unmarked SUVs skidded to a stop and the siren ceased. The four SIS officers, dressed in black raid gear, quickly emerged. Two used their open doors as shields as they aimed weapons at Middleton. The other two rushed him and took him down to the gravel.

Middleton was silent as his hands were cuffed behind his back by one officer while the other searched his pockets.

"What is this?" Young yelled. "What's going on?"

One of the men pointed toward the trash enclosure.

"Ma'am, stand over there," he ordered. "An officer will be with you in a moment."

Young did as she had been told as the cover officers holstered their weapons and approached the others. More SIS vehicles from the surveillance crew entered the lot. Ballard leaned down to the mic.

"Check his backpack," she said.

One man went to the backpack. He had the microphone stem from an earpiece and gave a running inventory as he put the contents of the pack on the hood of the Bronco.

"We've got one thermos," he said. "One wrapped sandwich. A second wrapped sandwich. One thirty-five-millimeter camera. A folded space blanket. Two—no, three PowerBars."

They could hear the zippers as the officer went through the other compartments of the pack and repeatedly said, "Nothing," until he opened an internal pocket.

"One conservancy ranger badge. That's it."

Stilwell was stunned.

"I'm going over there," he said.

"I'll drive," Ballard said.

38

BALLARD, LAFFONT, AND Stilwell got there in ten minutes. Ballard killed the siren as she pulled off the highway. The parking area was already a nest of police activity, as several more vehicles and officers had arrived.

Stilwell noticed that the doors of Middleton's rental car were open and the trunk lid was up.

"That's not good," Laffont said from the back seat.

Ballard and Stilwell remained silent, and they all got out.

Masser came out of the crowd and approached them. He had been riding with Captain Dawkins and the Mookie surveillance team. He looked like his dog had just died.

Ballard pointed at the rental.

"Paul, what the fuck?" she said. "You let them search the car? They needed a warrant."

"I know, I know," Masser said. "I couldn't stop them. They claimed exigent circumstances. But look, it doesn't matter. There's nothing in the car. We've got nothing, and we're going to have to cut him loose."

Ballard froze.

"Nothing?" Ballard said.

Laffont spread his hands wide. "How can that be?" he said.

"He knew," Stilwell said. "He made us."

Just as he said it, Stilwell saw Middleton behind the glass in the back seat of one of the unmarked cars. He was leaning forward because he was still cuffed. They locked eyes for a moment and Middleton smiled at him.

It was a *Fuck you* smile.

"How?" Laffont asked.

Stilwell looked at Laffont.

"What do you mean, how?" he said. "He saw us on the boat. He saw us in the restroom. It could've been you drying hands that weren't wet, or it could have been any number of—"

"Oh, so it's on me," Laffont said, squaring up in front of Stilwell.

"Guys," Ballard said. "Not here. Not now. Save that shit for later. We need to think this through. I have to go talk to the girl, and then we're going to huddle and figure out what to do to unfuck this situation."

She walked away with Laffont still staring at Stilwell.

"You know," he said, "Middleton wouldn't have found us in that restroom and I wouldn't have been drying my *unwet* hands if you hadn't stumbled into our surveillance."

"And I wouldn't have *stumbled* into your surveillance if I had been told he was on the move," Stilwell said.

"Guys, what did Renée just say?" Masser interjected. "We're all pissed off about this. But let's cool our jets and work this out."

"Fine," Laffont said.

He turned and stepped away, scuffing the gravel with the heel of his shoe.

Stilwell glanced back at the car, and this time Middleton gave him a slight nod as if to say, *I got you.*

Stilwell looked away and saw Ballard in a one-on-one with Molly Young by the front of the Bronco. He could not hear what was being said but guessed that Ballard was assuring her that she had never been in danger. The young woman had her chin down and her arms folded tightly across her chest. A classic defensive pose. Stilwell looked past her and toward the mountain chain rising in the distance. He started reviewing every detail he could remember about the past two days. He was looking for what they had missed.

By the time Ballard came back over to talk, he thought he had something.

She waved her team together in a huddle. "Okay, guys, what's our next move?" she said.

Masser and Laffont said nothing. Ballard looked at Stilwell.

"Stil?" she prompted.

"We need to hold him," Stilwell said. "Middleton."

"With what?" Laffont said. "He played us. We don't have a shred of evidence to hold him with."

"Actually..." Masser said.

"What, Paul?" Ballard said.

Masser looked at Stilwell.

"You're talking about a forty-eight-hour hold, right?" he asked. "Not actually charging him?"

"Yes, hold him while we find the evidence to charge him," Stilwell said.

Laffont made a snorting sound. Ballard held up her hand to quiet him.

"Paul?" she said. "Anything?"

Masser bumped a fist against his chin as he thought something through.

"Okay, just thinking out loud here," he began. "He brought her here under false pretenses. He used a false name. And he set up a phony second hiker. We have the evidence to support all of that."

"But none of that is technically illegal," Laffont said.

"But it shows intent," Masser said. "I think it gives us probable cause to arrest him for attempted abduction or attempted assault. I don't think either would stick. There's not enough there to ultimately file the charge, but you'd get your forty-eight hours."

Under California law, probable cause was needed for arrest and detainment. Evidence had to be presented to the district attorney and charges filed within forty-eight hours or the detainee had to be released.

"He could post bail and be out before the end of the day," Laffont said.

"But if we kick the attempted assault up to attempted rape, we can go for no bail until he appears in front of a judge," Ballard said. "That would give us till tomorrow."

Masser nodded. Ballard looked at Stilwell.

"Better than nothing," she said.

Stilwell nodded too and felt a charge of adrenaline hit his blood.

"He booked these hikes while he was still back on Catalina, right?" he said. "Before he knew about us. That means when he got on the Express and left the island, he had his abduction-and-murder kit with him."

"In his backpack," Masser said.

"Which I almost opened when he was in the restroom," Stilwell said.

"So he must have dumped it all after he made you guys," Ballard said.

Stilwell turned to Laffont and said, putting all animosity aside, "You guys had him from the boat to the state building," he said. "Where did he dump it?"

Laffont tucked his chin down as he mentally reviewed the surveillance of the day before.

"What stops did he make?" Ballard pressed.

"He went to the rental-car counter at the Express dock," Masser said. "I watched him while Tom got our car. He went to the rental lot and got in the car. Then he drove. Tom picked me up and we never lost sight of him."

"He did the drive-through at an In-N-Out," Laffont said. "He ate his hamburger in the car and— "

"Cheeseburger, actually," Masser said. "I saw it on the binos."

"Whatever," Laffont said. "He threw his trash out there, but it was one of those little cardboard boxes they give you. I don't think that was it."

"After that, he went straight up the one-ten to downtown and the Reagan Building," Masser said.

"And you kept eyes on him?" Ballard asked.

"One of us did at all times," Masser said. "Most of the time it was both— "

They were interrupted by the approach of Captain Dawkins.

"Ballard, are we cutting him loose?" he asked.

"No, we're not," Ballard said. "Can your guys take him over to Foothill and put him in an interview room? I'll get there eventually and see if he wants to chat. Then we'll book him."

"We can do that," Dawkins said.

"Thank you, Captain," Ballard said.

Dawkins walked off, issuing the order to one of his men to transport Middleton to the Foothill Division station.

Ballard turned back to the team, and Stilwell asked a question.

"Did Middleton have the backpack when he went into the state building?" Stilwell asked.

"Uh, yes, he did," Masser said. "I remember that."

Laffont snapped his fingers.

"The restroom," he said. "He went into the restroom on the fourth floor. We didn't go in. Too risky, especially after what happened on the boat."

"The restroom and when he was in the job interview at the state parks office," Masser said. "Those were the only times we didn't have eyes on him. Then SIS came and picked up the tail from there."

"They said he went straight to the hotel in Burbank," Ballard said. "He didn't leave his room until he headed here."

"I can write the warrant," Masser said. "You two go to the hotel; Renée and I will go to a judge."

"Forget it," Stilwell said. "It's not in his room. He'd figure we'd search his room. This guy thinks he's smarter than us. Otherwise, he wouldn't have run this whole charade. He wanted to taunt us. You can check his room but he wouldn't make a mistake like that."

Stilwell gestured toward the crowded parking lot.

"He thinks he's got this covered," he continued. "Hell, he just smiled at me."

"When?" Ballard asked.

"Five minutes ago," Stilwell said. "Handcuffed, back seat of a cop car, and he fucking smiles at me. He thinks this is a game and that he's already won it. Point is, he's too smart to leave any evidence in his room. I like the state building. It's somewhere there."

"I like it too," Ballard said. "Let's go."

39

BALLARD HAD CALLED ahead, and they were met by the chief of building security, a retired LAPD man named Mayfield. At Ballard's request, he had sealed the fourth-floor restroom and evacuated the branch office of the state department of parks and recreation. Mayfield had a maintenance supervisor named Teed on hand as well. They rode an elevator to the fourth floor and split up the search. Laffont and Stilwell, along with Teed, took the restroom, while Ballard and Masser went with Mayfield to the parks office.

The restroom had four toilet stalls, four urinals, and four sinks. There were two trash receptacles, one built into the wall next to the line of sinks and one an open can that was filled to the brim with crumpled paper towels, tissues, and other debris. The room had a basic government-grade drop ceiling made of two-by-two mineral-fiber panels held in place by metal gridwork.

Laffont spoke to Teed as he pulled on a pair of nitrile gloves.

"Do you know when these trash cans were last emptied?" he asked.

"Since the state budget cuts, the cleaners do this floor only Tuesday and Thursday nights," Teed said. "So Tuesday night."

"Then we're in luck," Laffont said.

Stilwell was going down the line of stalls, checking in each.

"You got another set of gloves, Tom?" he said.

"Sure," Laffont said.

He handed another set from his pocket to Stilwell.

"Peace offering," he said.

"Accepted," Stilwell said. "Thanks."

"I'll take the can."

While Laffont went to the can by the door, Stilwell pointed to the in-wall receptacle.

"Is there a trick to opening this?" he asked.

"Any key works," Teed said.

He walked over to the receptacle, pulling a key ring on a retractable chain off his belt. He stuck the key into a slot in the stainless-steel panel and opened it like a door, revealing a rectangular trash receptacle with a plastic bag liner.

"We're also going to need a stepladder to check the ceiling," Stilwell said.

"I'll go get it," Teed said.

"And a flashlight if you've got one," Laffont said.

"Sure," Teed said.

Teed left the restroom as Laffont turned the trash can over on the tile floor.

"Middleton wouldn't have had a ladder," he said. "If he used the ceiling, he probably stood on a toilet."

"You're right," Stilwell said. "I just thought if we were going to search up there, we'd want the ladder."

Laffont spoke while he used one foot to spread the debris from the can across the floor.

"You know, the way you put this together about Middleton dumping the evidence was pretty impressive," he said.

"You mean if I turn out to be right," Stilwell said.

Laffont said nothing, but it was another peace offering, Stilwell thought, as he pulled the trash liner out of the wall receptacle. It was so light, he knew right away it was not where Middleton had gotten rid of the contents of his backpack. Still, he put the bag down on the counter between two sinks and put a gloved hand into the bag to search through it. He found only one solid object amid the paper towels and tissue: a toothbrush. He wondered if Middleton brushed his teeth before going in for his interview.

"Middleton went in here before the interview, right?" he asked.

"Yeah, before," Laffont said. "Why?"

"Found a toothbrush."

"Even if it was his, we won't need it. We can get DNA directly from him."

"But then he'd know it."

"Well, the only way you'd be able to say the toothbrush was his would be to take his swab."

"True."

Stilwell dropped the toothbrush back into the bag.

"There's nothing here," he said.

"And nothing here," Laffont said.

He bent over and started gathering the debris spread on the floor and returning it to the trash can. Stilwell liked that he didn't leave it for Teed to handle. He stepped over and helped clean up.

Teed came back with a stepladder and a flashlight. Laffont said he'd do the honors. He set the ladder up in the center of the room, climbed three steps, and reached up to one of the mineral-fiber panels. He pushed it up and over, creating a two-by-two opening in the ceiling. Stilwell saw that there was about two feet of crawl space there, but it was crowded with piping from the building's fire-suppression system and cables from its computer network.

Laffont climbed to the top step of the ladder and put his head and shoulders through the opening. Stilwell turned on the flashlight and handed it up to him, then used both hands to hold the ladder steady while Laffont swept the light around in the crawl space.

"Nothing," he said. "No, wait, there's something in the corner. Looks like a bag."

He carefully climbed down and carried the ladder to the last stall. After positioning the ladder so its legs straddled the toilet, he climbed up again, removed the ceiling square, and reached into the opening. He retrieved a white plastic bag and handed it down to Stilwell.

Once Laffont was safely down off the ladder, they checked the bag's contents together. It contained four well-thumbed editions of *Hustler* magazine.

"Nice," Stilwell said.

"Looks like somebody's been using the stall to polish the knob," Laffont said. "That's pretty old-school when you can get your porn free on the web. You want to keep 'em, Stil? You're an old-school kind of guy."

"Is that another peace offering? I appreciate it, but I think I'll pass."

"Yeah, me too."

Laffont walked over and dropped the magazines into the trash can.

"Mr. Teed, thanks for your help," he said. "Could you put the ceiling back together for us?"

"I'll handle it," Teed said.

"Thank you," Stilwell said.

He and Laffont walked out into the hall.

"Well, that was a bust," Laffont said. "Let's see if Paul and Renée got lucky."

They walked down the corridor to the state parks office and got there just as Ballard and Masser were coming out.

"Anything?" Laffont said.

"Nothing," Ballard said. "We looked in every possible spot he had access to. There was nothing there."

"What about the drop ceiling?" Stilwell asked.

"The thing is, he was never alone in there," Ballard said. "I called the guy who interviewed him, and he said he was in reception and then in the interview room. So when would he have climbed up to the ceiling?"

Stilwell nodded. He felt the heat of failure on his scalp. He had been sure Middleton dumped the incriminating evidence somewhere along the way after leaving the boat.

"I think we're going to have to get a warrant and check his hotel room after all," Ballard said.

"I'll write it," Masser said.

It was a prime moment for Laffont to come down on Stilwell for the waste of time, but he said nothing.

They headed down the hall and got on the elevator. Mayfield kept offering names to Ballard, seeing who was still around from the old days when he was working cases.

As they descended, Stilwell tuned them out. A thought came to him.

"Wait a minute," he said. "Did Middleton take an elevator to or from his interview?"

"He did," Masser said. "Both ways."

"Was he alone?" Stilwell pressed.

"We didn't ride with him, obviously," Laffont said. "But he got on by himself and went right to the fourth floor. We watched from the lobby."

In unison, everyone looked up at the ceiling of the elevator. There was a two-by-two emergency escape panel.

"Do you remember which elevator he took?" Ballard asked.

"The other one," Masser said. "Coming and going."

While the others were still looking up, Stilwell looked down at the brushed-steel handrail that was on three walls of the elevator. Middleton could have used it as a foothold in climbing to the escape hatch.

"We need to get the stepladder back," Laffont said.

40

STILWELL FOLLOWED BALLARD into the interview room, carrying a cardboard evidence box. He put it down on the left side of the table and they took the two seats across from Middleton.

"What the fuck is this?" Middleton said angrily. "I've been waiting here three fucking hours. You need to charge me or let me go, and I know you can't charge me, because you don't have shit. Stop playing games, take your loss, and go home."

He jerked the chain that linked his handcuffs to an iron ring at the center of the table.

"Games?" Ballard said. "We're not the ones playing games. But we can talk about that after I take care of two pieces of business. The first is to tell you that you are being recorded in this room. Video and sound. The second is that I will give Sergeant Stilwell the honor of informing you of your constitutionally guaranteed rights."

Stilwell recited the Miranda advisement.

"Do you understand these rights as I have explained them to you?" he said after finishing.

"Oh, you're really scaring me now," Middleton said sarcastically, "with your rights and your mystery box. I hope there's a sandwich for me in there because those bozos out at the trail took mine and I'm fucking starved."

"Do you understand your rights as I have recited them?" Stilwell asked again.

"Yes, I understand my rights," Middleton said. "Okay? I took Law Enforcement 101, you know. You're just trying to scare me because you've got nothing. I'm supposed to be like 'Oh, what's in the box?'"

Ballard and Stilwell said nothing.

"You get the reference?" Middleton said. "*Seven*? Good movie. But it was about smart cops. You wouldn't know anything about that."

"You like serial-killer movies, Kent?" Ballard asked.

"Oh, you know the flick, then," Middleton said. "Spacey was awesome. Is that what this is? We're discussing serial-killer movies?"

"Mr. Middleton, you're under arrest for the murder of Angela Metier," Ballard said. "Now that you've heard your rights, do you wish to talk to us about it?"

Middleton threw his head back and laughed loudly, then leveled his eyes at Ballard. They were piercing with hate.

"You people are a fucking joke," he said. "You think you can bluff me? No chance, lady. You've got nothing."

"This is no bluff," Ballard said. "We are offering you the opportunity to tell us how it happened. I'm sure it's been a heavy burden to carry."

Middleton shook his head like he was dealing with a child.

"Honey, you need to polish your act if you want to talk to me," he said. "Because this is a joke. You're a joke."

Ballard looked at Stilwell and nodded. Then she looked back at Middleton.

"We found your stash," she said. "It makes sense that you'd put it in a place you knew you could go back to. You know, to retrieve it. But that really wasn't very smart."

Stilwell opened the box. He reached in, took out a sealed plastic evidence bag containing a spiral-bound notebook, and placed it on the table. He watched Middleton's face as he registered what it was and understood that there had been no bluff. They had indeed found the evidence he had hidden above the ceiling of the elevator.

For that fraction of a second, Stilwell saw recognition. It was the *game-over* look. But just as quickly, it was gone.

"What do you have there?" Middleton said, his bravado coming back. "A how-to manual on getting away with murder?"

"Close," Ballard said. "More like how to get caught by describing and sketching your kills. I guess it might be hard to remember where all the bodies are buried when you feel like visiting your victims."

She pointed at the notebook.

"What's really great about this is we hadn't been able to find anyone for the fifth key on the ring you left us. Now we have a map to her. Thanks for that. And as soon as we find her, we'll add that charge. We are going to be adding a lot of charges, Kent."

"I don't know what you're talking about," Middleton said. "I've never seen that before and you can't prove I have."

"Well, we've got this thing now called touch DNA," Ballard

said. "And we're going to get it off every page in that notebook. Every page."

"So what? It's not going to match me," Middleton countered.

But the fight had gone out of his voice. He knew what his future was.

"Sure it won't," Ballard said. "You keep telling yourself that."

Stilwell reached into the box and started taking out the other items. First a carton of nitrile gloves, the kind used by law enforcement.

"This is interesting," Ballard said. "Sergeant Stilwell called your boss out on the island a few minutes ago. What's his name, Stil?"

"Mick Dunaway."

"Right, Mick Dunaway. Stil—er, Sergeant Stilwell called him up and asked what brand of gloves you have out there in the rangers' supply closet. And guess what—they're True Blue too, the same brand we found in your stash. Mick was very helpful. He said he'd do an inventory for us and see if he's missing a box."

"Fuck you and fuck him," Middleton said.

Stilwell next brought out a roll of duct tape, followed by a rubber-banded coil of snap ties. After that came the black hood and the ball gag, the handcuffs, the knife, the slipknot garrote, and, last, the folding tactical shovel. Each item had been separately sealed in plastic.

"That shovel is cool," Ballard said. "Folds up and fits into a backpack. This is the most well-thought-out abduction-and-murder kit I've ever seen. I'm betting it gets written up in the *FBI Law Enforcement Bulletin*. That's big time."

Middleton just shook his head and looked down at the table.

"Reality got your tongue, Kent?" Ballard said. "You sure you don't want to tell us about how you used the garrote? I'm guessing you're the type who liked to choke them out, bring them back, choke them out again. Over and over till they begged you to end it. Was that your sick program?"

Middleton lunged at Ballard, but the chain went taut and he hit the table face-first. Ballard didn't even flinch. She'd been expecting it.

Middleton slid back into his seat. Blood ran down his face from his broken nose.

"I want a fucking lawyer!" he yelled.

"Sure, we'll get you a phone," Ballard said. "Make it a good one."

"And a goddamn doctor!"

"We'll get an EMT to take a look at you. We want you healthy for what's ahead. And pretty for the cameras. There are going to be a lot of cameras."

Ballard stood up. Stilwell did as well and started putting the evidence bags back in the box.

"I want you to remember this, Kent," Ballard said. "It was a woman who took you down."

"Just fuck off," Middleton said.

Ballard headed to the door. Stilwell finished packing the box and folded the top closed. He stared at Middleton as he picked it up to go.

"What are you looking at, motherfucker?" Middleton said.

"Nothing," Stilwell said. "I'm looking at nothing."

Outside the room, Laffont and Masser were at a desk where they had been watching the video feed from the interview. There were a few Foothill Division detectives standing behind them who had been watching as well. One of them clapped as Ballard approached. She nodded her thanks. Stilwell put the evidence box down on the desk.

"Can one of you go to the firehouse next door and get an EMT to come take a look at him?" she asked. "Somebody's gotta stuff some cotton up his nose."

"I'll go," Laffont said, heading out.

"After we get him fixed up we'll bring him downtown and book him," Ballard said. "Then I want to take the evidence directly to the lab. Hopefully Darcy will fast-track the DNA."

"You've got a lab go-to?" Stilwell asked.

Ballard turned to Stilwell.

"We do," she said. "Darcy Troy. You know her?"

"No," Stilwell said. "Catalina cases always go to the end of the line."

"Speaking of Catalina, when do you head back?"

"If you don't need me for anything more here, I think I'll go now."

"Actually, we need you over there."

Stilwell nodded. "Bird Park?" he asked.

"Right," Ballard said. "I'd like to seal the apartment and put the girlfriend in a hotel room."

"Thursday nights are busy at the Nickel," Stilwell said. "Means she'll be working tonight. I heard there are a couple rooms behind the bar for seasonal staff. I can probably get her into one of those if they're open."

"Good," Ballard said. "We'll get a search warrant tomorrow. We'll also need to interview her."

"I'll write the warrant tonight so we can hit up a judge first thing," Masser said.

"You want me to do any of it?" Stilwell asked. "The search or the interview? Or will you be coming over?"

"Let's see in the morning," Ballard said. "But if you can seal the apartment and handle the girlfriend tonight, that would be great."

"Consider it done," Stilwell said.

"Then I'll walk you out," Ballard said.

Stilwell held his hand out to Masser. They shook, and Stilwell asked him to tell Laffont he said goodbye as well.

Stilwell and Ballard walked out the back door of the station into the lot where Stilwell had parked the Bronco at five that morning.

"Now I just gotta hope I don't need a jump," he said.

"I'm sure we can get you a jump if you need it," Ballard said. "When's the last boat over?"

"I think it's at eight. I'll make it."

"Look, Stil, I need to tell you something. You heard me tell Middleton it was a girl who took him down, but that was just to bust his balls and get inside his head. I know it was you. We're here because of you. You found him. And when this hits the media, as I'm sure it will, I'll make sure you get the credit you deserve."

"Don't worry about that. You could probably use the credit more than me. A story like this might get you more volunteers."

"That would be nice. I wouldn't have to lean on Paul and Tom so much."

"Paul and Tom—there was a little friction between us, but they're good guys. They do good work."

"You do too. I'd even say you're a wasted talent out there on that little island, but man, you've got a lot of shit going down on Catalina."

"Small island, big crime, as they say."

Ballard nodded as they came to the Bronco.

"You know," she said, "I was thinking about the ironwood tree where we found Angela."

"And?" Stilwell prompted.

"I'm always going to think of you when I see that tree. Ironwood. I hope we cross paths again, Stil."

"Yeah, me too, Renée."

Stilwell shook her hand and got into the Bronco. She waited while he buckled up and turned the key. The engine came to life. He gave Ballard a thumbs-up. She gave a short wave in return.

"*Aloha, e ku'u hoaloha,*" she said.

Stilwell smiled.

"Goodbye, my friend," he said back.

He closed the door and watched Ballard walk back into the station.

41

IT WAS LATE by the time Stilwell got home. Handling Gwen Bassett turned into an issue, as she had trouble grappling with the news that her live-in boyfriend had been arrested for murder and that she would not be allowed to return to her apartment for the time being. Then Mack Fanning, her boss at the Nickel and the man from whom Middleton presumably got one of his aliases, became upset because it was the eve of a busy weekend and his lead bartender was incapacitated by the information Stilwell had delivered. He initially refused to let Bassett use the seasonal crew quarters, but eventually he relented and she was allowed to stay.

After that confrontation, Stilwell went up to Bird Park and crisscrossed the door to the apartment shared by Middleton and Bassett with yellow crime scene tape and a DO NOT ENTER sign. He posted Dawn Stabile, who was on second shift, at the complex until calls for service took her elsewhere.

His house was dark when he entered, but he could hear TV

noise from the bedroom. Then he heard Doris Day singing "Que Sera, Sera" in a duet with Arthur Godfrey and he knew Tash was watching *The Glass Bottom Boat.*

To Tash, the romantic comedy was comfort food. She had grown up in a family that took pride in the island and loved seeing it in movies and on television shows. Over the years Tash had curated a selection of DVDs of movies and shows that were either set on the island as part of the story or filmed there and presented as somewhere else. The collection included everything from *Captain Blood* to *Baywatch.* The most notable of the obscurely connected productions was the classic film *Jaws.* The underwater shots of the terrifying opening sequence of a young skinny-dipping woman being stalked by a great white shark were filmed in the clear waters off Catalina.

Tash insisted on having a movie night once a month, during which they shared a bottle of wine and discussed Catalina's role in that night's film. While Tash preferred romantic comedies like *The Glass Bottom Boat* and *Catalina Caper,* Stilwell really only engaged with suspenseful films like *Jaws* and *Chinatown,* the latter of which had used a club in Catalina as the setting for the shady Albacore Club.

Tash heard Stilwell come in and called his name.

"Be right there," he called back.

He left the go bag he kept in the Bronco by the door so he would remember to replenish it with a clean set of clothes. He went into the kitchen, put an ice cube in a glass, and liberally soaked it in Blanton's bourbon, then headed to the bedroom.

"*Que sera, sera,*" he said.

"You must be beat," Tash said.

"Definitely. Last night I stayed in this cheap motel on

Sepulveda up in the Valley. I got no sleep because of the people who use the place for their various businesses—if you know what I mean."

"I do. Why didn't you stay somewhere nicer?"

"Because we had a five o'clock start and I knew I'd only get a few hours in. Anyway, right now all I want to do is take a hot shower and crawl into bed."

"Good. I'll finish watching this while you're cleaning up."

He came around to her side of the bed, leaned down, and kissed her.

"How many times have you seen this outdated farce?" he asked.

"Too many to count," Tash said. "But I love it. I mean, how many times do you get Paul Lynde and Dom DeLuise in the same movie?"

"Uh, this is the one and only?"

"You are correct, sir."

"I'd still take *All Ashore* with Mickey Rooney over Doris any day."

"Very funny. We'll watch *All Ashore* again next movie night."

"Oh, you know what, I just found out I have to work that night."

"Not very funny. How did it go today?"

"Well, it looks like we got our man."

"*What?* When were you going to tell me?"

"I just did."

"And you're talking about the bones case, right?"

"Yeah, we arrested a guy. I'll be doing some follow-up stuff tomorrow."

"Who is it?"

"Gwen Bassett's boyfriend."

"The ranger? Oh my God, that is crazy."

"Yeah, well, he's crazy."

"Does she know?"

"Yeah, she knows. I came from the Nickel. She didn't take it too well."

"Well, congratulations, I guess. Always seems weird to say that about a murder case."

"I know what you mean."

"Take your shower, but then you have to tell me all about it."

"Uh, I just pretty much told you everything I can. We're trying to keep it on the down-low at the moment."

"What does that mean?"

"Just that we don't want to say much until charges are actually filed."

"You still think I'm Lionel's source, don't you?"

In his exhaustion, Stilwell had stumbled into the one spot of friction between them.

"No, Tash, I don't. We hashed that out a long time ago and I really don't. I'm just tired and said the wrong thing. I completely trust you on that."

"But not on other stuff?"

"God, no. I just can't seem to say the right thing here. I'm going to take a shower and then we can start over. Okay?"

"Okay, fine."

Stilwell took his glass of bourbon into the shower with him and put it on the shampoo shelf. He sipped it after dousing his head under the spray. He soon felt its burn start to work on the tightness between his shoulder blades and the angst between his ears.

When he came back to the bedroom, the movie was over and Tash had fallen asleep. That was okay with him. It was probably for the best, since he had messed up by saying the wrong thing earlier. He now wanted quiet so he could think. He knew there was still work to be done on the Middleton case but he was already disengaging and getting ready to go after something that was possibly more dangerous than a madman.

PART FOUR

Blue Smoke

42

STILWELL WAS AT his desk prepping for the seven a.m. roll call when he got the news. He held roll call on Fridays only because that was when he had four to six deputies on duty to handle the start of the weekend. It was preseason, so it would be only four this time. Stilwell was figuring out how to deploy them while still keeping at least one deputy on post at Bird Park until it was decided when the search of Kent Middleton's apartment would be and who would conduct it.

But everything changed when his cell phone buzzed. It was Ballard.

"Morning, Renée."

"He's gone, Stil."

"Who?"

"Middleton. They found him in his cell an hour ago. He's dead."

Stilwell's chin dropped. He leaned forward, elbows on the desk, one hand over one ear, the phone to the other.

"How?" he asked.

"He killed himself," Ballard said. "They're telling me he took the cotton pack out of his nose and the tape off his face and made some kind of ball with it. Then he swallowed it and choked to death."

Stilwell closed his eyes. He said nothing and a long silence went by.

"Stil?"

"He got away with it."

"No, we—"

"He spent one night in jail. For five women. Maybe more. Don't kid yourself—he got away with it."

Another silence before Ballard spoke.

"At least we stopped him. There would have been more than five if we hadn't."

Somehow that didn't make Stilwell feel any better.

"Where was he booked?" he asked. "Didn't they have him on suicide watch?"

"Metro City, and they tell me they did," Ballard said. "Tear-away blanket, no shoelaces, twenty-four-hour camera, lit cell, the whole nine yards. But they didn't see it. They thought he'd put the blanket over his head because of the light. So he could sleep. He did the whole thing under the blanket."

"They should have seen it coming."

"I don't know about that. You were in the interview. I think at first he thought he could beat this."

"No, I saw it. For just a moment when I pulled out the notebook, I saw it in his eyes. He knew. He knew what his future was and it was bleak. It was prison for the rest of his life. He had the *game-over* look."

Ballard didn't respond right away and Stilwell waited.

"You know, I should have seen it too," she finally said.

"You were asking the questions," Stilwell said. "You had to concentrate on that."

"No, I mean later when we were taking him to Metro. He said something that was almost a confession."

"What was it?"

"I was in the back seat with him. Laffont was driving and Paul was in the front passenger seat. At first I was just trying to bait him into an admission. I reminded him that he'd been flying completely under the radar until he started engaging with us. You know, taunting us. I asked what was up with that and he answered, but carefully. He said, 'The person you have me confused with probably realized that he had to raise the stakes, that he had to make it more dangerous.'"

"That doesn't seem very suicidal."

"Right, but then he went back to that movie *Seven* and said he would be remembered forever and that I wouldn't be remembered for anything."

Stilwell said nothing.

"It was like you said," Ballard continued. "He was thinking about the future. I even said to him, 'Is that a confession?' and he said, 'It was nothing.' I should have read it right."

"Do you think that means he broke his nose on purpose?" Stilwell asked. "Part of the endgame?"

"Whoa, that's a little bit of a stretch, don't you think?"

"Maybe. So what happens now?"

"Media relations still wants to do it up big," Ballard said. "A press briefing later this morning with the chief talking about closing the case. They'll invite the sheriff and you, if you want to come over."

"No, count me out. It's the start of the weekend, and I'm going to be busy here. You still going for a search warrant on the apartment?"

"No, we'll let that go for now and just wrap things up. I think he was smart enough not to leave evidence around for his girlfriend to find."

"You sure? He had that camera in his backpack. There might be photos, possible leads to other victims."

"His notebook will give us that. For now I think we leave things as they are. I need Masser to work on the summary report. A search warrant will have to wait."

Stilwell didn't think it was the right call but let it go. It was not his department. It was not his case.

"What about the girlfriend?" he asked. "Does that mean she's clear to go home?"

"If she wants," Ballard said. "And if we need to talk to her, I'll reach out to you to set it up. It will be interesting to see if she talks to the media. They're going to find her. I see Josh Mankiewicz and *Dateline* knocking on her door."

"You're sure she wasn't part of this with him?"

"All our victims were taken before he moved out to the island and met her, right?"

"Right."

"So that puts her in the clear."

"I take it she doesn't know yet that Middleton offed himself?"

"I don't think so. Only a few people know at the moment."

"Then I'd better go tell her before it hits the news."

"Sorry to stick you with that."

"It's okay. Eight years in homicide, I got used to it. When's the press conference?"

"Last night I was told to write something up for the chief to have by ten this morning. I don't know if they'll stay with that timing after what's happened."

"There's a local reporter out here I promised I'd keep in the loop. All right if I tell him? I'd just like to give him a heads-up so he can get over there."

"Is the paper online?"

"No, just print. People still read want ads out here. Keeps things local."

"A throwback. Yes, talk to your guy, only I didn't tell you that you could."

"Understood."

"I guess that's it, then. I'm sorry it turned out this way, Stil."

"Yeah, me too."

"Stay in touch."

Ballard disconnected, and Stilwell leaned back in his chair and tried to collect his thoughts. He didn't know what to feel about Middleton taking his own life. He sat there staring into space until he realized how angry he was. He felt cheated somehow. And he felt sorry for the families who had waited years for answers and would not have the full measure of justice—of hearing a jury or a judge pronounce Middleton guilty.

He took Middleton's suicide as a final *Fuck you.* As him saying, *You aren't going to drag me into court, display me to the world like an animal, and convict me.*

There was a knock on the door, and De Giorgio stuck his head in.

"We're all here, boss," he said.

"Good," Stilwell said. "I'll be right out."

Stilwell opened his phone and called Lionel McKey's cell. When he answered, Stilwell could tell he had woken him up.

"Lionel, get out of bed," he said. "You have to catch the first boat to overtown."

"What?" McKey said. "Why?"

"For the press conference on the bones case. You don't want to miss it. We got somebody."

"Okay, okay. You mean you made an actual arrest?"

"We did, yeah. So get up and get over there. I heard the press conference is at ten. Call me after and I'll fill in the blanks."

"Okay, I'm going."

"Good."

Stilwell disconnected and got up to meet with his deputies.

43

THE BUFFALO NICKEL was on Pebbly Beach Road by the freight docks, through which much of the island was supplied. Behind it was the heliport, where the better-heeled visitors arrived from the mainland. A helicopter got you to the island fifty minutes faster than the Express.

The Nickel didn't open until lunchtime but Stilwell wanted to get to Gwen Bassett before the news from the press conference overtown came ashore in Catalina. He walked around behind the bar and knocked on the door of the crew room, where he had left Bassett the previous night. It was nine a.m., which he believed was a reasonable time to knock.

The first knock got no response. The second and louder effort got a rebuke from inside.

"Go fuck yourself!"

"Gwen, it's Sergeant Stilwell. I need to speak with you."

There was silence. He knocked again, more gently this time, a reminder that he was waiting.

"All right, all right, I'm coming," he heard through the door. "Hold your fricking horses."

The door finally opened and Bassett peered out from darkness, squinting against the exterior light as she finished pulling a polo shirt with the bar's buffalo-head logo down over her hips.

"What?" she said.

"I'm here to tell you that you can return to your apartment," Stilwell said. "I said last night it was being sealed and then searched today. That won't be happening now."

"Why, because you realized how wrong you all are about Kent?"

"Uh, Gwen, I have some bad news about that. I'm very sorry to tell you this. Last night at the jail Kent Middleton took his own—"

"No! Don't say that. You're wrong. You're so fucking wrong."

"I'm sorry, Gwen. He's gone."

She held a hand over her eyes.

"He wouldn't have done that. Never."

"I'm afraid he did. I'm sorry for your loss."

"Don't you dare say that! If he's dead, it's because of you. He couldn't take the lies you told about him."

"They weren't lies, Gwen."

She dropped her hand and looked at him through tearful eyes.

"Yes, they were," she said. "Kent wouldn't do the things you say he did."

"I'll tell you what," Stilwell said. "Whenever you're up to it, come over to the substation and I'll sit down with you and we can go over the investigation and the evidence the police gathered. I think if you do that, you will realize that you probably dodged a bullet with him."

"Fuck . . . you."

"Would you like me to give you a ride up to Bird Park?"

She slammed the door. It sounded like a shot.

"I guess not," Stilwell said.

He stood there for a moment. He heard a door open behind him and turned to see that the slamming had drawn Mack Fanning out of the kitchen to see what was going on.

"Aw, shit," he said. "You gotta leave her alone, man. I need her today or I'm fucked."

"Good luck with that," Stilwell said. "Her boyfriend died."

"No shit?"

"No shit."

Stilwell started walking back to his ATV. Fanning called after him, "You're not helping much around here, bud," he said.

"Yeah, I get that a lot," Stilwell said.

Back at the sub, Stilwell grabbed the radio he had forgotten to take to the Nickel and used it to tell De Giorgio to go up to Bird Park and remove the crime scene tape from the door of Gwen Bassett's apartment. He then scooped the stack of crime reports out of the box on Mercy's desk and took them back to his office to review.

It was almost two days of reports, but it took Stilwell only fifteen minutes to go through them and determine that there was no need for investigative follow-up from him on any of them. It was the usual fare. There had been several calls to the bars the night before to handle drunk-and-disorderly patrons, some noise complaints from residents in the bar district of Avalon, and two DUIs—golf carts and automobiles fell under the same drunk-driving laws. Most of the reports in the first two categories had been handled or resolved on the scene and involved written citations requiring the accused to either pay a fine or appear in court to dispute the charge. Since most offenders were visitors to the island, they paid the fines to avoid having to come back for a court appearance.

The DUIs were a bit more complicated. The offenders were brought to the sub, fingerprinted, photographed, and booked, then RORed—released on their own recognizance—on the promise that they would not drive to their home or hotel. Once these cases were forwarded to the district attorney's office, offenders were offered a choice: They could enter a diversion program or go to court, which in Avalon was held only on Fridays and presided over by a traveling judge.

There were also a handful of reports of golf-cart thefts in the stack. All these had been resolved quickly on the scene as unintentional, since many of the carts looked identical, especially to someone inebriated or close to it. It was rare that locals took their keys out of the carts.

To Stilwell's relief, no reports in the stack had to do with graffiti on historic structures or vandalism up at the ABC vineyard.

Stilwell was now clear to work on other active cases, and he began by using his phone to sign into the county's intranet system. By using his cell, he avoided leaving a digital trail on his department-issued desktop computer. He navigated to the page for the sheriff's department and from there went to the personnel page. As a unit supervisor, he had low-level access to basic information about department employees. Since he had little to no involvement in choosing who was transferred to Catalina, he usually used his access only after the fact to see what he could learn about those who were coming in.

But now he had a different purpose. He typed *Gavin Lambert* into the search bar. Soon he was viewing the résumé Lambert had submitted to the department eighteen years earlier as part of his application.

The birth date on the résumé put Lambert currently at

forty-eight years old. It said he was born and raised in Riverside in the next county east. He attended classes at UC Riverside for one year before joining the US Marine Corps. In 2003 he was deployed with a regimental combat team that took part in the invasion of Iraq. He was deployed a second time the following year with his RCT and fought in Fallujah. He retired from the Marines in 2006 to pursue a career in law enforcement. According to the résumé, Lambert received a chestful of commendations while serving, including a Purple Heart, a Bronze Star for valor, and a Combat Action Ribbon, and he had been awarded a Hog's Tooth.

Stilwell was unfamiliar with the Hog's Tooth and typed it into his search engine on the desktop.

What he got back sent an ice-cold finger down his spine.

> A Hog's Tooth is a round presented to a US Marine upon graduating from the Marine Corps Scout Sniper school. It is traditionally a 7.62mm NATO round, the cartridge fired by an M40A3, the primary rifle used by Marine sharpshooters.

Stilwell now knew that Lambert was a sniper.

44

STILWELL DUG DEEPER and found a military site that revealed that the sniper round necklace was called a Hog's Tooth because *HOG* was an acronym for *hunter of gunmen*. This was derived from a military superstition that held that every soldier had a bullet out there with his or her name on it, and it was just a matter of time before that bullet was fired. But if a Marine sniper took out an enemy sniper and then took a round from the dead shooter's gun, he had retrieved the bullet with his name on it. If he wore it on a shoestring around his neck, he would be invincible. He couldn't be killed.

Stilwell went back to the Gavin Lambert résumé and learned that after he retired from the Marine Corps in 2006, he immediately joined Blackwater, the contract private-security force. He stayed in Iraq for another eighteen months, where he was assigned to protect diplomats and embassy employees. Stilwell assumed that the job could have included work as a sniper, running overwatch on motorcades and scanning rooftops for enemy combatants.

Stilwell had a better understanding of why Simon and Trestle had come back to the island for measurements. They were looking for ballistic evidence that might tie Lambert's past as a sniper to the ambush at the airstrip.

Stilwell took out his phone and called his friend Monty West, an investigator with the medical examiner's office. They had worked multiple cases together when Stilwell was in the sheriff's homicide unit. They also shared a lifelong allegiance to the Los Angeles Dodgers, the reigning World Series champions. They had once even journeyed to Arizona together to attend the Dodgers spring-training games.

As usual, West answered the call with a baseball reference, which Stilwell responded to in kind.

"I miss Clayton Kershaw already."

"Well, I still miss Vin Scully."

"What's up, Stil?"

"I want to ask you about the Alton Quigley autopsy."

"Which one is—oh, that's the deputy, right? Not my case."

"Then what did you hear about it?"

"Not much to it. Head shot. Large-caliber projectile."

"The projectile is what I'm interested in."

"I heard it went to metallurgy, but I don't know if they got anything back yet."

Stilwell was silent for a moment. He had heard nothing about metallurgic evidence or analysis from Simon but he had to act like he was in the loop.

"Can you punch it up on your screen and see if we're still waiting on the report?" he asked.

"I could but I'm not at my computer," West said. "I'm in the field making a pickup."

"That's cool. Can you check when you get back?"

"I'll call you."

West disconnected.

Stilwell put the phone down and thought about what he had seen that night at the airstrip. Coming back up the hill after chasing Kalas, he had been focused on Ramirez because she was still alive and he had to stop her from bleeding out. He had made a quick visual check on Quigley and knew right away that he was beyond help. The entire back of his head was gone. This meant that the projectile that hit him likely tumbled or shattered on impact, spreading the wound track and shredding his brain as it plowed through and then exited from the back of his skull. That the ME had asked for a metallurgy analysis suggested to Stilwell that the bullet had shattered and part of it had been recovered during autopsy.

Stilwell picked up his cell again and called Ernie Simon, but he didn't answer. Stilwell checked his call history and saw the burner number Simon had previously used. He called that number, and it also went to voicemail. He was about to leave a message when he was interrupted by an incoming call. He checked the screen and saw that it was Captain Corum, probably calling about the press conference. He sent the call to voicemail and left a message for Simon:

"Ernie, I know about the bullet fragment. Call me back."

Stilwell thought he had phrased the message in a way that would make Simon return the call. Stilwell sat back and wondered if he was going down a rabbit hole. The ME request for a metallurgic analysis was an effort to identify the type and manufacturer of the round that killed Quigley. That was good, thorough work, but what would it achieve? Identifying the manufacturer would be useful only if they could prove that a suspect had bought or possessed matching ammunition. The question was, could they?

Stilwell didn't know the answer, but Ernie Simon probably

did, and maybe that was why he hadn't picked up either of Stilwell's calls.

There was a single knock on the door and Mercy stuck her head in.

"Stil, Captain Corum just called me," she said. "He wants you to call him back ASAP."

"Did you tell him I was here?" Stilwell asked.

"Uh, yes. But he knew from the cameras, I guess. Was that wrong?"

"No, it's all right. How did he sound?"

"Sort of mad."

"Okay, I'll call him. You can shut the door."

Stilwell braced himself and made the call. As expected, Corum came in hot, not bothering with any salutation.

"Why am I hearing about this press conference from the sheriff's adjutant?" he said. "Why am I being asked to brief the sheriff on something I haven't been briefed on myself?"

"Sorry, Captain," Stilwell said. "I'm writing up the report now. I was going to get it to you before there was a press conference, but it's Friday and things are getting busy out here. A lot of weekenders landing."

"I don't have time to wait for you to write a report. Tell me right now what's going on and what I need to tell the sheriff so that he doesn't come off as a complete ass in front of the cameras."

It's always about the cameras, Stilwell thought. He spent the next ten minutes giving Corum a short summary of what had occurred in the past twenty-four hours on the Middleton and missing-hikers case. He ended it with a piece of information he knew Corum would like.

"The good news is he killed himself at Metropolitan," he said. "The city's jail, not ours. If anybody goes Epstein on this, LAPD has to deal with it, not us."

"Thank God for that," Corum said.

"Is that enough for the sheriff?" Stilwell asked.

"We'll see. You know, Stil, it looks like you did good work here, and the LAPD is going to give us a piece of the credit pie, but it still bothers me that I wasn't in the loop on this thing till it was all over but the shouting. You have a big problem with keeping me informed, and all I can tell you is that it's wearing thin. It's really wearing thin."

"All I can say, Cap, is that I will do better."

"You'd better do better. I have to go brief the sheriff now, but we need to talk about Kalas and how the fuck you let him escape."

"I didn't *let* him escape, Captain. He—"

"I don't have time for this now. But you're going to need me on your side when the shit hits the fan. Start acting like you want that."

He disconnected before Stilwell could respond. He was still holding the phone to his ear when Monty West called back.

"Whaddya got?"

"Jones said they haven't typed up a report yet."

"Who's Jones?"

"Hunter Jones. Our metal man. He's a subcontractor. He's writing the report now. You want to wait for that report or hear what he told me? I took notes."

"Go ahead. You tell me."

"Okay, first of all, it was a frangible projectile, basically built to disintegrate on impact. As it did in this case. But a small fragment was recovered from a piece of the skull collected at the scene. The fragment was embedded in the interior lining of the occipital bone. The report will have photos of all this."

"Can't wait."

"Let's see... what else? I can barely read my own writing.

Okay, it was an MIP round. That means metal-impregnated polymer. That's a polymer matrix mixed with metal particles—in this case, copper. The composition of the recovered fragment is consistent with MIP projectiles manufactured by a company called MIPCO Ammo. That's what I've got."

Stilwell was silent as he finished taking his own notes.

"Okay, this is good," he said. "I appreciate it. Let's go to a game soon."

"Anytime you want to get off that rock out there," West said, "I'm here."

Stilwell disconnected and looked down at his notes, then typed *MIPCO Ammo* into his search engine and clicked on the company's website.

There were several photos on the home page of men wearing military uniforms and brandishing assault rifles, presumably engaged in combat. Quotes from satisfied MIPCO customers recommended the polymer ammunition. The site listed the many virtues of the product, which was described as environmentally friendly because each round was lead-free.

The MIP round was deemed to be safer than traditional ammunition because the disintegration of the projectile upon impact reduced ricochets and overpenetration, which occurred when jacketed lead ammunition passed cleanly through a target and went on to cause unintended damage.

What was not extolled on the site was that the MIP ammunition was perfect for a sniper. It left widespread trauma that could make up for off-center impacts, and the reduced overpenetration and ricochets cut down on collateral damage.

The home page claimed that the ammunition could not be bought in a gun store anywhere in the world. It was available for purchase only through the website. Stilwell saw that the company was based in Temecula, which was in Riverside County, not far from where Gavin Lambert had grown up. This led Stilwell to go to the Who We Are page on the site to check out the owners and staff. He didn't see Lambert's name and didn't recognize any of the people listed, but he knew that many law enforcement officers were licensed gun dealers or had other side gigs in the gun trade. Considering Lambert's résumé, it would not be surprising for him to have a relationship with an ammunition manufacturer.

Stilwell realized that he was no longer behind Simon and Trestle on the case. He had moved ahead of them because they were still waiting on the metallurgy report. They would soon catch up, but Stilwell couldn't wait. He wanted to press forward. The logical next move would be to serve MIPCO with a warrant for any records of purchases by Lambert or business involvement with him, but Stilwell couldn't do that. It wasn't his case, and all warrants had to be approved by Corum, who would no doubt shut Stilwell down before he even finished making the request.

Stilwell picked up the phone and called the number listed at the bottom of the MIPCO home page for general inquiries. He then switched back to the Who We Are page and looked at the photo of Walter Bessemer, the founder and president of the company.

A female voice answered the call.

"MIPCO, how can I help you?"

"I'd like to speak to Walter."

"Who can I say is calling?"

"Gavin Lambert."

"Hold, please."

Twenty seconds went by and the call was transferred. It rang once and was picked up by a man who was clearly familiar with the person he thought was calling.

"Hey, Chopper, what's going on?"

Stilwell said nothing. He just listened.

"Gavin, you there?"

Stilwell disconnected. He went to his screen and clicked on Walter Bessemer's name. The bio it led to was short, but what was there was enough. Bessemer had been a Marine, had fought in Iraq, and won a Bronze Star for heroic action during the battle for Fallujah.

It was clear that the two men were well acquainted. The etymology of the nickname was easy for Stilwell to trace: Lambert becomes Lamb Chop. Lamb Chop becomes Chopper. No doubt Lambert and Bessemer were foxhole buddies.

Stilwell felt that he was now another step ahead of Simon and Trestle. And he knew that being out front was a lonely place to be.

45

STILWELL'S INVESTIGATION OF Gavin Lambert was built on a hunch with evidence as thin as the strands of a spiderweb. It was completely circumstantial. Some smoke but no fire—yet. It also wasn't Stilwell's case to pursue. But none of that mattered. He had been there that night when his two deputies were ambushed by a sniper. He felt a responsibility to them and a responsibility to make sure justice prevailed. He couldn't trust that the investigators assigned to the case would accomplish that. So he remained a dog with a bone, unable to let it go.

Stilwell had always trusted his instincts. Lambert was a trained killer who had shot at people from a distance during a war. Stilwell knew from his own experience that taking a life, in combat or not, from afar or not, carried a burden. But the burden lessened the next time it happened. You had already crossed a border within yourself. Killing, no matter what the circumstance, became easier. His instincts told him that Lambert would have no boundaries when it came to taking a life to head off a career-threatening scandal.

He was aware of what he was missing—the case could jump from the circumstantial to solid ground if he could prove that Gavin Lambert was on the island at the time of the shooting. He knew that a sniper treasures his weapon the way a violinist treasures a Stradivarius. He would bet his house that Lambert had kept the gun. He had used disintegrating ammunition so that there could be no ties to it. It might be hidden somewhere, but Stilwell knew he still had it.

Finding the gun would be a key part of the puzzle, even if ballistics would not.

The rest of Friday went down easy, although the island was beginning to fill with visitors for the weekend. Stilwell got home before Tash, who always worked till dark on Fridays, as a fleet of private boats came in and moored in the harbor. Stilwell used the head start to cook dinner, hoping it would serve as an apology for his missteps of the night before. He made one of her favorites from his limited culinary repertoire, his mother's Irish stew with fresh bread from the bakery at Vons for dipping.

On Saturday morning Stilwell followed Tash to the harbormaster's tower, where she once again set him up at a monitor so he could view the footage from cameras positioned around Avalon Harbor. This time he was interested in one camera in particular, the one that months earlier he had repositioned to capture a better view of the Express docks. It now recorded every person who stepped off a ferry and came to the island.

Watching the footage was tedious. He didn't want to move too quickly through the hours of video leading up to the last arrival before the shooting at the airstrip. He kept the playback on real time as each boat came in and its passengers disembarked, fast-forwarding only between dockings. This meant taking twenty minutes to get through each hour of video.

He suspected that if Lambert arrived by ferry, he might have worn some sort of disguise. But the one thing he would not be able to camouflage was the forty-five-inch length of an M40A3 sniper rifle. Stilwell had researched the weapon's dimensions and learned that it was not collapsible. He had looked at various carrying cases sold online, and now, while reviewing video of the Express docks, he wasn't looking at people but at luggage. Every guitar case and rucksack drew his attention. He had seen Lambert only at Quigley's funeral, but since Lambert gave the eulogy, he'd had Stilwell's attention for a solid ten minutes while he spoke so eloquently about his fallen comrade and then afterward when he was talking to a gathering of his troops. Stilwell felt confident he would be able to identify him, even in a disguise, once drawn to him by the bag he was carrying.

But four hours of video-watching went by without Stilwell spotting a single contender. He also kept an eye out for the arrival of Gonzalo Kalas, but by the end of his review, he was certain that neither man had come to the island by ferry. Stilwell thought it would have been a mistake for Lambert to come by public transportation, but he'd felt he had to eliminate that possibility. Now Stilwell had to decide whether he should commit the rest of his afternoon to watching video from the day after the shooting in case Lambert had boarded a ferry to leave the island. He was temporarily relieved of having to make the decision when Tash came over and invited him to lunch.

"You can leave?" he asked.

"Yes," Tash said. "Audrey can cover. It will be good experience for her. Besides, all our reservations are in. She'll only have to deal with stragglers."

Audrey Goodson was the interim assistant harbormaster who'd been hired when Tash moved up to interim harbormaster.

"Where to?" Stilwell said.

"I made a rez at Bluewater," Tash said.

"Going fancy, huh?"

"Why not? Plus it's close if Audrey needs me."

"Let's do it."

Stilwell stood up from the desk where she had set him up to watch video. He had trouble focusing because he had just sat for four hours looking at a screen two feet away.

"You okay?" Tash asked.

"Yeah, just too much screen time."

"That will do it to you. You want to sit down?"

"No, I'm good. I have to remember to take breaks and walk around when I come back."

"How much more do you have?"

"I'm about halfway through."

"Ooh. You're going to have a whopper of a headache tonight."

"We'll see."

It was a two-minute walk down the pier and then right on Crescent to the Bluewater. Tash ordered the lobster roll, while Stilwell went with the sand dabs. Stilwell had not explained why he had to review video from the camera focused on the Express docks, but when he told her the date he wanted her to cue up, she knew it was related to the airstrip case.

"Is there anything I can do to help?" she asked.

"Nah, it's kind of a fool's errand," Stilwell said. "But something I need to do to cover all the bases."

"For the detectives overtown?"

"Not really. More for myself. But if I get something, I'll share it with them. If they ever call me back."

"What's that about?"

"To tell you the truth, I don't know. I thought Ernie Simon was keeping me in the loop. But I left messages yesterday and today and haven't heard back. Something's going on with him."

He noticed the worry line crease her forehead.

"Not a big deal," he said. "He's probably just taking the weekend off. He's been running on this thing from the start."

The truth was, Stilwell was beginning to think something or someone was blocking Simon from making contact. He had decided to give it till Monday morning before he did something about it.

"Are you going to be able to stay here for a while?" Tash asked.

"I have no plans to leave the island," Stilwell said.

The crease was now gone.

"You want to watch a movie tonight?" he asked.

"Yeah," she said. "If you'll be home."

"Planning on it."

"*Chinatown*?"

"What happened to *All Ashore*?"

"After last night's dinner, you can have *Chinatown*."

"I'll have to cook more often."

The waitress brought their food, and without speaking, Tash cut her lobster roll in two and put half on Stilwell's plate at the same time as he forked half of his sand dabs onto her plate. Then they laughed at each other.

When they got back to the tower, Stilwell tried Ernie Simon on his burner and regular cell phone. Both calls went to voicemail. He didn't bother leaving a message. After that, he got back in front of the screen and went to work on the video review, moving to the morning after the shooting. He continued looking at the packs and suitcases people were carrying as they arrived to board the Express ferry. Then he saw himself in the video. He had forgotten that he went to the dock to hunt for the man he had chased on the mountain the night before. Watching it now, he felt like it had occurred a year ago, not just a couple of weeks.

He watched for another four hours but didn't see a case that might have held a sniper rifle. Nor did he see any passenger resembling Lambert. The day had been a bust. But at least it told him that if Lambert was the shooter, he had used a different way to get on and off the island—most likely a private boat.

Stilwell went over to the command post where Tash sat with a 360-degree view of the harbor.

"I'm going to head out," he told her.

"Did you find anything?" she asked.

"No, but I had to do it. You want me to pick up dinner?"

"How about Mrs. T's?"

"Sounds good. What do you want?"

"Want to split kung pao chicken?"

"Sure."

"And shrimp fried rice."

"Got it. See you at the house."

Stilwell left the tower and walked down the pier and over to the sub. He unlocked the door and entered an empty substation. The second shift had started at six p.m. and both deputies were out on patrol. Stilwell dropped the two-way he was carrying into the wall charger and grabbed a fresh one. He then checked his desk to see if there were any message slips left for him by the deputies. There were none.

He looked at his watch. It was six thirty and he knew that Tash would be another hour buttoning up things. He grabbed the key to his ATV and headed out, locking the door behind him.

He drove south toward the industrial area of the island, then took Wrigley Road over the shoulder of the mountain and down to Pebbly Beach Road. He cruised by the Buffalo Nickel and over to the Avalon boatyard.

The boatyard was where most locals kept their small

watercraft. All vessels were dry-docked—that is, stored on wooden cradles lined in rows like a parking lot. Customers leased spaces, and a forklift picked the boats up and put them in the water at the floating dock. An owner could call ahead and have their boat in the water by the time they arrived. The cost for dry storage was dramatically lower than the cost of keeping a boat floating in the harbor full-time.

The boatyard was privately owned and operated. It appeared to be closed for the night by the time Stilwell got there. It was surrounded by a fence topped with razor wire. The gate was closed across the entrance but could be opened with a combination on a keypad. Leaseholders were given the combo so they could access their boats after hours. The sheriff's office and the fire department also had the combination for emergency access. Stilwell looked up the five-digit number on his phone, punched it in, and drove the ATV through once the gate rolled open.

Stilwell drove down the center aisle, boats lined up on both sides, to a small office and bait shop by the floating dock. He was hoping to find someone still at work, but the windows of the shack were dark. He looked around to see if there had been any cameras installed since the last time he was in the yard. He had recommended cameras after a series of thefts from boats stored in the yard were reported. But the boatyard's owner had been reluctant, and Stilwell guessed that was because some of his customers might be involved in criminal activities. That was why there were no cameras before the thefts and he supposed that was why he didn't see any now.

Stilwell knew the boatyard was only one of many places on the island where a boat drop could be made. Descanso Beach on the north side of the harbor was a good location as well. But the boatyard would turn up in an online search for a boat ramp or drop-off point. It would be the likely choice for an overlander who wanted to avoid arriving in the harbor with his sniper rifle.

This was another dead end.

Stilwell took out his phone and called Mrs. T's Chinese Kitchen to order dinner. He then turned the ATV around and went to get it.

46

STILWELL LIKED GETTING to the sub early on Mondays. It was the calm after the storm of the weekend. He would read the crime reports that had come in during the busy days, decide what needed his attention, update the schedule of who was working and when, and generally set up things for the week ahead. It was basic busywork, but the routine of it created a normalcy he enjoyed. He also enjoyed the quiet time with a latte and croissant from Catalina Coffee & Cookie, which was on his way from the house.

But he was only a half hour into the routine when his cell buzzed with a text from Carol Najera telling him to call her as soon as he got up. She was the major crimes prosecutor assigned to the Douglas Allen case. He called her right away.

"I've been up," he said. "What's going on?"

"Allen filed an electronic motion over the weekend accusing you of harassing his family," she said.

Stilwell had to take a moment to get his focus back on the Allen case and figure out what this was about.

"He's calling *not* arresting his son harassment?" he finally said.

"I don't know the details but they're using whatever happened to try to remove you from the witness list," Najera said.

"Yeah, well, it's bullshit."

Stilwell spent the next ten minutes recounting the graffiti investigation that had led to his sit-down with the ex-mayor's son.

"Can you get on a boat and come over here?" Najera asked. "I need you to tell all this to the judge. Allen's really grasping at straws at this point."

"I guess so," Stilwell said. "When?"

"This morning. Right now. Allen's lawyer has asked for a hearing on it."

Stilwell looked at his watch. He could catch the eight a.m. ferry if he hurried and if there was room. The first boat back on Mondays was often packed with tourists returning home after the weekend.

"Okay, I'll try to grab the next boat. Meet at the courthouse?"

"Come to my office. But listen, his son might be coming on the same boat to testify. If you see him, don't go near him. You understand?"

"Got it."

"Okay, see you soon."

Stilwell left a handwritten note on Mercy's desk saying only that he had gone to the mainland for a court appearance.

The eight o'clock boat was sold out and the waiting list was in double digits, but Kim Krabill was in the captain's chair and got him on board standing room only. He stood outside the open door of the pilothouse. It was a good spot for viewing the flying fish that leaped from the water in front of the bow as it cut through the waves toward Long Beach. Stilwell thought he would never grow tired of seeing the dolphins and flying fish and the occasional whale on the ride to and from the island. Krabill had once told him that hitting a whale was her biggest nightmare as a captain.

Along the way he got another text from Najera, saying that the judge had set the hearing for eleven. That gave Stilwell some breathing room, but factoring in the boat ride back, it meant most of his day would be taken up by this distraction.

At one point during the seventy-minute cruise, he took a walk around the boat decks, surreptitiously checking to see if Matt Allen was aboard. If he was, Stilwell didn't see him, and he returned to his spot by the pilothouse door.

By 9:45, Stilwell was seated in the waiting area of the Long Beach branch of the district attorney's office. He had texted Najera before entering the building to let her know he'd made it.

There was no one else waiting to see a prosecutor. Stilwell called Ernie Simon again. For the sixth time his call went unanswered. Fed up with his supposed friend and colleague ducking him, Stilwell called the main line for the homicide unit. The call was picked up by Dulce Camarena, the office assistant. She had been in the position for years. No last names were needed.

"Dulce, it's Stil. It's been a while."

"It certainly has. How are you, Stil?"

"I'm good. I have a question for you. I'm trying to reach Ernie Simon. Do you see him in the bullpen?"

"Uh, Ernie is no longer here."

Stilwell was taken aback.

"You mean he transferred?" he asked.

"No, he retired," Camarena said.

"When was this?"

"Friday was his last day."

"Well, when did he give notice that he was retiring?"

"I think that happened Friday too, but you'd have to ask Captain Corum."

Stilwell was stunned by this timing. His immediate conclusion was that Simon had been forced out to avoid something that threatened more than his job.

"Is Trestle there, Dulce?" he asked. "I need to talk to him."

"He's on vacation this week," she said. "Actually, for two weeks. I'm looking at the vacations calendar here. I heard he went on a cruise."

"Well, who's handling the Quigley case while he's gone if Simon's retired?"

"I'm not sure, but the captain told me to send all inquiries to him. Should I see if he's free?"

"No, I'll call back later. Thanks, Dulce."

He disconnected and dropped so deeply into dark thoughts about this that he did not hear the receptionist trying to get his attention until she nearly yelled his name.

He finally looked up.

"Carol can see you now," she said.

The hearing with the judge was held in chambers because of the sensitivity of the claim involving a juvenile. Superior court judge Greta Galvez was presiding. Douglas Allen was there along with his two attorneys, Martin Klein and Avril Gardner.

"I have read the defense motion to dismiss Sergeant Stilwell as a witness," Galvez began. "It makes serious accusations and I would like to hear the state's response."

"Yes, Your Honor," Najera said. "The state's response is that this is a spurious claim and a desperate effort to undermine the case before it has even gone to trial. As you can see, I have

Sergeant Stilwell here and he is ready to present testimony and evidence as to what really occurred involving the defendant's son."

"Very well," Galvez said. "Sergeant Stilwell, I am going to put you under oath."

Stilwell raised his hand and took the oath to tell nothing but the truth. The judge told Najera to proceed.

"Sergeant Stilwell, can you tell the court what brought you into contact with Matthew Allen last week?" she asked.

"Happy to," Stilwell said. "My office on Catalina was contacted by multiple citizens reporting that two of Avalon's most important historic structures, the chimes tower and the casino, had been defaced with graffiti. I investigated and confirmed the reports."

From there, Stilwell recounted under questioning the investigation that led to his identifying Matt Allen as the suspect. He shared the photos he had taken of the graffiti and the stills from the video at the casino.

"Who mentioned the name Matt Allen first?" Najera asked. "You or Olester Bryant?"

"It was Bryant," Stilwell said. "He recognized the letters *FSID* and told me there was a group of kids at the school who used it as a name for their informal club."

"Did he look at the photo you have shown us?"

"He did and he said it was Matt Allen. He agreed to set up a meeting with Matt the next morning. We had that meeting, and Matt arrived wearing a hoodie that matched the one the suspect was wearing in the surveillance video. It also had blue paint on the sleeve."

"Did you accuse him of the crime?"

"No, I didn't need to. It was obvious to me and I didn't think my purpose there was to make an arrest. I just told him the graffiti needed to stop, and if it did, I would let it go."

"Did you at any point threaten him with arrest or try to coerce him into revealing information about his father?"

"No, not at all."

"Did you talk about his father?"

"I didn't, but he did."

"And what did he say?"

Klein objected to Stilwell giving an answer, saying it would be hearsay. Najera argued that what Matt Allen said should be allowed under the excited-utterance exception.

"I'll hear what he said and consider the objection after," Galvez said. "You may answer, Sergeant."

"He called his father a crook and then he called me stupid for taking so long to get him on anything," Stilwell said.

"Did he say anything else about his father?" Najera asked.

"No, that was it."

"Now, was there any witness to this conversation?"

"Yes, Bryant was there the whole time. It's a rule that when you talk to a juvenile during an investigation, you have to have another adult present. I asked Bryant to stay and he did."

"Did you record the conversation?"

"I did, yes, on my phone."

"And did you bring that recording with you?"

"Yes."

Najera asked the judge for permission to play the recording. Klein objected and seemed surprised to learn there was a recording. The judge overruled the objection, and Stilwell played the short conversation he'd had with Matt Allen in its entirety. Najera asked no questions afterward.

"I have nothing further, Your Honor," she said.

It was the defense's turn, and Klein launched a weak effort to attack Stilwell's credibility, noting that he had not filed any reports on the two acts of vandalism.

"Were you trying to conceal the fact that you had put the mayor's son in a room and pressured him to confess?" he asked.

"Uh, first of all, he's not the mayor anymore," Stilwell said. "And second, by choosing not to file a report, I was using my discretion and doing Matthew Allen a favor. A reporter was already calling me about the graffiti. We keep the names of juveniles private, but anything can leak, and I didn't want that for Matt. I thought his intentions were good, just misguided."

"But that was against the rules, right?" Klein insisted. "You broke department regulations. Where else have you broken the regulations?"

"It was a judgment call," Stilwell said. "And, Mr. Klein, I make them every day."

"I'm going to step in here," Galvez said. "If you want to ask Sergeant Stilwell about rules and regulations, you can do that at trial, Mr. Klein. Because he will be allowed to be a witness. The motion is denied and I would think twice about wasting the court's time in the future. Good day to you all."

47

STILWELL DIDN'T GET back to the island until almost three o'clock. The whole way back on the Express, he mulled over Ernie Simon's sudden retirement and Bob Trestle's impromptu two-week cruise. Added to that was the order that all inquiries about the airstrip case were to go through Corum, and Stilwell had no doubt that the captain was shuttering the entire thing. It would remain open for appearance's sake, but there would be no continuing investigation. The question was why. If Gavin Lambert was the key suspect, the cover-up had to be for a more important and dangerous reason than to avoid a scandal over one deputy killing another because of a tawdry extramarital affair. There was something bigger involving Lambert—and possibly Corum—that needed to be contained, something in addition to the affair that could have come out when Quigley and others testified under oath in a divorce trial.

It had to be something that would do more than damage the sheriff's reelection campaign. Stilwell believed it was something that could send people—important people—to prison.

The divorce case would only have been the conduit for Quigley to go public with it. Divorcing couples often threw exaggerated and outlandish accusations at each other in pretrial motions. But it became put-up-or-shut-up time when they got to court, raised their hands, and took the oath to tell the truth. Quigley had kids, and by all accounts he had been close to them. If he was fighting for custody, he would have had to destroy his wife, and one way to do that was to claim that her actions through an affair with Lambert had somehow put the kids in danger.

He decided to change direction. Instead of trying to find the spot where Lambert arrived on the island, he would look for the mode of transport he took to get there. When the Express docked, he went back to the substation, checked in with Mercy, and closed himself in his office.

In the state of California, motor-operated vessels were treated similarly to automobiles. Every boat with an engine of any size had to be registered and licensed. Every operator of a boat with an engine had to have a boater card, which was much like a driver's license and carried the same information about its holder. As with autos, all this was under the control of the Department of Motor Vehicles.

Stilwell used his DMV access to enter the state's boating records and quickly determined that Lambert did not own a registered boat or have a boating card in his name.

Stilwell knew that many in law enforcement liked to fish or sail as a means of getting away from the job. He had gone through a heavy boating-and-fishing period himself before transferring to Catalina and still liked to go out on a boat with Tash from time to time and drop a line. He switched over to the department's database and used his access to identify every deputy on Lambert's drug team. He also wrote down the names of any spouses listed in their mini-bios, because he knew that most cops, especially those assigned to drug units, were hesitant about putting their IDs and addresses into databases.

Lambert's major narcotics unit had twelve members. After switching back to the DMV database, Stilwell went through the list of names one by one to see if any of the deputies under Lambert's command owned a boat.

He went through all twelve names and got no hits. He started running the names of the spouses, and on the fourth try, he got a hit. According to the DMV, Deborah Blackmore, wife of Deputy Daniel Blackmore, had registered a 2005 Bayliner in her name in 2018.

The boat was named *Rapsody in Blue*. Stilwell assumed the misspelling of *rhapsody* was intentional. He remembered something Quigley had said in passing soon after his transfer to Catalina. He mentioned that a member of the drug unit he had just left often performed rap songs at get-togethers outside of work. Stilwell guessed that deputy was Blackmore, that he'd named the boat with references to both his music and his job as a cop on the thin blue line.

The Bayliner registered to Blackmore's wife was only seventeen feet long and could be trailered instead of kept in the water. In California, boat trailers had to be registered with the DMV separately from the boats they carried. Stilwell went back to the DMV database and ran Deborah Blackmore's name. Sure enough, in addition to her driver's license, she had a boat-trailer registration.

But Stilwell suspected he had gone down the wrong rabbit hole with the Blackmores. The Bayliner was a little small for ocean use, and the registration showed that they lived in San Dimas, which was in the eastern part of the county and far from the coast. He guessed that the Bayliner was a lake boat used out at Big Bear Lake. It wasn't the boat he was looking for.

Stilwell ran the rest of the spouses' names through the DMV for boat registrations and got no more hits. He sat back in his chair and rubbed his eyes as he tried to think about what he might have missed. He suddenly leaned forward and on a hunch typed MIPCO president *Walter Bessemer* into the search engine.

He got a hit. Bessemer owned a thirty-six-foot Beneteau Gran Turismo called the *Bullet*. Stilwell had never heard of the brand and googled the boat. It was a sleek cruiser with twin 300-horsepower outboards. A hybrid of comfort and speed, it retailed for over half a million dollars. It was also at the extreme end in terms of length to transport on a trailer. To be sure, he checked Bessemer's name for a trailer license and came up empty. He now knew the boat was in the water somewhere and he had to find it.

Bessemer didn't enjoy the same anonymity as law enforcement officers when it came to DMV registration. His boat was registered to an address on Grand Canal in the L.A. suburb of Venice. His driver's license put him there as well. Venice was far from where MIPCO was located, in Riverside County, but L.A. County had very restrictive regulations on manufacturing ammunition. Stilwell guessed that Bessemer enjoyed the good life in Venice while his disintegrating bullets were made out in the desert.

The search for the *Bullet* had an obvious starting point. Venice was adjacent to Marina del Rey, the largest man-made harbor for recreational boats on the continent. It was home to several private yacht clubs and offered some of the most expensive dockage in California—hence the name Marina del Rey, which translated to "the King's Dock." The likelihood was high that Stilwell would find Bessemer's boat in the marina. The only issue was that there were five thousand other boats floating there with it.

What Stilwell had going for him in his search was that Marina del Rey was owned by the county and therefore fell under the jurisdiction of the sheriff's department. The marina had hundreds of live-aboards and was surrounded by high-end condo towers and commercial businesses. The MDR substation was much larger in terms of personnel than the Avalon sub, and Stilwell had strong connections there because so many of the boaters from MDR put Avalon Harbor on their itineraries. There had been much intel sharing and many cross investigations in the time Stilwell had been posted on Catalina.

He called Sergeant Dave Akins, his counterpart at the MDR sub.

"I got a boat in the marina I need to find," Stilwell said. "And hopefully some video of its comings and goings for the past week or so."

"Not a problem," Akins said. "Give it to me."

"The boat's called the *Bullet.* It's a thirty-six-foot Ben— "

"I know it. Nice boat."

"How do you know it?"

"The name sort of stood out to me when that boat showed up. Turns out it's actually owned by an ammunition guy, but I didn't know that until we checked it out. Before that, I was wondering if we had some made guy or a gangbanger wanting to get into the marina."

"How long ago was this?"

"Maybe two years."

"And you've talked to the owner?"

"Yeah, briefly. I've got his card somewhere here."

"Walter Bessemer?"

"Could be. Sounds right."

"Do you know where he docks it?"

"Yeah, he's in the PMYC basin."

"What's PMYC?"

"Pacific Mariners Yacht Club."

"They got cameras on the boats there?"

"Oh yeah, they got cameras up the ying-yang."

"They cooperate, or are we talking a warrant?"

"Oh no, they go along to get along. Tell me what you need."

"I want to come over and look at video of the *Bullet* going back eight days."

"Okay, what else?"

"Can you send somebody over there and shoot me a photo of the boat?"

"Not a problem. I'll do that when I go talk to them about you coming in."

"Perfect."

"Now, do I want to know what this is about?"

"No, you don't. And you want to keep all this to yourself. For now."

"I got ya. I'll call you back in about twenty."

"Good deal. Call me on my cell."

They disconnected. Stilwell looked at the photos of the boat model on his screen. He scrolled down and read that Beneteau boats were built in France and that the company was a hundred and forty years old. He wondered about Bessemer choosing this particular company and boat. He guessed that Bessemer was the kind of guy who wanted a boat nobody else in L.A. had. That said something about him that might be useful down the line.

48

STILWELL NEEDED TO know more about the connection between Bessemer and Lambert. He had linked them together simply because of the familiarity he'd heard in Bessemer's tone when he mistakenly thought he was speaking to Lambert. They knew each other. Stilwell was sure of that. Bessemer's biography on his company's website revealed the connecting points of the Marine Corps and Fallujah. But there had to be more.

Since his days in the homicide unit, Stilwell had a LinkedIn account under a false name that he used for investigative purposes. He pulled up Bessemer's profile and found additional details, potential connections to Lambert that could not be ignored. According to LinkedIn, Bessemer had also grown up in Riverside and joined Blackwater after serving in the Marines. The profile said he'd founded MIPCO with funding from the private security firm and contracted to provide munitions for Blackwater.

Stilwell was interrupted by a call on his cell. But it wasn't Akins calling him back. It was Carol Najera, the prosecutor.

"You won't be testifying against Allen after all," she said.

"What?" Stilwell said. "The judge reversed her ruling?"

"No. You won't testify because there won't be a trial. Allen is going to take a deal."

"And plead to what?"

"A single count of bribery. He'll probably do four years."

"Is that enough for what he did over here?"

"I'm not handling the negotiation. I'm a trial attorney. His offering to take a plea bumped it over to a negotiations team. So, to answer your question, no, it's not enough. But it's not my call."

"Shit."

"I know what they're doing—avoiding the risk of going to trial. They're getting something instead of rolling the dice and maybe getting nothing."

"Is he pleading guilty or no contest?"

"No contest."

"So he doesn't even have to admit guilt. This is fucked up. We should go to trial and nail him to the wall."

"We should, but we're not. This deal has been signed off on by the DA herself. It avoids a costly trial that was by no means a slam dunk. At least he'll be going away for a while."

"When is the sentencing?"

"It hasn't been set. Once he goes into court and enters the plea, the judge will put it on the calendar."

Stilwell's phone buzzed with another call.

"Look, I'm not happy about this," he said. "But I need to go. When does he go to court to enter the plea?"

"Probably Friday," Najera said. "I'll let you know. You should be there."

"Okay, I'll talk to you before then."

"Look, it's a conviction. That's all that matters. And he'll never hold office again."

"Right."

He disconnected and immediately connected to the other call. It was Dave Akins.

"Listen, I'm here and the boat's not in its slip," he said.

"Anybody there know when it left?" Stilwell asked.

"Yeah, just a few hours ago. The guys here saw two people on it, Bessemer and a second guy they didn't know."

"Will they let you look at video?"

"They're bringing it up for me right now."

"Good."

"Hang on."

Stilwell overheard Akins talking with somebody, but the sound was muffled and he couldn't make out what was said. Akins came back to the call.

"Okay, I'm looking at it," he said.

Stilwell waited.

"It's two guys," Akins said. "They're getting on the boat and getting it ready to go out."

"Did they bring anything on board?" Stilwell asked.

"Uh, one has a backpack."

"How big?"

"Just standard size. The one that had the backpack just got the lines and pushed off. The other's in the helm driving. They're heading to the channel."

"Can you take a photo of them and text it to me?"

"Stand by."

This time Stilwell heard Akins tell someone to back up the video, then freeze it. A few seconds later his phone dinged with a text and he took it away from his ear to look at the photo Akins had sent.

The photo was grainy, which was to be expected, and appeared to be from a camera that was at least a hundred feet away from the boat. It showed two men standing on a dock next to a boat with *Bullet* painted in script across the stern. Stilwell used his thumb and forefinger to expand the shot and get a closer look at the two men. One of them was facing the camera. It was Lambert.

A stab of fear went through Stilwell's chest. Not fear for himself, even though he instinctively knew that they were coming for him.

"Hey, isn't that one guy with us?" Akins said. "He's in narcotics, I think."

"That's him," Stilwell said. "But he's not with us. Not anymore."

"What's going on, Stil?"

"I'll tell you when I can. What time was that on the video? When they left. The time code is blurred on this."

"Uh . . . the time code shows three ten."

"Then they're already here."

"Where? Catalina? How do you know they were going—"

"Because I made a mistake and now they're coming for me."

"What mistake?"

"I made a call I shouldn't have made. I need to go, but can you ask them to show you video from two Mondays ago? I want to see when that boat left and when it came back."

"Two Mondays ago, you got it. But are you sure I—"

"Call me back. Thanks."

Stilwell disconnected and immediately called Tash. He knew he might be overreacting. There was nothing suggesting that Tash was under threat. But he had missed signs last year when one of his investigations put her in danger. He was not going to make that mistake again.

She didn't pick up right away.

"Come on, come on, come on," he said.

He was getting ready to leave the sub and run down the pier to the tower when she answered.

"Hey, what's up?"

"Uh, are you wrapping up early today?"

"Thinking about it. The harbor's empty and there's not much to do."

"Okay, Tash, I need you to trust me and do what I ask. Can you do that?"

"Is something wrong?"

"Yeah, it might be. So I want you to stay in the tower. Lock the door and stay there until you hear from me."

"What's going on, Stil?"

"I can't get into it right now. I just need to know that you will lock the door and wait there for me. It's important, Tash."

"Okay, okay, but is someone coming here or— "

"You're safe there. You just can't go home. You understand? Not till you hear from me."

"They're coming for you?"

"Look, Tash, I have to go. I'll explain everything later. Just stay there. Okay?"

"All right, I'm staying right here. And I'll lock the doors."

"Good. I love you."

"Stil— "

He disconnected. Lambert believed he had the element of surprise on his side. But he was wrong. He also thought that Corum and the cameras would give him the advantage in the sub, so this was where he would come. But he was wrong again.

Stilwell quickly came up with a plan of action that used the sub to his advantage. He then stepped out into the squad room to show himself to the cameras. As he'd expected, the room was empty. Mercy had gone home for the night and the second-shift deputies were out on patrol. He went to his locker in the bunk room and got the two extra ammo magazines he kept there. He stuffed them into a back pocket, then pulled his Glock from its holster, racked the slide, and chambered a round. He was ready.

He went back into his office, closing the door behind him. He set up the desktop computer and pulled up the sub's cameras on his cell phone. Then he opened the office window, removed the screen, and climbed out into the dark.

49

HUDDLED AGAINST AN outside wall of the civic center and using the hedge as a blind, Stilwell pulled up the exterior-cam package and expanded the video. The camera was located in the entry courtyard shared by the substation, the town library, and the single courtroom. He watched and waited, guessing that Lambert wouldn't make a move until Corum gave him the all-clear. He would tell him that Mercy had left and the second-shift deputies were out on patrol, leaving only Stilwell in his office.

Ten minutes went by and Stilwell started to wonder if he had it all wrong. He went through the suppositions that had led him to be hiding behind a hedge outside his office and waiting for a killer to come looking for him. He started with the phone call he had made to MIPCO and his using Lambert's name to get to Bessemer. If Bessemer thought the hang-up call was suspicious, he would have told Lambert about it. If he provided Lambert with the number the call had been made from, that would have led to the substation and Stilwell. But Lambert could not have pushed Simon and Trestle out of the way. He would have needed Corum for that, and that tied the captain in.

Stilwell finished the mental review feeling confident in his conclusions and his plan. He just needed to be patient. He knew Lambert was coming for him. It was just a question of when.

Stilwell called Akins.

"You check the video from two Mondays ago?" he whispered.

"Just finished," Akins said. "The same two guys took the boat out at five that day. It was daylight then, so you could see them clearly. Then I fast-forwarded, and when the light came up on Tuesday, I saw the boat was back and I'd missed it coming in. So I went back and found it. The boat came back about three that morning. Two guys got off but it was too dark to see if it was the same two."

"Were they carrying anything, either going out or coming back?"

"Yeah, like a backpack, but it was tall. It went above the back of the guy's head. Kind of looked like an electric guitar case. Or a gun case. And he had it coming and going."

Stilwell nodded to himself. He had been right about Lambert wanting to keep his sniper rifle. Otherwise he would have thrown it into the Pacific on the way back from killing Quigley.

"Can you get me a photo of that?" he asked.

"Sure I can," Akins said. "But what's going on, Stil? You're whispering like you're hiding or something. Are these guys coming for you?"

"I'm whispering because I can't talk right now. Can you send the photo?"

"I just did."

"Okay, now delete it, and don't tell anybody about this."

"I don't know what you're into, brother, but are you sure you don't need my help? I could be there in an hour."

"I appreciate that, but I have a feeling an hour will be too late. If you don't hear from me by tomorrow, send out the troops."

Just as he said it, Stilwell saw a figure enter the courtyard on his phone screen. It was Lambert.

"Jesus, man," Akins said. "I think you—"

"Dave," Stilwell said, cutting him off, "I gotta go."

He disconnected and started moving. Phone in one hand, and now his Glock in the other, Stilwell moved along the wall to the corner, made the turn, then advanced out in the open to the entrance of the courtyard. He paused, and on his screen he watched Lambert go into the substation. He went into the courtyard himself and crossed to the door to the courtroom. He pulled his keys, unlocked the door, and entered the darkened interior.

A short hall directly connected the courtroom to the substation jail so that detained offenders could be delivered securely to court. Stilwell moved down it quickly and stopped before entering the jail to switch his phone to the interior-camera package. He could see Lambert in the squad room approaching the closed door to Stilwell's office.

50

AS STILWELL WATCHED, Lambert turned his head and leaned his left ear to the door to listen to the voices inside. Stilwell saw that he was holding a gun in a standard combat grip.

As Lambert took a step back from the door and readied to breach it, Stilwell pocketed his phone, raised his own weapon in two hands, and moved quietly out of the hallway and into the jail. He moved toward the squad room on a line leading directly toward Lambert's back. He was closing in on him when Lambert raised a leg and kicked the office door open; his momentum carried him into the room with his gun up.

The room was empty. Stilwell's recorded interview of Gonzalo Kalas was playing on the computer screen.

Stilwell moved in swiftly and put the muzzle of his Glock to the back of Lambert's neck.

"Put the gun on the desk," he said calmly, "or I'm going to put your lights out."

"Okay, okay," Lambert said. "I thought something was wrong. I was just trying to help."

"Sure you were. Just put the gun on the desk and slide it to the other side. Now."

"I'm doing it, man. Don't worry. There. I slid it over. Can we talk now?"

Stilwell kept his gun hard on Lambert's neck. With his free hand, he reached under Lambert's windbreaker and ran his fingers along his belt line until he found his cuffs. He yanked them out of the clip-on holster, reached around, and tossed them onto the desk.

"Okay, without turning around, I want you to cuff your right hand and then reach it back to me," he ordered.

"Are you sure you want to do this, Stilwell?" Lambert said.

"Do it. Now."

"All right, all right, your call."

"Yeah, it's my call. Do it."

Stilwell heard the snick sound of the cuff's teeth as it closed. Lambert slowly reached his arm back as instructed. But then he started to turn with the motion.

"No!" Stilwell yelled.

He threw his weight into Lambert and bent him down over the desk. Lambert's gun was now within his reach and Stilwell swiped it off the desk. It clattered to the floor.

"Give me your fucking left hand," he ordered. "Now."

Lambert complied.

"I wasn't going to do anything, man," he said. "I still think we can talk this out."

"Just stay down!"

Stilwell took his weight off Lambert and grabbed his left wrist. He yanked it behind him, put the gun down on his back, and quickly snapped the second cuff on. He tightened both cuffs and picked up his gun. Lambert was secured.

"Come on, man, they're too tight," he protested.

"That's too bad," Stilwell said. "Are you carrying any other weapons?"

"No. I mean, yes. I've got a pocketknife, front right pocket."

"Stay where you are."

Stilwell holstered his weapon, then put one hand on Lambert's back to hold him in place while he reached around with the other to check the pocket. He pulled out the knife and dropped it to the floor. He then proceeded with a standard pat-down, finding a badge wallet, a clip of cash, and burner phones in his pants and jacket pockets. He put them all down on the desk. When he moved down Lambert's legs, he felt a hard object above his right ankle.

"You forget to mention the boot gun?" he said.

He pulled up the cuff and pulled a zip-lock bag containing a small handgun out of Lambert's sock. He stood up and looked at it through the plastic. It was a two-shot derringer.

"Huh, not a boot gun, exactly," Stilwell said. "And not really a throw-down. You brought this for me, right? That's why you have it in plastic. I was going to be a suicide. Was that the plan?"

"I don't know what you're talking about," Lambert said. "I came over here to pay my respects to my man Quigley—who you didn't protect, by the way."

"Of course you did. Get up. Let's go."

Stilwell grabbed the chain between the cuffs and yanked Lambert up off the desk.

"Ow, man," he protested. "Take it easy. I told you these are too fucking tight. I can't feel my hands already."

"Then why'd you say *ow*?" Stilwell asked.

He used his grip on the cuffs and one hand on the back of Lambert's collar to pivot him toward the door and walk him out of the office, through the squad room, and into the jail. He marched him into the first cell and closed it. It was an old-fashioned cell with a key lock. He pulled out his keys and secured the cell door.

"You're making a huge fucking mistake here," Lambert said.

"Well, it's mine to make," Stilwell said. "Turn around and back up and I'll take off the cuffs."

Lambert did as instructed, and Stilwell used his universal cuff key to release his wrists. Lambert immediately started rubbing his hands to get the circulation going again.

"I'll be back," Stilwell said.

He headed toward the squad room.

"You can't do this to me!" Lambert called after him. "Your career, what was left of it, is fucking over!"

"Yeah, yeah, yeah," Stilwell said to himself. "I've heard that before."

He went back to his office, collected the weapons off the floor, and put them on the desk. He held up the baggie containing the two-shot derringer. He was sure that the plan had been for Lambert to use it on him and then build a suicide scenario.

He placed the weapon down on the desk and picked up the burner. He opened it but saw it was password-protected. He put it down and called Tash on the desk phone.

"Are you all right?" she asked.

"Yes, everything's fine," he said. "You can go home but I need a favor first."

"Anything. What do you need?"

"You have the radar still on?"

"No, I shut it down, but I can turn it back on."

"Okay, I'm looking for a thirty-six-foot-long boat that is going to be anchored close to shore on the south end. Probably near the boatyard or the cargo dock. I need its exact GPS coordinates. Can you get that?"

"I'm on it."

"Good. Call me back."

"Will do. And Stil, I love you too."

"I knew that."

He went back into the jail and looked into the cell. He held up the burner.

"You want to give me the password so I can tell your pal Bessemer to come ashore for the pickup?"

Lambert said nothing. Stilwell could read the shock on his face. He'd had no idea how much Stilwell knew.

"I didn't think so," Stilwell said. "For the record, you are under arrest for murder and conspiracy to commit murder. Do I really need to read you your rights? I'm sure you can say them in your sleep."

"Fuck you, Stilwell. This is going exactly nowhere. You'll get a call in a minute, and you'll be told to cut me loose. Then you're going to have to look over your shoulder for me for the rest of your fucking life."

"I'm totally—"

Stilwell's phone started buzzing.

"I told you," Lambert said. "Now who's in the cage? You or me?"

But it was Tash calling back. She said she had located the boat anchored near the cargo dock.

"Can you text me the coordinates?" he asked.

"They're on the way," she said. "Anything else?"

"That's it. Go home, and I'll get there as soon as I can."

Stilwell hung up and called Akins. He answered right away.

"You still want to help?" Stilwell asked.

"You bet," Akins said. "What do you need?"

"I'm going to send you the coordinates for where the *Bullet* is anchored. It will be south of the harbor here. I need you to go grab that boat and hold the guy you'll find waiting on it. Walter Bessemer."

"Hold him on what?"

"Conspiracy to commit murder."

"I'll be on the water in ten minutes. Send me the coordinates. I'll call you when we have him. Is this still top secret?"

"Not for long."

Stilwell sent a copy of Tash's text with the GPS coordinates to Akins. He then looked at Lambert through the bars. He had made the call to Akins in front of him to get his wheels turning.

"So, your pal Bessemer," Stilwell said. "How do you think he's going to hold up under the lights? A guy like that... I mean, once he was a warrior, but now he's living the good life. Boat worth half a mil, house on the Grand Canal in Venice. You think he'll stand up and lose all that just for his pal Chopper? I don't know, man. I'm thinking he's going to flip like a bug on a hot plate first chance he gets."

"Fuck you, Stilwell. You have no idea the shit that's about to rain down on you."

"You really got me shaking, Chopper. How high up does this thing go in the department? Is it about cartel payoffs? Is that what Quigley was going to reveal in his divorce? That his kids might end up living with a cartel bagman?"

Lambert didn't reply. He stared at Stilwell through the bars with dark, hateful eyes.

The moment was broken by the buzz of the phone in Stilwell's hand. He looked at the screen. It was Captain Corum. When he looked back up, he saw that Lambert was smiling at him.

Stilwell took the call.

"Captain?"

"Stil, I'm looking at the camera feed from the jail out there and I see we have a big problem."

Stilwell glanced up at the camera mounted in the upper corner of the room.

"What kind of problem, Captain?" he said.

"I don't think I need to explain it to you, Stil. What I need is for you to let Lambert go. You keep his weapons so everybody's safe, and you let him walk out the door."

"He came here to kill me and make it look like a suicide."

"I am sure that's a misunderstanding. How about we talk this out in the morning? After you let him go."

"What were you going to do about the camera feed? Just erase it all? I guess with you in charge of the investigation, it wouldn't really matter."

"You're talking nonsense, Stil. You have to listen to me. You let Lambert walk. I'll send a helicopter for him tonight. He's off the island and everybody's safe."

"And what if I don't let him go?"

There was a long moment of silence before Corum responded.

"Your career is on the line here, Stil," he said. "You know that, right? You know what I have on my desk here? A report that holds you responsible for the escape of a prisoner suspected in the shooting of two deputies, one fatally. That's a career killer. You know that. Now, I can file it and let it take its course. Or I can shred it. What do you want me to do, Stil?"

Stilwell said nothing. He walked out of the jail and into the squad room. He opened the door to the audio/visual equipment closet and hit the main power switch, shutting down the cameras and every screen in the office.

"Come on, Stil, I want to see what's happening," Corum said.

Stilwell maintained his silence. He walked back into the jail.

"Talk to me, Stil," Corum said. "How do you want me to handle this? Don't you want to stay out there on your island with your pretty little girlfriend and your happy life? Or do you want it all to go away?"

"Like the way you made Simon and Trestle go away?" Stilwell responded.

"Simon retired, and Trestle's on a cruise to Hawaii. Nothing's happened to them. What we need to do is fix the situation at hand. Can we do that, Stil? It would be best for everybody."

Stilwell realized he was pacing in front of Lambert's cell. He also realized he was at a point of no return. If he didn't stand down now and let Lambert go, he could lose everything he had built for himself on the island.

"Captain, I gotta go," he said.

"Stilwell, don't hang up on me," Corum said.

Stilwell disconnected and looked into the cell at the man who had killed Alton Quigley and ruined Ilsa Ramirez's future.

"What are you going to do?" Lambert asked.

"The right thing," Stilwell said.

He walked out of the holding area and back to his office. He sat down behind his desk and contemplated things for a long moment before raising his cell phone and punching a name. It was answered right away.

"This is Lionel McKey at the *Catalina Call*. How can I help you?"

"Lionel, it's Stilwell. Are you busy? I have another story for you."

ACKNOWLEDGMENTS

Many thanks to Judge Carol Najera for the stories and the lore. The author also gratefully acknowledges Asya Muchnick, Emad Akhtar, Bill Massey, Jane Davis, Heather Rizzo, Tracy Roe, Betsy Uhrig, Pamela Marshall, Dennis Wojciechowski, Rick Jackson, and Mitzi Roberts.

ABOUT THE AUTHOR

Michael Connelly is the author of forty-one previous novels, among them the *New York Times* bestsellers *The Proving Ground, Nightshade,* and *The Waiting*. His books, which include the Harry Bosch series, the Lincoln Lawyer series, and the Renée Ballard series, have sold more than eighty-nine million copies worldwide. Connelly is a former newspaper reporter who has won numerous awards for his journalism and his novels. He is the executive producer of four television series: *Bosch; Bosch: Legacy; The Lincoln Lawyer;* and *Ballard*. He spends his time in California and Florida.

RAISING READERS

Books Build Bright Futures

Thank you for reading this book and for being a reader of books in general. We are so grateful to share being part of a community of readers with you, and we hope you will join us in passing our love of books on to the next generation of readers.

Did you know that reading for enjoyment is the single biggest predictor of a child's future happiness and success?

More than family circumstances, parents' educational background, or income, reading impacts a child's future academic performance, emotional well-being, communication skills, economic security, ambition, and happiness.

Studies show that kids reading for enjoyment in the US is in rapid decline:

- In 2012, 53% of 9-year-olds read almost every day. Just 10 years later, in 2022, the number had fallen to 39%.
- In 2012, 27% of 13-year-olds read for fun daily. By 2023, that number was just 14%.

Together, we can commit to **Raising Readers** and change this trend. How?

- Read to children in your life daily.
- Model reading as a fun activity.
- Reduce screen time.
- Start a family, school, or community book club.
- Visit bookstores and libraries regularly.
- Listen to audiobooks.
- Read the book before you see the movie.
- Encourage your child to read aloud to a pet or stuffed animal.
- Give books as gifts.
- Donate books to families and communities in need.

BOB1217

Books build bright futures, and **Raising Readers** is our shared responsibility.

For more information, visit **JoinRaisingReaders.com**

Sources: National Endowment for the Arts, National Assessment of Educational Progress, WorldBookDay.com, Nielsen BookData's 2023 "Understanding the Children's Book Consumer"